SLEEPER

T.J.HAWKINS

This book is a work of fiction and, except for historical fact, any resemblance to actual persons, living or dead, is purely coincidental.

ISBN: 9798808904217

To Dad

Dedicated to you for being such a fantastic father.

lots of love

Jamie

For Sarah.

ACKNOWLEDGEMENTS

To my wife. My rock and best friend. Thank you for putting up with me.

I would like to thank all those friends and relatives who have let me use them as sounding boards and who must be so grateful that this book has now eventually been published.

For Dad, who has always supported me. The most decent person that I know.

Special thanks to Iona Havard, freelance graphic designer from VisIONAry Ink, who illustrated the cover and has shown just how talented she is.

SLEEPER

CHAPTER ONE

Tom and Luna Rivers were, they always felt, just an average family. They lived in a fairly small three-hundred-year-old country cottage, situated down the end of an unmade lane. The house was typical for the period, with a slate roof, beamed ceilings and a huge inglenook fireplace that occupied half of one wall in the sitting room. 'Chocolate box' was the phrase that everyone used to describe it as but, at the end of the day, it was still just a small cottage. Though they could never be described as rich, they did consider themselves to be financially comfortably off and instead placed a greater importance on their good health, which they put down to keeping fit and maintaining a decent diet. Tom and Luna had twin girls who had both just started at the same university and were, without doubt, the most important thing in their parents' lives. They were then a happy, albeit unremarkable, family.

Tom certainly wasn't expecting any change to the safe routine that was his life. He found himself gazing out of the window and trying his best to enjoy the sunny countryside views, as the train sped its way towards London. He always rather enjoyed travelling by rail but it really didn't make up for having to endure a mind-numbing four-day conference on the subject of 'Sustainability in Modern Architecture' that his company had seen fit to send him on. Four whole days. *Urghhh. What a pain in the ass* - as his American wife, Luna, had so eloquently described it. He was pretty sure that he nodded off and started snoring at the last conference that he went to and that was a marginally more interesting topic than this one. *How to stay awake and look interested at the same time? Difficult one. Maybe copious cups of coffee beforehand would do the trick?* Tom started doodling on the pad in his folder.

The only ray of sunshine in what looked like a miserable trip was his planned early morning visit to see his baby. Not a literal baby, of course, but nevertheless something beautiful that he had helped conceive. A new multi-storey retail and office building of steel and glass in the heart of London which had recently started construction. As he had been the principal architect in its design, Tom was sure that visiting his creation would be the most interesting part of his day but it would definitely be all down-hill from thereon.

He looked out through the window again and it became clear that the train had now reached the outskirts of the capital, highlighted by a seemingly never-ending line of assorted concrete buildings facing the railway line. His thoughts turned to his wife. Lovely Luna. Her unusual first name was owed to the presence of a 'super-moon' on the night of her birth and her mother had always told her that her name was a reminder of how special she was. He simply couldn't argue with that.

Tom really hated being away from her and he wondered if he was prone to the same sort of separation anxiety that an animal feels. This feeling was probably compounded by his guilt over the 'little spat' that he had with her the night before. His habit of working out the plots of TV thrillers before they were fully revealed was one thing that his wife found really irritating. He knew this but, yet again, seemed unable to help himself and identified the killer and probable motive half-way through the first episode of a new series that they had decided to watch.

'Why would you do that? What is wrong with you?' Luna had barked at him and then, completely incensed, stomped off to the kitchen grumbling to herself.

'Come on, Luna. The script writer's the one that should have been shot. At least that would have been less obvious. All the killer needed was a neon sign above his head saying *it was me*,' he had shouted after her.

'Oh my God, you're so annoying,' his wife yelled back.

Tom knew that her assessment of him was absolutely correct but he was also sure that these vexing traits of his meant that she would never find him boring. That would be a much bigger threat to their relationship. He was also sure that, though she probably wouldn't admit it, Luna would miss him now that he had started his trip away.

Tom took his keys out of his pocket and unfastened the leather key fob to reveal the family photo inside. He smiled. *Mind you, she's not without guilt.* The only benefit that he could think of for attending this conference was that at least he got a break from her relentless teasing over the grey hairs that had started appearing on the sides of his thick head of brown hair. *It was evidence of who was getting all the stress in the relationship*, he had previously retorted. Annoyingly, despite them both being in their early forties, Luna's blond hair had still to gain its first grey and he knew she would remind him of that fact on a very regular basis. The truth was, however, that deep down he actually quite enjoyed the teasing and banter with his wife. Her vivacious personality and a 'give as much as you get' type attitude were some of the qualities that he found attractive about her in the first place.

Tom's thoughts were rudely interrupted by the train tannoy system announcing his stop, followed by the end of the platform coming into view. *Right, quick trip on the tube which then gave him an hour and a half spare with the clients before he would need to get off to the conference.*

At precisely 8am and exactly on time, Tom walked into the lobby of the twenty-storey building for his meeting and was promptly greeted by two men in their early thirties, smartly dressed in tailored blue suits.

'Good morning,' he said.

'You must be Tom. I'm Peter Davis and this is Paul Harrison,' said the shorter of the two, with both men then shaking his hand.

Soft hands, Tom observed. *What is the world coming to when construction managers have soft, manicured hands?*

'Please come this way. As you know, we are in the early stages with this project but we just wanted to run through a few things with you before we can all have a look around the upper floors.

Tom looked around the lobby area and nodded. Just as he had designed it and looking every bit as good as the artist's impression – if not better. Large plate glass windows and entrance doors leading into the spacious lobby area. Huge ceramic marble effect floor tiles and a dramatic centre lighting piece, which he had sourced from Milan, added to the decadent and contemporary look.

His director had stressed to him the importance of McInnis Construction as a client and that their satisfaction with this project would mean a great deal of repeat business. He was not about to let the company or his boss down. *Who knows perhaps a promotion and pay rise will be on the cards?*

Tom followed his clients into a meeting room located behind the lobby area but as he was doing so, he couldn't help but think that there was something slightly odd about them. He just couldn't put his finger on it. Tom sat down in the chair indicated to him by Davis, at the end of the table.

'Perhaps, I should get these out first,' said Tom refocusing his thoughts and then taking some plans out of a black tube that he had been carrying under his arm. 'I understand that you have particular concerns over the layout of the office units?'

'Yes, that's correct. It's really this section on the first floor,' replied Davis, circling the area on the plans with his finger. 'I know that they're only partition walls and can be altered but we would prefer to get it right first time if we can. We're concerned about the flow around these offices – there appears to be some pinch points.'

'OK. No problem. I can certainly give you some alternatives that would probably solve that,' said Tom nodding.

'Before we get started, I bet you could do with a coffee?' said Davis. 'I know I could.'

As Davis walked back towards the door, Tom couldn't help but notice his perfectly polished shoes.

'Thanks,' said Tom, as Davis exited the room behind him.

'So, Tom. Did you have a good trip up?' asked Harrison.

'Yes, thanks,' replied Tom, noticing that a very small amount of perspiration was now visible on Harrison's top lip.

'Have you been an architect for long?'

'About fifteen years,' replied Tom. 'Have you been doing this long? I imagine that you were a tradesman at some point? Every construction manager I meet seems to have started that way.'

'Err … yes. I was a bricklayer,' said Harrison.

Tom noticed that his carefully targeted question moved Harrison from having a slight air of nervousness to being very uncomfortable.

'Were you? I've always admired the skill of a good bricky. You know I was looking at a site the other day which was due for redevelopment and the whole terraced row of houses was built in a rat-trap bond. You don't see many of those these days, do you? Just out of interest, what would you say is the main issue with that type?' asked Tom, frowning slightly.

Harrison looked like a rabbit stuck in the headlights but, to his relief, the awkward moment was interrupted as Davis walked back into the room.

'Here you go, Tom,' said Davis leaning over his shoulder and placing a cup of coffee in front of him.

As Tom picked up his coffee cup, he felt a sharp scratch to the side of his neck. He had barely enough time to react before his vision had blurred and a feeling of complete intoxication quickly followed. The cup fell and smashed to the ground. Though Tom still tried to stand up, his legs seemed to have lost all strength and he dropped back into his chair. He turned his head towards Davis just briefly before it then dropped and his eyes closed.

'Thank Christ for that,' said Harrison. 'He knew something was wrong. Don't know how - but he did.'

'Well it doesn't matter now, does it? Stop looking so nervous, will you? It's done.'

'Why us? Couldn't someone else have been sent? They have a reputation you know?' said Harrison. 'Please tell me that you put plenty of that into him?' He nodded at the empty syringe in his colleague's hand.

'More than enough. That was twice the amount needed for a normal person,' said Davis leaning down. Calm down, for God's sake – he's as …'

A swift elbow to the face stopped Davis's sentence abruptly as Tom then sharply pulled his head down and smacked it hard into the desk. Davis fell backwards and collapsed to the ground. Harrison responded by lunging towards Tom's arms in an attempt to restrain him but, even though he was still disorientated, Tom grabbed his attacker's neck in a vice-like grip. Harrison writhed around, desperately gasping for breath until slowly Tom's hold began to loosen and eventually, his arms dropped to his side and he slumped back in his seat. Harrison, now coughing and panting, looked across at his colleague who was bleeding from a cut to the forehead. Davis held up an empty second syringe and, in unison, both men loudly exhaled.

CHAPTER TWO

Tom struggled to open his eyes. He felt groggy. It reminded him of his younger years, when he had woken up in the morning with a really bad hangover but at the same time knew that he was also still drunk. He tried to focus his eyes and then sit up but it quickly became apparent that he was paralysed from head to toe. His eyes darted around the white room that he found himself in. When he looked down, he realised that he was lying in a bed and that he was wearing a blue hospital gown. Attached to his arm was what appeared to be an intravenous drip.

'Good morning, Tom,' said the woman in a white coat with a set of stethoscopes around her neck, who had just entered the room.

'What happened to me? Where am I?'

'You're in a specialist ward. I'm a doctor here.'

'Why can't I move?'

'Please don't panic. I understand how this will be really confusing and upsetting for you. Your main motor functions are temporarily disabled but I can assure you these will return shortly.'

Tom stared at the person now standing over him. She was slim and petite with pronounced cheek bones and a little nose with equally small round glasses.

'Last thing that I remember was being in a meeting with some clients. No wait … that's right. I think they tried poisoning me. I remember them talking about it.'

'Well, you're in safe hands now. You really need to rest.'

'Can I phone my wife and let her know that I'm OK? It's really important. I don't want her worrying.'

'I'm afraid, that won't be possible. Tom, what I'm about to tell you will be quite a shock and you might struggle to come to terms with it.'

'What do you mean? Has something happened to Luna?'

'No, she's fine, don't worry. It's about you. There's no easy way to tell you, so I'm just going to come out with it. You probably won't believe me but here we go. About twenty-five years ago, you were recruited to MI5. You willingly signed up to a new program that we had developed, where exceptional agents were placed in a type of sleeper state and their memories were suppressed. Now a critical threat to the country has emerged and we need to restore you to active service.'

'Well, yes. I'm a secret agent. Of course, I am,' Tom whispered. 'James Bond, that's me.'

Tom lowered his head back down on to the pillow. *Dear God, I'm hallucinating or dreaming or something. Perhaps it was the fish that Luna cooked last night?* He closed his eyes and hoped that when he opened them again everything would be back to normal. Once more he drifted off to sleep.

Tom had no idea how long he had been asleep this time but just as the doctor had suggested, it seemed that some function had returned to his limbs. He sat up and swung his legs around on the bed. It was clear that he was in the same room as before but there was no sign of the doctor. *Perhaps that bit was all in my head – along with the 'by the way you're an MI5 agent.' Strange hospital room. Very minimalist,* Tom thought as he looked around. He noticed a phone on the desk in the corner and tried standing up. His legs felt like jelly and Tom realised that he was not going to be able to make it to the other side of the room without falling over. He promptly sat back down as the doctor returned to the room.

'What were you doing, Tom?'
'Oh, so you are real then. Thought it was all in my head. I was just going to call my wife and let her know that I'm alright. It's fine though. I guess it can wait.'
'It's probably best if you rest some more. You must still feel tired.'
Tom knew this was good advice. He was really struggling to keep his eyes open and within seconds of lying flat on the bed, Tom was asleep again.
Hours could have passed by but with the lack of a clock or even a window in the room, it was difficult for Tom to know.
'How are you feeling?' asked the doctor.
Tom raised his head off the pillow.
'Do you remember anything from your past, Tom?'
'Yeah, I think so. I sort of remember <u>you</u> actually. You're Dr. Patel, aren't you?'

'Well done, Tom. Let's see how much more you can recall. When we first met, I told you a lot about myself. Have a think and see if you can remember any of it.'

Tom pushed himself up on his elbows and looked straight at Prisha Patel.

'I'm sure you said you used to be a professor at Harvard. And before that at University College in London. You're a neuroscientist, aren't you? It seems to be coming back to me.'

'Well done. Anything else? I told you some personal stuff as well.'

'Was your father killed in a bomb blast in London? I think your mother was badly injured too. That's when MI5 recruited you.'

'That's well remembered, Tom. You're doing brilliantly. I want you to have a little more rest now,' said Patel, adjusting the switch on the drip feed attached to Tom's arm.

Tom slumped back down in the bed and his eyes closed.

'Good evening, Tom,' said Dr Patel, standing at his bed side.

Tom immediately opened his eyes and sat up. The tiredness had gone and he was feeling alert and wired.

'Do you remember anything about your recruitment into MI5?' asked Patel.

'Yeah, I do actually. It's quite weird. Feels like yesterday but I know it's not. The guy who recruited me was a Scot called Iain McGregor. Really nice bloke. I remember we had some very late drinking sessions which involved some serious amounts of whisky.'

'Oh right,' said Patel, raising an eyebrow. 'Anything else?'

'Yes. Everything. My induction, all my training … it's all coming back to me.'

'I'm delighted. You're making great progress. We need to finish the restoration of your memory and then I believe you have a meeting pencilled in with an old friend. Do you still need to call your wife by the way? There's a phone on the desk,' said Dr Patel.

'My wife? No, that's alright. I'm sure she's fine.'

CHAPTER THREE

MI5 Deputy Director MacGregor repositioned, ever so slightly, his white spotted blue tie and then checked his slicked back black hair in the picture-in-picture on his laptop, as he waited for an update from the head of Special Science Projects, Doctor Prisha Patel. *Appearance rules the world,* his father always quoted at him - which in retrospect seemed quite odd coming from someone who spent his whole working life welding ships at the shipyards in Glasgow with a cigarette hanging out of his mouth.

'Morning Prisha', said Mac answering the video call. 'How are you and, forgive me for saying it, more importantly how's our boy?'

'Good morning, Mac. Don't worry, no offence taken,' replied Dr Patel with a grin. 'Simply amazing is the short answer to your question. We have moved him into Stage Two of his restoration, so at the moment he's emotionally detached from everything. Zombie mode as we call it. In fact, I'm pretty sure he wouldn't even recognise you at the moment.'

'Probably a good thing. Not sure he would appreciate being pulled out of his lovely family life.'

'Well, he will remember everything when we put him through his final stage tomorrow,' said Patel.

Mac shifted around in his seat and re-adjusted his tie for a second time.

'Should I be worried? He did volunteer for this programme, you know. Albeit twenty-five years ago … and OK he didn't have a wife and family. A lot's happened in his life since then. God, I hope he's alright about this.'

'He will be absolutely fine, Mac, I can assure you. Having just completed Stage One, which is the psychological element if you remember, his loyalty and devotion to his country are absolutely front of his mind – almost to a fanatical level, I would say. And you, by the way, he holds in great esteem.'

'Thank goodness for that. We did get on really well when I recruited him back in the day. Quite glad that he remembered that. OK, let's have the low down then Prisha – is he the right man for the job?'

'So. As we have done previously, Tom's superior genes were manipulated when we first recruited him, so that he would be the best possible version of himself.'

'Yeah, I still don't understand how you do that but as a wise man once said to me *you don't need to understand how the sausage is made,*' said Mac.

'Yes … quite. Now Tom being placed in a *Sleeper* state for so long is unusual but we are confident that when his reactivation is complete, then he will be fully restored to his previous levels.'

'That's excellent news, Prisha.'

'Well, it's fair to say that Tom started at an exceptional level before we even did anything. For example, he has an incredible constitution.'

'Yes, I *do* know that. He broke the nose of one of my best officers and throttled the other when they tried to subdue him. The amount of our special cocktail that they had to inject into him would have killed a normal person. They told me that they were in fear of their lives.'

Mac's laptop screen changed to a picture of a graph and he noted that each annotation along the bottom of the chart had a pair of bars above it - one green and the other red.

'These are Tom's psychological test results. As you can see, they are all way above that of an average MI5 officer. You will also have probably noted that there are a few that really stand out.'

'Yes, I can see that. Intelligence, perception, empathy and logic. All of them pretty well off the chart,' said Mac.

'So, to answer your original question – yes, he is absolutely the right man for the job. If you want to understand what the bad guys are thinking and what they may do next then you need Tom. Ignore his advice at your peril.'

'OK, Prisha, that's understood. What about the more physical skills?'

'I've got some reels for you.'

As the video started, Mac found himself watching dash-cam footage from the inside of a Ford Focus RS. He sat wide-eyed as Tom raced the car around a disused scrap yard, skilfully weaving between the carcasses of various wrecked vehicles at what felt like breakneck speeds and then sliding sideways out of an old warehouse with plumes of dust in his wake. When the clip ended, Mac realised that he had been gripping the sides of his office chair so tightly that he had left indentations.

Before he had a chance to get his breath back, the next video started. Tom was lying on the ground in an army cine-range, armed with a standard SA80 rifle. The 180-degree cinema was showing an urban scene with enemy combatants advancing towards him. Tom fired his first shot and the film was frozen. A white light from behind the screen showed where the bullet had struck – exactly in the middle of the forehead of a soldier who had peered over the top of a car bonnet. The next two shots were fired in quick succession and again the film was paused. One enemy was shot in the chest and the other, who was peering over his shoulder, received a head wound. Just two minutes more and the army observer announced that all hostiles had been eliminated.

Thirteen dead in three minutes – that had to be a record, thought Mac.

'And finally, if you're ready Mac,' said Dr Patel rhetorically as the last video clip started.

The footage showed a top-down camera view of a large judo mat with Tom standing in the middle wearing white martial arts gi clothing and surrounded by three opponents. Each one attacked in turn and, with apparent ease, every strike was easily deflected. With a double hand clap from the referee, all opponents then attacked at the same time. As Tom finished

16

incapacitating the last of his opponents, Mac sat back in his chair and nodded.

'Wow. Sort of reminded me of watching *The Matrix*,' said Mac.

'Never looked out of control, did he? All of them were MI5 officers who held black belts in their respective martial art, by the way.'

'Very impressive, Prisha. We do still need to talk about the elephant in the room, of course. We've never had an agent who has been kept in a sleeper state for quite this long before and who has a wife and with kids who are all grown up. Is his family bond going to be an issue?

First point, we can't have him making his wife aware of who he really is. And secondly, it's critical that he doesn't get distracted on a mission where so much and so many will depend on him.'

'The problem you have Mac, is that his dedication and devotion to his family come from the same part of his psyche that is connected to his patriotic feelings. We have suppressed his feelings towards them as much as we can by using various techniques including hypnosis and cerebral suggestion. His priorities, shall we say, have been tweaked. But you want a super agent whose passion for defending his country makes him relentless. The emotions between family and country are essentially the same. There's a limit to what we can do but we'll have a better idea tomorrow once the final part of his restoration from sleeper status is completed.'

CHAPTER FOUR

'Good morning, Tom,' said a man's voice with a deep gravelly Glaswegian accent.

Tom Rivers awoke on a long black leather couch in the sort of sparsely furnished room that you would normally find at the doctor's surgery. The voice sounded familiar and as he opened his eyes and started focusing on the person sat in front of him, Tom then recognised the face. Older and with more facial lines, yes, but still very distinctive - Iain McGregor. And as he was twenty-five years previously, dressed in a pin-stripe suit. *I wonder if he has a huge wardrobe just full of them?* Tom thought.

'Good morning, Mac,' Tom replied as he sat up on the couch. He made a quick visual scan of the room which had a number of medical diagrams on the wall, other related objects on some shelves and decorated in standard magnolia paint. The recovery room at MI5 headquarters he assumed from previous conversations with Dr Patel.

'How are you feeling?' asked Mac.

'I feel ... supercharged. Strong, sharp, powerful ... it's really difficult to describe. It's sort of like I've had a huge dose of caffeine and then some. It's good to see you again, Mac. Can I still call you Mac? I imagine you've climbed to some dizzying heights in MI5 by now?'

'Well, actually I'm now the Deputy Director General,' Mac replied with a smile on his face. 'And in line for the top job when Sir Nicholas Meads retires next year. Normally you would have to call me *sir* but as it's you Tom, I think it's ok for you to still call me Mac,' he continued with a genuine tone of affection in his voice.

'You only say that because you think that as you're probably about to send me on a one-way mission - who's going to know!' Tom replied with a chuckle. 'Blimey look at you! Sounds like you've come a long way from the youthful looking section deputy chief that I met all those years ago and convinced me to join his new program.'

Mac looked at Tom and he felt his stomach turn. Tom's joke about it being a one-way trip was not so far off the truth in many cases, as these types of agents typically had a low survival rate due to the extreme danger that they would face. The two of them had built up a good relationship all those years ago and if things had been different, he had no doubt they would have ended up as best of friends. At the back of his mind, Mac had always wondered if he had resisted sending Tom on a mission before because it would have felt like sending a friend to their death. He always countered this by reminding himself that he was a professional and didn't show favour between his agents. Previous missions didn't really fit

Tom's profile but this one did, unfortunately, as Tom's numerous abilities and pure determination to win gave MI5 the best chance of success - plus he was perfectly positioned with his 'normal' job to catch the enemy by surprise.

'Well, I'm not sure I ever looked youthful, but I do get some comfort from knowing that I have less grey hair than you do now!' Mac laughed.

Tom smiled back. 'Ha! No greys at all from what I can see, Mac! So, you either don't have enough stress in your life or you've decided to get help in the form of a little plastic bottle.'

'I can't believe you would suggest that I'm so vain as to resort to colouring my hair!' Mac laughed.

It almost felt like a former life when Mac had approached a fresh-faced Tom Rivers at the end of his Royal Marines potential officer's course all those years ago. The results had been passed to him from the Special Science Projects team which confirmed his genetic make-up. But it was more than that. Tom was different to most, with such a high level of integrity which is rarely found in the modern age. He was the sort that would stand with others, even if it meant his certain death. Honour was his code. Patriotic and completely dedicated to protecting the innocent. In fact, Mac remembered thinking at the time that Tom had been born in the wrong era. The Middle Ages, where knights followed a code of chivalry would have been his perfect time. It was this part of Tom's profile that Mac knew would make his new project so appealing. Once he had told Tom that he was setting up a special section for MI5, where the agents would one day be called on to save hundreds or perhaps even thousands of lives, he was confident that Tom would be signing up to it. 'Sure', he had said to Tom, 'you could go and fight for country in the armed forces, which is a very brave and admirable thing to do. Or you could be the person that will stand between the bad guys and the slaughter of countless British civilians on our own soil - innocent men, women and children.' Mac knew what to say to hook Tom and reel him in.

'So, does Sir Nicholas know about your special agents?' asked Tom.

'He knows that we have agents like you but no, he doesn't actually know your identity or details of the missions. He made a conscious decision not to know,' replied Mac.

'Ah, the plausible deniability claim. So, if I cock it up then he can say that he knew nothing about it. Very political'.

'Yes indeed. I am aware, however, that my head *is* on the chopping block along with my career if you do make a mess of it, Tom. If this goes wrong, then the implications could be horrendous. So, get it right or I will tell your wife that you were giving away state secrets to some little twenty-year-old Russian agent that you were seeing on the side!' Mac said with a grin.

'Harsh Mac, that's harsh.'

The door to the room opened and a familiar looking woman walked into the room dressed in a smart grey suit with white blouse.

'How are you feeling?' asked Dr Prisha Patel.

21

'Strong and focused,' Tom said with a steely look in his eyes. 'Strong and focused.'

Mac was always taken aback by how Tom could flip so easily between the two sides of his personality. It was almost like flicking a switch between the good, humoured family man and the single-minded killer but fortunately his 'Mr Hyde' was always kept under control. *'Thank God he's on our side,'* thought Mac.

'Well Tom, I have been told by Doctor Patel here that you are now fully restored.'

Dr Patel smiled at Tom and then turned toward Mac. 'We have now finished performing the tests on Tom and as we had hoped, he is still 98% of the physical and mental level he was when we recruited him twenty-five years ago.'

'Exceptional.' said Mac. '98%! Well, when you have the starting physical level of a silverback gorilla then that's pretty impressive!' he joked. An exaggeration for sure but Mac also knew that this still meant that Tom was far stronger than any terrorist would reasonably expect from someone who just looked like an average middle-aged man. Bright, tenacious and resourceful too. Mac knew that Tom was going to need every advantage that nature had given him if he was going to succeed in a mission which so much and so many depended on. 'I'm afraid time is not on our side, Tom,' he continued. 'We would normally have spent a couple of weeks taking you through the re-awakening process but we have received intelligence that our targets have moved up their schedule and so we can't afford a delay from our end. Sorry Tom but we are going to have to throw you in at the deep end.'

'I see,' said Tom. 'Well, we better get on with it then.'

'Before we go to the briefing room Tom, you need to know that this mission is particularly dangerous,' said Mac.

'I wouldn't have expected anything else, Mac. That's why you pay me the big bucks. Oh, no wait a minute ... you don't, sorry. For a moment there, I got confused with my normal job where I get well paid for no risk to my personal health.' Tom's face turned from lighthearted to gravely serious and he looked Mac dead in the eye. 'I know what I signed up for and the risks involved. I also know that you would not have brought me in if there wasn't a serious threat. I will stop them, and I will do whatever it takes. If I make it through, then great. If I don't ... well, I trust you to look after my family.'

Mac nodded. 'Of course.' He paused briefly but then thought it was best not to dwell on that outcome any longer. 'As you say Tom, you wouldn't have been brought in if there wasn't a serious threat and I think it is fair to say that they don't get much more serious than this one.'

'So, what do you have for me, Mac?' asked Tom.

'Well, we have a terrorist group determined to kill civilians. That doesn't sound particularly unusual, does it?'

Tom shook his head. 'Why do I get the feeling that there's a bit more to it than that?' he asked.

'Very perceptive.' Mac said wryly. 'This terrorist group happens to have a technical scientific genius in their ranks who has developed a device which has the potential to turn Britain into a third world country for years and at the same time murder countless people. This is by far the biggest threat that we have ever faced in peacetime.'

'How the hell did they get all the elements to build such a thing?' asked Tom

'A little assistance from a certain foreign power that would be delighted to see us become helpless. We are also a useful dry run for them.'

'Dry run? Do you mean for America?' Tom asked with a slight frown.

'Exactly. Can you imagine the change in world order with America and Britain being sent backwards hundreds of years in their technology? Even with America's might, it would take a very long time for them to recover. In the meantime, one country would emerge as being the supreme world power.'

'Russia. Oh my God!' Tom exclaimed now realising the severity of the situation. 'They would be able to do whatever they wanted, and no one could stop them.'

Mac nodded. 'Tell me Tom, what do you know about Electromagnetic Bombs or EMP effects?'

Tom frowned but before he could speak Mac pointed at the corner of the room.

'Have a think but in the meantime there's a basin and mirror over there,' he continued. 'Get yourself together and when you're ready make your way across the corridor to the Operations Room and I'll introduce you to the team,' he continued before walking out of the room.

Tom looked at himself in the mirror. He looked fresh and his brown eyes, which usually looked and felt so tired after a day at work, now had a sparkle to them. Whatever Dr Patel had done to him, he now felt Herculean ... and his mind ... his mind felt so alert and focussed. After splashing some water on his face, Tom slipped his black leather shoes on and grabbed his black suit jacket off the nearby coat peg. One last look in the mirror to check his sharply pressed suit trousers and open white shirt and he was good to go. *Not quite where he had imagined he would be when he had left his house for a four-day business conference in London,* he thought to himself before striding out towards the meeting room

CHAPTER FIVE

MI5's Operations Room was huge with a large black and very modern boardroom type table in the middle and some sixteen leather-faced, chrome framed chairs. On the periphery of the room, a whole wall was covered with photos, maps and drawings as well as a bank of large monitor screens all currently showing the words 'MI5' underneath the agency's logo. On the other side of the room, by the corridor, the wall was almost completely made of dark tinted glass. Mac beckoned Tom to sit down at the end of the table.

Already sat at the table were two police officers and also two soldiers dressed in urban camouflage clothing and both with their berets lying on the table in front of them. Tom had always been a keen scholar of soldiering and immediately recognised their cap badges and rank insignias. The first was a black beret with the badge of the Royal Army Ordinance Corps, the army's bomb disposal specialists. The soldier who sat behind it was a white stocky man in his mid twenties with crew cut ginger hair and had the rank insignia of a Staff Sergeant. The second beret was fawn in colour and with one the most famous army badges in the world. The winged dagger of the Special Air Service. The man who sat behind it was black, late twenties in age, slim and could even be described as wiry in build, which Tom had correlated to the level of fitness that he must have attained. His face was narrow with pronounced cheek bones. The three pips on his rank insignia indicated that he was a Captain.

Though Tom couldn't help but be impressed by being in the company of the SAS, for some reason he didn't feel out of place or intimidated by them - even though he knew logically he should be. These guys had reached the pinnacle of soldiering - they were the finest in the world. He was just an architect who had lived a normal life by comparison. And yet it felt perfectly natural that he was sitting with them and moreover felt that they should be taking his lead and not the other way around. Tom reached for a buttermint sweet from a bowl on the table, at the same time raising a slight smile as he remembered telling Mac when they first met that they helped him think better.

'Tom, I would like you to meet Commander Amir Malik and Superintendent Shelley Carson. Commander Malik is Head of the Metropolitan Police Anti-Terrorist Unit and Superintendent Carson is the Ground Incident Commander for any attacks. From the Army, this is Captain Aaron Jax and Staff Sergeant Andy Lang,' said Mac. Everyone at the table simultaneously nodded at Tom. 'The mission is called '*Volta*', by the way.'

'After Alessandro Volta, I assume - the inventor of the electric battery?' said Tom.

Mac nodded and picked up a remote control, which he then used to lower a large presentation screen from the ceiling.

'So, Tom. EMPs?'

'Well, EMPs are not really my area of expertise to be honest but if I remember correctly, these are the devices that fry electrical circuits if they go off?'

'Staff Sergeant Lang. Perhaps you could give us your background briefing on these devices?' continued Mac.

'I guess that's a reasonable summary, Tom,' said Sergeant Lang in a broad east London accent. 'To give you a bit of background, ElectroMagnetic Pulse effects were originally noticed when the first nuclear weapons were tested. Basically, when one of those goes off, it sends out a powerful electromagnetic field which can produce an intense period of thousands of volts - a bit like a lightning bolt. This is likely to result in temporary or possibly even permanent damage to nearby electrical equipment.'

Mac pressed the play button on the video remote control and Tom watched the screen as a small EMP detonates and then every light and computer monitor in a nearby building fails.

'The building was the control tower for a small airport in East Africa which had been targeted by Al-Shebaab. The result was potentially catastrophic with a complete failure of every piece of electrical equipment in the tower,' continued Andy Lang. 'Fortunately, the pilots managed to land their planes safely, but it was clear that a larger EMP would have been able to disable multiple targets in one go, including aircraft, and also compromise the ability of the emergency services to respond. That was just a little EMP by the way - about the size of a small holdall bag. The one we believe is being built is substantially larger to the extent that they will need a transit van to be able to transport it to their target,' said Mac.

Tom raised his eyebrows. 'What's the definition of nearby in the case of a bomb this big?' he asked.

'Well that also depends on what type is used. We believe that the terrorists intend to assemble what is known as an FCG or, to give it it's full name, an explosively pumped Flux Compression Generator. It is probably the most effective of its type, so the immediate effects could be felt say a mile radius from the blast - maybe more. It will be my job to disarm the device, but we thought that it would still be a good idea for you to understand more about the target of the mission. Let me show you,' said Lang who then stood up and walked over to the area of wall covered in diagrams and specifications to then be joined by the others. 'So, here it is,' he said pointing at an A1 size drawing. 'You can see that in the centre is an area of explosives packed into an armature tube. Not conventional explosives by the way. This type of bomb needs the high velocity type. That is then surrounded by heavy wire, typically copper, which is wound around the explosive. A small start current device is used to produce an initial pulse. Once it has been completely assembled, then it needs to be contained in a non-metallic jacket or else it won't be stable and could be set off prematurely. Typically, something like concrete is used though fibreglass would be more lightweight. When the bomb detonates it can produce a wave of energy that is tens of Terawatts. To give you an idea of what this means, a large FCG can produce a current ten to a thousand times more than a lighting strike.'

'That's impressive,' said Tom. 'When you say explosives, I am assuming you mean conventional explosives not like the nuclear bomb which you mentioned before?'

'No. Our sources tell us that it will use conventional explosives. Apart from the major powers, most countries would struggle to get a nuclear bomb together, let alone a small group of terrorists,' said Mac.

'The nuclear version would most likely be used during the course of an attack by one of the big military states. It would be detonated at higher altitude to spread the effect further. The intensity would be less than one at ground level, but it would impact a huge area. The one we are going to be dealing with would still have a devastating effect once detonated and be more intense,' continued Lang, 'but the effect would be more localised.'

'What sort of electrics would it fry?' asked Tom.

'Well, basically anything with an electrical circuit. So just think for a minute about all the electrical things that you use which you can't when you get a power cut. Then think of all the other things which aren't dependent on the electrical mains but still have a circuit - for example modern cars. All of these will be rendered completely useless - possibly permanently. When the EMP goes off there will be a direct impact to all nearby circuits and the wires that most of them use will act like an antenna. Commercial computer equipment such as those used by the banks are easily damaged or destroyed because they tend to use Metal Oxide Semiconductors. If this goes off within range of their head offices where the main servers are located, then the banks will be rendered useless which means a failure in the financial system across the country and who knows how long that will take to resolve. Many months and possibly years - no one really knows,' continued Lang.

'So, you're saying that we could end up in a situation where people won't be able to access their money for maybe years? How are they going to live?'

'Difficult to imagine isn't it. You would hope that the government would sort some emergency money out with the other banks that weren't affected but until that's done then I guess some sort of ration voucher scheme will become the norm for everyone - a bit like during the Second World War,' said Mac.

'Then there are buildings where we are literally talking about life and death - such as hospitals. Imagine all the emergency equipment in a hospital failing. No heart monitors, ventilators or scanning equipment. Other elements such as signalling equipment for road and rail, airport equipment and airplane flight controls and most forms of communication includes phones, TVs and the internet will also be disabled. But it also has the potential to impact a wider area. The pulse will travel straight along the cables to the electric grid, and anything plugged in at home or at work for example could get destroyed. So, fridges and freezers for example could burn out. Not just at home but all the supermarkets and food suppliers as well, creating a food crisis. With a current of say a thousand times that of a lightening strike, the grid will be disabled, and it will most likely take many months to fix, maybe a year or even longer - we really don't know. London would effectively be sent back to the Stone Age,' continued Lang.

'Good God!' exclaimed Tom. 'This sounds like the apocalypse. Planes dropping from the sky, cars piling into each other on the roads, non-functional hospitals, no communications, no financial system and a food crisis.'

'The frightening thing is that this has a very good chance of becoming reality if we don't stop them. This is without doubt the biggest threat to the country since the nuclear arms race of the Cold War with the Soviet Union,' Mac said with the grim face of someone facing imminent disaster.

'I assume that the government have planned for this and that any critical electrics are protected?' asked Tom, reaching for another buttermint.

'Well, not really. Even with shielding, anything that has a cable going into it would be at risk. Even some military stuff,' said Lang. 'So, you can add to the list a disabled police and intelligence service as well.'

'Where the hell did they get all the explosives for this? I imagine that this special type isn't the sort that you can just pick up from an urban gang along with a handgun?' Tom asked.

'You're quite right. Let's say that a non friendly nation is helping out behind the scenes or at least a faction of it. There was a car bombing recently in Belfast that hit the news,' said Mac.

'The one where those three loyalist paramilitaries were killed who had just got off a murder trial?' asked Tom.

'That's the one. In fact, the person that they had murdered was the father of one of our terrorists.'

'The plot thickens' said Tom. 'Don't tell me, there was evidence pointing to the use of Russian made materials?'

Mac nodded and then pulled out a seat to sit down beside Captain Jax.

'So, it's safe to say that the terrorists have access to top notch equipment. Having said that, the materials might be Russian made but it's not them supplying it,' said Mac.

'Really? That's surprising,' Tom said raising his eyebrows.

'Well, the Russian government wouldn't be too upset if Britain was decimated by a huge EMP explosion, I think it's fair to say, but it's a step too far for them to be directly involved. Iran, however, has a less of a problem with it and feels it has little to lose. They won't shy away from telling the world that they were involved in inflicting the deep wound on the UK that brought it to its knees and that they have the means to do the same to America, unless they show more respect. They don't believe that Britain will retaliate militarily even with that amount of provocation,' Mac continued.

'You know, this could escalate quite easily into a World War, don't you?' said Jax. 'Russia stands by Iran and then the USA stands by the UK. Look at the First World War. Ended up as a World War because all the major powers were in alliances. One assassination of a country's leader and the rest, as they say, is history. This could move from being a disaster for Britain to being a disaster for the world.'

Mac looked down and then put his hands together, making a sort of triangle with his fingers. He continued staring at the tabletop and slowly nodded again.

'Your prediction, Captain, may not be as far away as you imagine. There's a meeting going on right now at Downing Street with the Prime Minister and Cabinet discussing what

Britain's response will be if the attack on London is successful. I wouldn't rule out a nuclear response against Iran.'

CHAPTER SIX

'Anyway, all the construction elements of the EMP bomb are identified on the drawing Tom, so I suggest you study them later. Now before I ask Captain Jax to brief you on the operational aspects of *Volta*, let's look at the group that you will be dealing with. Their name is *Adalah* and they were formed three years ago from despondent elements of various extremist organisations. Their name means 'Justice' in Arabic or 'God's Justice'. Not to be confused with other organisations that take the same name such as the one that represents the minority rights of Arabs in Israel, this one is made up of radicals who believe that certain countries around the world need to be punished for their crimes. There is also a fine but very important point to note here. The group is not an Islamic terrorist group per se. In fact, a number of them aren't even originally from the Islamic faith. They claim that their *raisin d'etra* is to deliver justice rather than because they feel that they are just fighting for a particular religion. Very unusual and quite concerning is that they have drawn in people from different faiths and backgrounds and promised them that under their type of Islam, they will receive the justice that they deserve.'

'Can I just point out that this isn't Islam,' said Police Commander Malik. 'I am a Muslim and can tell you that this is not Islam. It's a distorted view that they are peddling. Islam is a religion that forbids doing harm to others - unless it is in self defence. They are using this to justify their actions, but the killing of innocents is strictly forbidden in the Qur'an.'

Tom looked at the two police officers at the table, not really having paid them much attention before with the massive influx of information having taken over his thoughts. Commander Malik was slim, immaculately dressed in his well pressed police uniform and obviously took very good care of his appearance. Quietly spoken but must have an inner strength in order to have risen to his high rank despite any prejudices linked to his Asian background, Tom concluded. Superintendent Shelley Carson was also immaculate in her appearance but best described as being indistinctive in looks with short dark hair and the use of little or no make-up.

'That's true, Commander. We are also pretty sure that the leader of the group, Mohammed Baqri, isn't a dedicated Islamist but pretends to be and uses it as a way to draw others in,' Mac replied.

'So, they are sort of like a vigilante group then?' said Tom.

'Something like that. Many of their members are from the Islamic faith, of course, as there have been so many conflicts involving those countries. So, they feel that they are the ones that will carry out God's will and be the instrument of justice. This objective of dealing out justice means that they have actually managed to attract some key members from the other groups as well as some who have never been in an extremist group before - including some talented and well qualified scientists. It would be easy to think of them as just a bunch of mindless psychopaths but don't forget several of them have been taught at some of the world's finest universities and achieved great academic success. This in turn has provided them with the skills to develop the sort of technology which we are now facing. They also understand the countries that they are looking to terrorise as many of them have lived there and even been brought up there.' Mac pressed another button on the remote control and the wall mounted monitors changed from the MI5 logo to photographs with text down the side of each one.

'We believe that we are dealing with a cell of six terrorists for this attack,' he continued 'and they have all lived and worked or studied in this country. Home grown extremists. On the first monitor you will see the leader of the group, Mohammed Baqri. Born in London in 1988 and the third son of Yemeni immigrants. His father was a doctor, and he had a privileged upbringing. Degree educated in Middle Eastern history. A former Lieutenant of Osama Bin Laden, he is on the most wanted list in the US but had disappeared off the grid for the last couple of years. Highly manipulative and influencing character type,' continued Mac.

In other words, has a talent for being able to brain wash others into thinking what they are doing is acceptable, thought Tom.

'On the second monitor is the photo of Alim Farooqi or Doctor Alim Farooqi to give him his proper title. The technical brains of their unit and the person responsible for building the EMP. Born in 1975 in Pakistan, Dr Farooqi received Bachelors and Masters degrees from Oxford University before gaining his Doctorate from Imperial College, London. A fantastically talented academic according to those who knew him during his university years. We do know that members of his family were killed in a drone attack, which I imagine is his motivation.'

'The third one is an interesting case,' Mac continued. 'His name is Connor Morgan. He grew up on a large council estate in Birmingham. His father was an alcoholic and died when he was just five years old. His mother really struggled bringing up Connor and his three siblings on her own and ended up suffering from clinical depression. Her children were eventually taken off her by the local authority and put into foster homes. She then killed herself, believing that there was nothing to live for, as the authorities had banned her from seeing her children. Connor became a very angry young man - particularly with the state. He ended up going from one foster home to another and inevitably turned to a life of crime. Ever since the death of his mother, he has been looking to find a way in which he can take vengeance.'

'Setting off a large EMP that cripples the country that caused the death of his mother, would tick that box I imagine,' said Tom.

'Indeed. On the following monitors are Brigid Doyle, Usman Salah and then Asif Farooqi. The other person to be aware of is our inside man, Kalim Khan. He's one of your protégées, isn't he Amir?'

Commander Malik nodded. 'Kalim's an incredibly brave young man. Only twenty years old. He comes from the same area that I was brought up in and had started going down the wrong path in life. Along with the local Imam, we managed to explain to him the cost to the Muslim community of those that preached hatred and committed terrible acts - which they claimed was all in the name of God. I invited him to join the good fight and protect the innocent from harm. Since then, he's been working undercover for us, joining various gangs and providing useful intelligence, even though it was generally only concerning fairly minor crimes.'

'At the moment, his mother thinks he is just a small-time gangster and considers him to be a big disappointment,' said Superintendent Carson.

'Kalim finds that particularly painful, of course. It's a sad thing that his mother may never know that her son was involved in saving hundreds if not thousands of lives,' said Malik.

'He's not a member of *Adalah* by the way but is a member of the group that has supplied the explosives to them. He is the source of our information so far,' said Mac.

'I thought that the Iranians were supplying the explosives?' said Tom.

'They are...but not directly, of course. They can't be seen to be directly sponsoring terrorism just in case it goes pear-shaped, so all the explosives and other equipment plus intel is provided through this intermediary group. If the attack all goes to plan, then you can be sure that Iran will take the credit but if it goes wrong, then their reaction will be *nothing to do with me gov*,' replied Mac.

Tom examined the photographs on the screens. Dr Alim Farooqi looked just like he expected an academic to look, with small square glasses, neat black side parted hair and a face that somehow conveyed the feeling that he was an extremely clever and learned man. By comparison, Mohammed Baqri had an indistinctive face and if you had walked past him in the street, you would never have been able to provide a good description. He looked Middle Eastern, with short curly black hair and neatly trimmed goatee beard but no features that made him particularly stand out. *Being inconspicuous in an ethnically diverse country like Britain probably suited his goals*, Tom thought. Connor, however, was very distinctive in looks. White, bald and with a large scar down the right side of his face which was no doubt the result of his previous criminal activities. He also looked like he had spent a great deal of time in the gym with a very thick neck and pronounced triangular trapezius muscles.

Tom quickly scanned the statistics listed down the side of the photograph. Just under two metres tall or six feet five inches in old money and eighteen stone. '*Big lump*,' thought Tom '*but it won't help him.*' Then he looked at the profile of Brigid Doyle. A very attractive looking woman, fair skinned with shoulder length red hair and vibrant blue eyes. Twenty years of age.

'Connor's girlfriend,' Mac said, noticing that Tom was paying her photo particular attention.

'I recognise her. What's her gripe then? Or is she just in it because her boyfriend is?' asked Tom.

'No, she has a problem with the British authorities and has been trying to find a way to get back at them for years. All relates to the death of her father and her brothers. She's the one we mentioned earlier, whose father had been murdered by three loyalist paramilitaries.'

'OK, so she's got a revenge motive like Dr Farooqi and Connor Morgan. What's Mohammed Baqri's issue then?'

'Well, his main issue is that he's an unhinged sadistic head case,' Mac replied in a matter-of-fact way. 'A psychiatrist could probably write a whole book on the reasons why he is like he is. All we know is that he really enjoys inflicting pain and misery on others and that it is accompanied by an above average level of intelligence with a very eccentric yet charismatic personality type. He knows exactly which buttons to push to get the disaffected to join his cause. Perhaps it's just a power thing for him, because on the face of it, he doesn't seem to have much of a revenge motive like Doyle, Morgan and Farooqi. We did have him in custody for a while though, when he was with Al-Qaeda but had to hand him over to the CIA as things at the time were becoming a little bit uncomfortable at home thanks to a human rights investigation. Didn't want to add fuel to the fire if you see what I mean, so we passed him on to the Americans.'

'This is Asif Farooqi,' Mac continued, tapping one of the screens. 'He is Dr Farooqi's younger brother, by the way, and is probably the most normal and least extreme of the group. Quite a timid and quiet person but also easily led and was a simple target for Baqri to brainwash into following his ideology. And lastly, we have Usman Salah. A dedicated extremist, who believes a glorious death and place in heaven awaits him by killing those that have offended God. Ironically, this one we managed to make ourselves by sending him to prison. Originally just a petty but violent criminal, *Sal* as he likes to be called, was radicalised in prison. Then once released, he has made every effort to make himself infamous through social media with graphic videos of beheadings and torture during his time with the Islamic State. Completely loyal to Baqri and rarely leaves his side.'

Tom looked carefully at the photo of Sal. Wispy thin dark hair, which was brushed straight back, black beard and a thin gaunt face with very deep-set eyes that somehow conveyed only hatred. *If death had a face*, thought Tom, *then it would look like that.*

'I've met the girl recently and I also recognise the other two.' Tom frowned. 'Her hair was different to the photo. Still red but in a short bob style. She's also got a tattoo at the base of her neck if I remember correctly.'

'Yes, it's called a *Serch Bythol.* An ancient symbol of two Celtic knots intertwined - depicting eternal love. For Connor, I guess,' replied Mac.

'They all work in the same location as I do - the Sovereign Business Park. I had a brief chat with her when they moved into their business unit and even smiled and waved at them when I've seen them getting into their van.' He paused for a few seconds. 'Oh, so you're the reason behind how I managed to get such a great well-paid job there. So, when the man from the recruitment agency phoned and told me about a job that would be impossible to turn down, you were just putting me in the right place?'

'Yes, I'm afraid so. When we had word that they were going to be renting premises on that park, we needed to look at the businesses that currently operated there and then look at the agents that we had available. We only had a few days before they arrived, and we had to have someone in place before then. Your current employer *Allinson, Cooper and Collier* are architects already based there. You could fit in with little suspicion and if the terrorists decided to check you out, they would find someone who has a long history of doing that job and had spent years of studying before that. To be honest Tom, we also thought that you would be hard to stop and if anyone had the sheer relentless dogged mindset to complete the mission at any cost it would be you.'

'Thanks ... I think. I knew one of my traits that my wife finds most irritating would be useful one day. So, did you just pay my current boss a visit and tell him to take me on?'

'Pretty much. We got him to sign the necessary Official Secrets documents, of course, and then told him that he needed to interview you as a matter of urgency and offer you the job straight away on the basis that they had gained some major clients recently. He was to offer you outstanding pay and conditions - basically whatever it took for you to say yes. At the same time, we also met with your previous employer and told them that they needed to let you leave immediately. When the Adalah group took over their premises, you were already there at the building two units along from theirs and being your usual pleasant, friendly self. Your behavior was completely natural, of course, as you didn't know any different. They have been used to seeing you come and go with rolls of drawings under your arms, and this means that you should now be able to approach their building without them getting too nervous,' said Mac.

'Why doesn't the SAS just storm the building?'

'Well, the problem is we don't exactly know how far along they are with making the bomb. We believe that the last components are being collected tomorrow morning, but we don't know how critical they are. The danger is that, for all we know, the bomb may already be capable of detonation and, as Sergeant Lang mentioned, the device is potentially unstable until it has been put into a jacket. We can't take the risk that it will detonate either accidentally or deliberately, so we must leave our move against them until we think the EMP is in a stable condition. As you probably know Tom, Guy's Hospital is less than a mile from the business park as well as one of London's major roads, the A2, which has a 50 mile an hour speed limit on it. Imagine the carnage when the controls on all those cars fail and imagine the consequences when one of the country's biggest hospitals loses power and all its equipment gets fried. At the same time, we can't risk the terrorists moving the bomb further into central London. So, we feel the best chance of success is a stealth mission at its current location tomorrow morning, when we believe the bomb will be in a stabilising jacket. The other issue Tom is that there is only one way into the building. This is where you come in.'

CHAPTER SEVEN

'Captain Jax, could you brief Tom on the operational side please?' said Mac.

Jax - That's a hell of a name, thought Tom. *Sounds like he should be a wrestler or something.*

'Tom, I am sure you recognise this building,' Jax said, walking over to the next section of the wall. His voice was a lot deeper than Tom was expecting. For some reason, in his mind, it didn't seem to match a man with such a slim build. Well spoken though with no hint of an accent.

Numerous satellite photos of the business park where Tom worked, as well as photos of every side of the building now occupied by the terrorist cell, along with floor plans and the original construction schedule covered this area of the wall.

'As you know Tom, and can also see here on the site plan, the target building is Unit 24 which is located at the very end of the Sovereign Business Park and facing up the service road. So, it's a good choice of building for them with their lookouts being able to clearly see anyone approaching from a decent distance. The building's walls are constructed of concrete block and the roof is corrugated steel,' Jax said pointing with an open hand at a photo of the building. 'There is a fire escape to the rear serving the first floor, but the fire door has been removed and blocked up.'

'They clearly wanted to make sure that the front was the only way in or out of the building,' said Tom.

'Correct. Now, if you would look at this floor plan, please,' said Jax gesturing to an A1 drawing on one of the boards. 'You can see the entrance to the building here at the front and a roller shutter door beside it for deliveries. If you go through the main front door, you then have a room immediately on your right. This is where the main cctv monitoring equipment is and one of the terrorists will, we are sure, be based in there at all times. There are cameras all around the building including one covering the main door, one looking up the service road and another on the delivery entrance. Just past the cctv room you can see an inner door immediately in front and a staircase to the right,' he said tapping at the floor plan. 'On the first floor there is an open plan office approximately half the area of the ground floor with two toilets down the far end. You will note this line of windows,' said Jax, running his finger across the front line of the building.

Tom nodded in response, helped by the fact the building was so familiar to him.

'They are the only ones in the building and note that they also face to the front. Our reconnaissance has identified that another one of their cell will be there, keeping lookout. Back on the ground floor, you can see that the inner door by the staircase leads through to a large open deliveries area, which has the shutter doors. We expect that a third member of their cell will be there with another bank of cctv monitors, so that they can keep an eye on the front. Beyond that is a further inner door which leads through to the area where we believe that they are constructing the bomb. Of course, the key members of the group are still likely to be going between the areas as well, so don't assume that you are only going to run into the foot soldiers. There is no easy way in for us to this building or shall I say not without making some noise and then increasing the risk of the bomb being detonated. In addition to the cameras there also appears to be motion detectors around the perimeter.'

'Can you not go through the roof or something?' asked Tom.
'Not a chance. Trying to walk across a metal roof like that quietly and then cut through it without the guy below hearing anything is a bit of a tall order. The same obviously applies to trying to go through the first-floor windows. You've got to remember that anything that makes them suspicious could result in detonation of the bomb and, as Mr McGregor mentioned, the number of civilian casualties will be significant. Stealth and surprise is the way forward,' replied Jax.

Tom studied the plan carefully. 'So, I guess that means going through the front door then?'
'That's right. We've looked at all the options and the one that carries the least risk, and the greatest chance of success is,

strangely enough, the one where we go straight through the front door. Your role will be critical though. If you fail, then the mission will fail and people will die - it's as simple as that,' said Jax.

'I understand,' Tom said with the same steely determined look in his eyes that Mac had noticed earlier.

'So, assuming that our informant gives us the thumbs up, this is the plan.' continued Jax. 'We are going to arrange for a parcel to be delivered to you. Tomorrow morning, you will leave your office and walk to your car where you will collect some more drawings from out the back of it. The terrorists will be used to seeing you do this over the previous few days, so nothing new there. An MI5 operative will then arrive dressed as a courier and in a branded courier van. He will give you a parcel. The courier driver will appear to be in a rush and, as he hops into his cab, you notice that the parcel is addressed to Unit 24 - which, as you know, is where the terrorists are. You try to get his attention and point at the correct building. Make sure you point a few times to ensure that the lookout on the first floor has seen you. The courier driver waves you away as if he hasn't got time to speak to you and rapidly moves off in his van. You need to appear irritated by his attitude and then walk the parcel over to Unit 24. As you get near the front door the courier driver will reverse back down, having 'realised' that he has the correct parcel for your business unit still on board. A member of staff, who is another agent of course, will come out of your offices to take the delivery. This should now have diverted the attention of the lookout on the first floor, to some degree.'

Jax took a step sideways in order to stand directly in front of the front elevation plan and then tapped his finger on the first-floor area. He then moved his finger down to the front door and tapped again.

'You will knock on the front door with parcel in hand and at the same time the courier will try leaving but 'accidentally' hit one of the parked cars. This should fully distract the guard upstairs with the fracas going on outside your offices. At this point, you will need to quickly deal with the front door guard, and I would suggest that you move them back out of range of the camera. If you are lucky, the person in the deliveries area on the other side of the inner door wasn't watching the monitor covering the entrance at the time you approached the front. The likelihood is that they would also be watching the disturbance outside your offices. You will have to assume, however, that they weren't, and this means time is of the essence before they start wondering why you haven't started walking back to your office and then go to investigate. Next step is to interrupt the cctv signal. Let me show you this.'

Jax walked over to a table with a black box the size of a smart phone on top, picked it up and then handed it to Tom.

'This device is completely self contained,' continued Jax 'and all you need to do is flick the switch on the right upwards and place it on top of the CCTV control box. This will replay images on a loop and will appear as if it is still a live feed. That, in turn, will allow my team to approach the front. Before we do that, of course, we need you to move upstairs and take out the first-floor lookout. I understand from Mr McGregor that you are highly proficient in the use of the Glock 17 9mm with silencer and laser sight?'

Tom reached for another buttermint and nodded.

'Good. That should be your weapon of choice,' Jax continued. 'To stress the point again, time is critical so take the guard out and call in your status. Then all you need to do is get back downstairs and open the door. My team will move in and clear the way for Sergeant Lang to deal with the bomb. Any questions?'

'What happens if they decide not to open the door to me?'

'In that case you need to use an electronic lock pick,' said Mac, walking over with a small square black plastic box in his hands. 'Place this over the lock and within seconds you will be in. Magnets hold it in place by the way. The parcel actually contains the CCTV blocking device and has been carefully designed with a Glock 17 pistol and silencer concealed into the bottom on the right-hand side and a space for the lock pick on the left hand side. That way you can hold the parcel in your right hand and remove the lock pick without being seen by the camera.'

'Very 007, Mac,' said Tom.

'The great thing is that even if you walk in after using the lock pick, as you are carrying a parcel, you really won't appear threatening to them and they'll be off guard,' said Jax. 'No pressure but a lot of lives are depending on this plan working.'

CHAPTER EIGHT

It was 5am on the 6th June and the *Adalah* cell were all sitting around a table situated at the back of the first floor of Unit 24, near the toilets, with just Brigid Doyle keeping a lookout to the front but still within hearing distance of the conversation. Mohammed Baqri was seated at the head of the table and in keeping with his inconspicuous image was wearing blue jeans and a plain white T-shirt with a black casual cotton jacket neatly folded over the backrest of the seat beside him. Dr Farooqi sat directly opposite, in his white coat which was not only practical for what he was doing but also reminded him that he was, at the end of the day, a scientist. The room itself was typical for a commercial unit with matt white painted walls and just a map of London pinned to the partition wall.

It had already been a very long day for Doctor Alim Farooqi and he was feeling exhausted. More work ahead of him but he knew that once done, he had the chance to take revenge on those who had been responsible for the death of his little girl and his wife with their cowardly drone attack in Pakistan the year before. Their technology had sentenced him to eternal pain and suffering and now he would show them that there are people like him who can also use technology to make them pay for their crimes. He closed his eyes and remembered the day that changed his life forever.

His wife and daughter were simply making their way over to see his mother when they were killed. The British Army said it was 'unfortunate and regrettable' and blamed his little girl for suddenly changing the direction that she was walking and then running down a side road after her toy which was rapidly bouncing down some steps. His wife had run after her. By the time the drone operator had realised that civilians had entered the blast radius it was too late, and the drone could not be stopped. They said that two of their top targets were also killed in the blast and these men had been responsible for the deaths of countless British and American soldiers and civilians and were planning more attacks on innocent people. Well, his wife and daughter were innocent. Why should there not be justice for their deaths? How was it right that they should be robbed of their lives, and no one is held accountable? Well, the British were going to be made to pay for their mistake. His brother Asif, who was already friends with Baqri, had persuaded him to join a new group called *Adalah. Perfect,* he thought - *Justice.*

'Alim,' said Mohammed Baqri, interrupting his thoughts. 'Where are you up to on the bomb? You *will* be ready on time, won't you? It must be ready this morning, you do understand that don't you? No more delays and problems, right?' he continued without taking a breath between questions and with more than just a hint of stress in his voice.

Farooqi calmly waited until the machine gun of questions from Baqri had finished before taking off his glasses, placing them on the table and then proceeding to rub the area on either side of his nose where his glasses had been resting with his thumb and fore finger.

'My friend,' Farooqi said calmly, 'I am not building a toy here.'

'I know Alim and I'm sorry. I don't mean to cause you more stress, but I have to know that you will be ready.'

'This takes time and, may I say, some skill to ensure that it performs as we hope. The main part of the EMP is complete.' Farooqi used a pen from his top pocket and drew a diagram on an A4 piece of paper. 'The copper cylinder here acts as the armature tube and I have PBX in the middle.' continued Farooqi.

'PBX?' asked Sal.

'PBX. Polymer Bonded Explosive. I have used this type because the EMP requires a high velocity type. As you are aware, we will also be acquiring extra explosives later. Specifically, we need an element called a lens. This has been the most difficult part of the EMP to source because it is made up of layered explosives and has taken longer than expected to get our hands on. The lens will be placed here along with the starter device.'

Farooqi drew a lens shape to the end of the casement. 'The explosion starts with the lens and then travels through the armature tube in a conical shape,' he said drawing arrows to the side and upwards. 'Not to be too technical but the force expands the tube and when contact is made with the copper coil a compressed magnetic field is formed. It's a little more complicated than that but hopefully you understand the basics. The EMP will only be operational though once I have that lens.'

'I understand Alim. Thank you. Before I go through the plan, I first want to make clear, my friends, that we are not suicide bombers. There is not enough of us for that and once we do this mission then we will re-group and move on to another target. Having said that, if it's a choice between being captured by them or dying for our cause, then I choose to die,' Baqri said looking around the table as everyone nodded their agreement.

'One more thing that is very important. If, for whatever reason, you are unable to get the van to the target point, then you are to set off the EMP anyway. It will still have a significant effect but the closer to the target, the better. My friends, we have the beginnings of something great here. *Adalah* is more than a group of people. We are a family of brothers and sisters across the world, who have come together from different religious backgrounds but united now under one faith. We do not follow some extreme version of Islam like some groups but understand how our religion helps us focus on punishing those who have inflicted injustices on others. It is right, it is just, and it is God's will. Some of you like Alim and Brigid have lost loved ones and some of you have not but understand that what has happened is wrong. For you Connor, this is your moment to cripple the corrupt system which took your mother from you,' said Baqri in a manner more akin to a political speech. He looked at Connor and then at all the others who, in turn, then smiled and nodded in return.

'So, what is the target then?' asked Connor.

'OK. The target. I want you, Brigid and Alim to drive the EMP to this location, arriving at 5.45pm.'

Baqri picked up a ball point pen from the table, rose to his feet and walked over to the map of London. He then proceeded to circle St Paul's Cathedral and then excitedly tapped the church icon on the map again and again and finally with enough pressure to put a hole through the map.

'When you are sure it is ready then call me first before you set the timer for fifteen minutes and make your way to here where you will find a twenty-year-old red Toyota Camry. To be clear, the EMP is to detonate at 6pm.' Baqri again tapped at the map. 'This car is old enough not to have the electrical circuits that will render more modern cars completely useless when the bomb goes off. Make your way to the safe house. I will be taking a different route in another vehicle with Sal.

'Why St. Paul's?' asked Brigid.

Baqri put down the pen and then picked up a piece of string with a drawing pin on one end and a pencil on the other. He placed the drawing pin in the centre of the icon for St. Paul's cathedral and then drew a circle around it using the string.

'Alim reckons that the EMP will have an immediate effective radius of about a mile but for those buildings that have commercial computer equipment, they may be affected even further out than that. You see that there are number of high-profile financial targets that will instantly and directly be made completely nonfunctional. The Bank of England, the Stock Exchange and hundreds of other banks in the City of London will be shut down,' Baqri said pointing to them around the map. 'You can also see that within this mile radius are three hospitals - Guy's Hospital, London Bridge Hospital and the Royal London. All electrical functions in these hospitals will cease and chaos will ensue. Of course, that's not all of it. We should see the EMP pulse travel across the National Grid and affect electrical devices much further out than a mile. We are hoping to see the destruction or complete shut down of anything that has an electrical circuit across the whole of London and this should include the police and security services.'

'Won't the timer be affected by the EMP?' asked Connor.

'No, the timer is completely mechanical. No electronic parts,' replied Alim.

'At twenty minutes before 6pm, our brothers and sisters in *Adalah* will have sent out messages via social media of what is about to happen and that the police will be rendered impotent. They will encourage anarchy with rioting and looting. The heart of Britain will be ripped out and we will turn it into a third world country,' Baqri said with a smirk on his face.

Brigid nodded in appreciation. 'Amen to that.'

CHAPTER NINE

Brigid Doyle was born and bred in Northern Ireland during an era known as 'The Troubles'. The only girl of five children born into a Catholic family. Her mother ran the local pub and her father, Declan, was a local politician and member of the Republican Party, Sinn Fein. Brigid had been more than just close to her father - she completely adored him, as he did her. She was definitely 'daddy's little girl' and he spoilt her whenever he got the opportunity - much to the annoyance of her mother. Declan had a huge gregarious personality, with the sort of voice that just boomed, without any sort of volume control. There was no mistaking Declan Doyle for anyone else. Along with his large personality came his large physique - but not in a flattering way. It wasn't his fondness of good Irish food that had provided him with a substantial waistline but his great love of the black stuff - Guinness.

It was, however, Declan's work and outspoken comments about the end of British influence and the potential for a united Ireland at any cost that ultimately resulted in tragedy for the family. Not known for his subtlety, Declan Doyle took every opportunity to promote his ideas and beliefs on television and radio. He was, however, often heavily criticised for his reluctance to condemn violent actions by Republican extremists, to the extent that he seemed to almost encourage it. At the same time, he was scathing of any similar action taken by the mainly Protestant Loyalist paramilitaries. He had been warned by his own Party on numerous occasions that the content of his dialogue with the media was unacceptable in a country that was on the verge of finding peace with itself and at the same time gaining self-rule from the rest of the UK. He was 'fanning the flames of violence' his party leader had told him 'in a time when their aim was to snuff out that flame altogether.' Declan, however, still believed that any talks with the unionists would ultimately fail, so he refused to tone down his rhetoric and instead became even more controversial with his comments. He continued to upset large numbers of his fellow countrymen with his opinions but felt the end justified the means.

Then one day, the Republican extremists planted a bomb in a bin which was intended for a passing British Army patrol. A phone call was made to notify the authorities that there was a bomb in the area, in order for them to clear any innocent civilians but tragically the bomb exploded prematurely before the police had time to move everyone away. The terrible result was the killing of four children and the horrific maiming of two others, who were simply making their way home from school. Unsurprisingly, complete outrage followed - not only in Northern Ireland but in the rest of the UK and around the world.

The British Prime Minister called it 'a despicable, callous and cowardly act that deprived these completely innocent children of their futures' and promised that the killers would be brought to justice. The American President joined the condemnation and described the perpetrators as being 'the lowest of the low' and expressed a sincere hope that they would be found, and justice would prevail. Every major country around the world made similar comments but, as usual, Declan failed to criticise those that had planted the bomb. He did express his sincere sadness at the tragedy but laid the blame for the killings at the foot of the British government, saying that it was their actions that forced others into taking extreme measures, which in this case had resulted in the terrible loss of young lives.

His words were not only an embarrassment for his Party but also outraged most of their Catholic core member base as well. Despite trying to distance themselves from him, the Party continued to be inundated with complaints, as Declan not only failed to apologise but went even further in his remarks during interviews across the media. In one interview, he claimed that the bombers had committed no crime and that the British Government were the murderers and then in another one on national television even suggested that the British Army had probably planted the device in order to blame the Republicans. The target was now well and truly painted on Declan Doyle as he became a lightening post for the hatred of the Protestant community. It was not long until the seventeen-year-old Brigid witnessed a horrifying event that scarred her mentally forever and started her journey to the welcoming arms of Mohammed Baqri and *Adalah*.

It was a bright sunny Saturday afternoon in May and the local pub was busy with patrons enjoying an international rugby match on television between Ireland and Wales. The green, white and orange colours of the Irish flag were draped all around the part wooden panelled walls, as well as painted on the face of a particularly enthusiastic member of bar staff. Declan's wife, Eileen, was as usual serving behind the bar but finding it extremely difficult to hear with the customers cheering every time the Irish team moved the ball further down the field towards the Welsh line. Declan was sat in a corner bay seating area with Brigid and his brother, Joseph, and had been joining in with the cheering - fuelled by five pints of Guinness.

'That's strange,' said Brigid in raised voice. 'Gerry Flanagan just walked into the pub, looked at you and then just walked out again.'

'Well, there you go Declan,' said Joseph, 'proof right there, that you are bad for Eileen's business.'

'How the hell do you remember him, Brigid? You only met him once and that was about three years ago. Jesus, you have an incredible memory. Do your poor old father a favour and get another pint of Guinness for me and your uncle Joseph will you?' Declan boomed in his strong Northern Irish accent.

Brigid gave him a typical teenager face of both irritation and reluctant acceptance, which if she had spoken would have been the word 'really?' After letting out a deliberate and obvious sigh, Brigid stood up and started weaving her way through the crowd to the bar.

'Declan, I'm worried about you,' said Joseph. 'You've got to be more careful in what you say. You're upsetting a lot of people - a lot of the wrong people. Even the IRA has distanced itself from you.'

'Joseph,' replied Declan, 'I really don't give a shit. Some things need to be said. This peace that they are looking for between Catholics and Protestants won't work. Only violence will set us free.'

Meanwhile, Brigid had fought her way into a gap at the bar and through a combination of waving and shouting at the top of her voice, managed to catch her mother's attention.

'Don't tell me,' Eileen shouted across the bar to Brigid, 'your father looks like he's going to die of thirst if he doesn't get another Guinness down his throat?' she said with a broad smile on her face.

'You know what he's like. Keeps him happy but the more he drinks, the worse his jokes get, and they really aren't funny,' shouted Brigid back across the bar.

'He thinks they are. That's the sad thing,' Eileen replied as she started to pour the first pint.

At that point, three men burst through the pub's front door dressed in camouflage jackets and with their faces covered with black balaclavas. The first two of them were holding pistols at their sides and the last one had a sawn-off double-barrelled shotgun. The pub went quiet, and customers quickly parted out the way as the three men strode up to the table where Declan and Joseph were seated. The Doyle brothers were leaning slightly forwards at the table, intensely discussing Declan's popularity issues, as the men approached. The brothers looked up and without even a pause, the man with the shotgun lifted the weapon and fired both barrels into Declan's chest. The force of the blast threw Declan back into the bench seating and his head dropped backwards. One of the other paramilitaries then raised his pistol and fired a single shot into Declan's forehead. The sound of hysteria filled the pub to a deafening level but even then, above all that noise, Eileen's chilling scream cut through it all and seemed to just go on and on and on.

'Daddy!' cried Brigid as she tried running towards her father, only to be held back by two of the pub's regular customers.

'Jesus, no. Please no,' Eileen shrieked.

The third paramilitary pressed his pistol against Joseph's forehead and then pressed it even harder, pushing his head back with it. The area of his head that had the gun's barrel pressed up against it had gone white with a red discolouration around it and then the paramilitary pulled back the hammer on his pistol and just held it there for a few seconds. Then, unexpectedly, the gun's hammer was slowly lowered back to its starting position and the three men turned on their heels and calmly walked out of the pub.

The execution had been completed in a clinical manner but also in a deliberately public way. Joseph remained fixed in exactly the same seated position as when he had been talking to Declan, his face and clothes now heavily splattered with his brother's blood. Unable to move, he just stared through wide eyes at a space on the other side of the pub. Brigid pulled herself away from those holding her and scrambled across the bench seating, grabbing her father by his jacket and then attempting to pull him up from his slouched position. Other patrons in the pub quickly moved in and dragged her away, handing her over to her mother who had by now made her way to the front of the bar. Brigid stood in front of Eileen with tears streaming down her face and looked at her blood covered hands - her father's blood.

She held her hands up so that her palms were facing her mother and screamed.

CHAPTER TEN

If Brigid had been hoping that revenge for her father's brutal death would come at the hands of the IRA, then she was to be sorely disappointed. Orders had already been given by their political masters that there should be no response to the execution of Declan Doyle. The peace process being negotiated between the Protestant and Catholic factions in Northern Ireland was far too important to be put at risk for the sake of one loudmouth who had managed to upset so many people on both sides. This meant that the Doyle family had little choice but to hope that the Royal Ulster Constabulary, who were investigating the murder, would bring the killers to justice.

Three weeks had gone by and much to the surprise of the Doyle family, the police had made good progress. Three men had been arrested, questioned and then released on bail whilst the police continued their investigations. Detective Chief Inspector Patrick O'Neill, who was leading the investigation, had visited the Doyle family home and assured them that everything that could be done, was being done. He had explained that the evidence against the suspects was strong and significant material had been found in a search of the suspects' homes.

Within a few months, the suspects were in court on charges of murder. Brigid and Eileen sat through every day of the trial and the evidence against the men seemed overwhelming. Then disaster struck when it emerged that the police had failed to follow the correct procedure on several points during their investigation from the treatment of physical evidence to the questioning of suspects without legal representation being present. The case was dismissed by the Judge on a technicality, even though it was apparent to everyone present in court that the men were guilty of Declan's murder. As the Judge read out his decision, Brigid and Eileen just sat motionless in their seats, completely stunned by what had just happened. Then as the three men turned to each other and smiled, Brigid jumped to her feet.

'Murderers! Murderers!' she screamed at them. Then she turned her anger towards the judge. 'Do you call this justice? Do you? They've murdered my father and you've let them go free!' she shouted.

After being told to sit down by the judge and warned that she could be held in contempt of court, Brigid looked at her mother who then also stood up, grabbing her daughter by the arm.

'C'mon love,' Eileen said and then strode out of the courtroom looking straight ahead and without looking at anyone. Brigid followed but did manage to make eye contact with one of the accused men, who was now grinning at her. She felt a complete rage consume her and tried rushing at the man but was held back by a court bailiff. Brigid could only manage to scream the word 'Murderers' at them one more time before being led out of the courtroom.

Later that evening at their home in West Belfast, the Doyle family sat together and watched the evening news on television. As expected, the lead news article was the acquittal of the three men and showed footage of them standing outside on the steps of the court laughing and waving their hands in the air to their supporters. A reporter asked the men what they intended to do next and predictably one of them answered 'celebrate'. Brigid's three older brothers, Gerry, Sean and Liam all looked at each other and then Gerry nodded. Eileen had not seen this but Brigid had and knew that her brothers were not prepared to just let the murder of their father simply pass by. Brigid put her arm around her younger brother Declan Jr. who was sat beside her on the sofa and he then, in turn, rested his head on her shoulder.

The move by the Doyle brothers had, however, already been anticipated. DCI O'Neill paid a visit to the family home immediately after the end of the trial and expressed his sincere regret at the failures of the police service that had resulted in the judgement. He assured them, however, that the police were not going to give up and stressed the importance of not trying to take the law into their own hands. The same message came from Declan's party leadership but at the end of the day, everyone knew that the Doyles would not be able to just leave it. A little bit of asking around and the brothers knew which pub the 'celebration' would be taking place. Poetic justice they felt as they execute the men who did the same to their father.

But when the brothers arrived outside *The Railway* public house, armed police were ready for them. The brothers never even managed to see their targets before being surrounded and instructed to lay down their weapons. The gun battle that ensued was short and brutal.

Once more, DCI O'Neill visited the Doyle household. Not that he had to, but because he felt some sort of moral need. To describe it as being a difficult conversation was no understatement. How do you tell a woman who has recently seen her husband murdered in front of her that she has now also lost three of her sons - this time to the security forces? O'Neill attempted the impossible task. He explained that the police unit had tried to persuade them to give up but instead the brothers opened fire and injured one officer. The other officers had no choice but to return fire and put them down.

The reaction from Eileen and Brigid couldn't have been more different. Eileen was, understandably, overcome with grief but thought that solace would come from her remaining two children and through her faith. Brigid, however, felt that both the community and the Catholic Church had abandoned her family. Instead of grief, she found that she was overcome with an all-consuming fury - an overwhelming desperation and determination to invoke revenge. Not just on the three men that had murdered her father and caused the death of her three brothers but on the authorities and system that had failed them. She knew that the police were likely to be watching her and that her fiery temper had not gone unnoticed. To kill the men on her own would be difficult, if not impossible. She would have to bide her time but somehow she knew that her day would come.

Then, a year later, she met Connor Morgan in a Belfast bar. At first any sort of common ground seemed unlikely. After all, he was English and a protestant. Then she discovered that he had as much reason to hate the authorities as she did. Most men before him, had been completely besotted by her good looks and flamboyant personality but Connor wasn't easily manipulated and had a physical and mental strength that she came to admire and respect. They were good for each other. He was also very protective of her to an extent that Freud might have concluded that there was also a fatherly role being filled by him, which had been absent in her life. After just a short time into their relationship, Brigid felt able to tell him not only the terrible events that she had endured but also her desperate need for revenge.

'Revenge?' Connor had asked. 'Or justice?'

'Is there a difference?' she had replied.

'Well, often they are the same thing, I guess. But you are looking to right a wrong. To me, that's justice that you are after.'

Then Connor went on to explain that when he had been moved to Birmingham's category 'B' Prison after nearly beating a fellow in-mate to death, he had been approached to join a new group called '*Adalah*'. They promised him the justice that he *so* desperately wanted against the system that *so* completely failed his mother. There was just one compromise - the group was Islamic based. For Connor, this wasn't really much of a compromise. After all, his own religion had failed him and with that there was more common ground with Brigid who also felt that moving away from Catholicism was refreshing and empowering.

The leader of the group, Mohammed Baqri, met with them both and had promised two things. Firstly, that they would get the justice which they both so desperately wanted and secondly that they would become part of something powerful and world changing. Baqri explained that the group was different to other Islamic organisations in that its purpose was not to kill or punish those that did not conform to its perception of what Islam should be. Instead, its purpose was to bring together like minded people who were committed to punishing those criminals that had escaped justice - whether they were individuals or governments. Islam was just the instrument that would bring them together and would also be the glue that would bind them all as one family.

'Whereas Christianity talks of turning the other cheek, justice is an obligation in the Qur'an which says 'God commands justice and fair dealing. For those that carry it out in the name of God, a place in heaven awaits,' Baqri had explained.

In order to underline his point, he had asked Brigid to sit down in front of a tablet. On it, a live video was being streamed. She recognised the location - *The Railway* public house in Belfast. She watched as a silver BMW pulled up outside the pub. The camera zoomed in, and Brigid recognised the driver as the man who had grinned at her in the courtroom at the trial of her father's murder. Immediately, she felt complete and overwhelming hatred. She continued to watch as the other two men who had been on trial got into the car.

'These are the men who killed your father?' Baqri asked.
Brigid nodded.

At that, Baqri placed his mobile phone in front of her,
smiled and gestured towards the 'send' button. Brigid looked
at Baqri and realised what he was implying. As she pressed the
button an enormous blast ripped the car apart, completely dis-
assembling it and throwing the bonnet twenty feet into the air.
What remained of the car was engulfed in fire and the blast
had been so strong that a small crater had formed under it.

'God has granted you justice this day, Brigid,' said Baqri in
a soft voice.

A feeling of total euphoria swept over Brigid - a feeling
almost orgasmic and of such complete satisfaction that she had
never before felt in her life. She slumped back in her chair, at
the same time letting out a sigh but continuing to watch the
screen as if mesmerised by the flames. Connor looked at her
and smiled.

At that point, Baqri knew that Brigid and Connor were his
and he had plans for them both.

CHAPTER ELEVEN

At precisely 9.15am on the 6th June, the electric loading
bay shutters opened at the front of Unit 24 on the Sovereign
Business Park in London and Asif Farooqi drove a white Ford
Transit van out into bright sunshine, continuing away from
London and up the M1 motorway towards the north. His trip
was entirely expected by the Counter Terrorist Team following
a message from their informant, Alim Khan who confirmed
that Asif was collecting the missing items for the EMP -
though exactly which items he was not sure. All the
intelligence agencies knew the stakes could not have been
higher and what the potentially devastating consequences
could be if they failed to carefully monitor the *Adalah* terrorist
cell. Meticulous and thorough surveillance of every movement
in and out of the terrorist's base on the business park had been
treated as absolutely critical. Every time a member of the cell
had left to collect groceries, they were tracked by ground,
satellite and cctv surveillance until they returned. Details
including who left the building, when and where they went,
what they did and when they returned were all carefully logged.
No chances were now going to be taken at such a critical
moment in the operation and so Asif Farooqi's identity was

verified, and his every movement was carefully monitored. Even the CIA were following his van with one of their satellites.

At MI5 headquarters, the Counter Terrorist Team were watching the satellite images intensely and at just before 12 p.m. the white transit van arrived at a disused and neglected light industrial estate outside Birmingham. They continued watching as Asif Farooqi stepped out of the van, to be greeted by a group of nine men in two rows. The four men in the second row appeared to be armed with automatic weapons and from the front row, one man stepped forward and shook Asif's hand - a short stocky man with black crew cut hair but smartly dressed in a black suit with open white shirt.

'Can you get a close-up on him please?' Mac ordered to one of the MI5 support team. 'Benny the Bomb,' said Mac, as the camera zoomed in and focussed on the heavily lined face with a distinctive boxer's nose.

'Sorry? Did you say *Benny the Bomb*?' Tom asked quizzically as if he had mis-heard.

'Benny Erickson. I've been trying to get this guy for *so* many years that I developed a nickname for him. Scandinavian by birth and one of the world's foremost arms brokers. I've called him *The Bomb* because he specialises in supplying explosives, strangely enough. I really didn't expect him to have made a personal appearance though. Normally far too risky for someone at his level. I guess it shows how serious this is. He will have arranged the acquisition from the Iranians and that means the explosives will be top Russian made gear. He has a reputation to uphold, after all,' Mac continued with a contemptuous tone to his voice.

'How come you've never managed to catch him?' asked Tom.

'Difficult to arrest someone who lives on board a super yacht in International Waters under a Russian flag and has been given Russian citizenship. Their navy keeps a careful watch over him, as he has proved so useful to their goals. Having said that, this could now be the best chance that we have ever had to get him. A great opportunity for our secret service.'

'Looks like a couple of them are about to move the van,' interrupted Captain Jax. 'Into one of the industrial units by the looks of it,' he continued. 'Loading up the missing parts, I would imagine.'

'But which parts, is the sixty-four million dollar question?' said Sergeant Lang.

'Hopefully, we'll get a message from our man Khan about that one and then we will be in a better position to know what action to take next,' replied Mac.

The police informant within the group supplying the explosives, Kalim Khan, had already been notified by the surveillance team back in London of the van leaving *Adalah's* base on the business park. He knew that his mission to identify and report back what part or parts were being collected was critical to whether the security services waited until the EMP was made stable or to move against the terrorists now, knowing that the EMP could not be detonated.

73

As the van moved into one of the derelict industrial warehouse units, the terrorist group including Khan started walking towards a small office building.

'Come Asif. While they load up your van, have some refreshments with me,' Benny said, gesturing towards the door. 'I have a very nice bottle of Chateau Lafite Rothschild which I have been saving for a special occasion. I think this fits that definition - don't you? Or are you strict in your avoidance of alcohol?'

Asif laughed. 'Well, actually, I'm a lot less strict than many people I know. So, just the one glass would be very welcome. Thank you.'

After twenty minutes of wine and conversation later, the two men who had been loading the van opened the door and entered the office unit.

'It is loaded on the van and ready,' one of them said.

'Kalim.' Benny said pointing at Khan. 'Can you take Asif back to his van? Now the lens is on board, I imagine you will want to get on your way now, Asif?' Benny said re-directing his pointing finger to the general direction of the commercial unit that the van had moved into.

'Of course,' replied Khan and started walking back over with Asif behind him. As he was doing so, Khan realised the implication of what he had just been told - they didn't yet have a lens explosive for the EMP. His previous briefing with the security services had explained the workings of the EMP to him. *So*, he thought to himself, *this means that the EMP in*

London cannot yet be detonated. He felt excitement and fear at the same time. He had to get a message back as soon as possible.

Kalim watched as Asif Farooqi pulled the van out of the warehouse into the bright sunshine, driving out of the industrial estate and heading back down towards London. Time was of the essence. He now felt a huge burden on his shoulders and his stomach was doing summersaults. He quickly moved to a far corner of the warehouse to send a message back to MI5. Panic then set in, and he decided that this information was too important not to be received. Kalim took the risk to make a phone call. But just as he finished his call, he heard footsteps from the shadows and several figures walked out into the light.

'You disappoint me, Kalim,' said Benny. 'Did you not think that I know everything about everyone? Do you really think that I didn't know about you. That you are the little worm that would try and sell me out?' he continued angrily.

'Benny. I was just ...' Khan said, frantically trying to think of something.

'Oh ... no ... no ... no, Benny. Don't curse the boy. As it happens, he has completed his task ... perfectly,' said a man's voice coming from the shadows. Khan watched as a figure proceeded to flamboyantly walk, almost dance, around the corner as if he was a showman walking on to the stage. The man smiled at him, but it was still too dark for Khan to make out his face properly.

'He doesn't look like he knows who I am, Benny. Well, that's very disappointing,' he continued mockingly.

Khan looked confused and yet, at the same time, was more scared than he had ever been before in his life.

'Has Commander Malik not mentioned me at all? Your friend and mentor who managed to get you this job? Bet he has.'

Khan's face dropped as the man's face moved into the light.

'Dan-ahhh! Ding, ding, ding! He's just worked it out, Benny. You know who I am now, don't you?' The man said menacingly, with a broad grin on his face.

Khan slowly nodded in response. 'Yes,' he whispered.

'There you go. Or you can just call me ... the puppet master!' exclaimed the man, flinging his arms out to his side as if he was going to take a round of applause.

'But how...?'

'How? The Art of War, Kalim. The Art of War.'

CHAPTER TWELVE

It was now 1 p.m. and the anti-terrorist team had just received the message that Asif Farooqi was returning to London with an explosive lens.

'Something's not right,' said Tom looking down at the table in front of him.

Everyone looked at Tom and frowned. All except Mac, whose faced had more of an expression of concern than anything else.

'What do you mean Tom?' asked Mac.

'Something's not right,' Tom repeated. 'I've got a twitchy nose about this whole thing,' he continued as he watched the live satellite images of the terrorist's van being driven back down the motorway by Asif.

'One of Tom's many abilities, everyone, is his outstanding psycho-analytical abilities,' Mac said looking at the two soldiers and the two police officers. 'He has an exceptional talent of being able to get inside people's heads - a greater understanding of what makes people tick. So, when his *nose twitches*, then I get very nervous. Any idea what's behind this, Tom?'

'I don't know.' Tom said looking up. 'It's Baqri, I think. I've managed to find a little time to study him, in order to try and understand how his brain works. I know that you described him as being *unhinged*, Mac, which I would agree with to some extent - in that he clearly has some psychopathic tendencies. But he's also highly intelligent and is a very careful planner. He's a strategist at heart and one thing I found out, that was particularly interesting, is that he was a very highly respected chess player when he was younger. I have also discovered that he is a great scholar of history and in particular military campaigns and leaders. Yet, with this attack he has put all his eggs in one basket. He must know that there is a risk that it could fail and, if it does, then he has lost everything. There are very few people in the world with the ability to build such a large EMP as Dr Alim Farooqi. So, if the good doctor is caught or killed then they will become just another terrorist organisation. And Baqri wants it to be more than that. He wants to be the leader of an organisation that is known and feared throughout the world.'

'So, what are you getting at?' asked Commander Malik.

'I'm not really sure.' Tom paused and briefly looked down at the desk again while he thought. 'So, Baqri sends just one of his group to Birmingham to collect the explosive lens? The person he chooses is Asif Farooqi - the most passive person in their team and the least likely to be able to take care of himself if the collection turns nasty. Wouldn't you have sent someone like Connor or Sal with him?'

'Perhaps Baqri thought that keeping the majority of the group with the EMP in London was the priority?' said Superintendent Carson.

'Perhaps,' said Tom, popping yet another buttermint sweet into his mouth. 'But I'm not sure that's it. We're missing something. Baqri is the sort that has a reason for everything he does. So, when our man Kalim Khan sent a message back after Asif collected the explosives, what exactly did he say?'

'Well, he just confirmed that Asif had collected a lens explosive and was on his way back to London,' Mac replied.

'So, at the moment, we believe that Baqri's masterplan was to send Asif to collect the lens explosive from Birmingham and return to London. Farooqi then finishes the EMP and they all drive into central London to set it off?' Tom said frowning. 'Baqri has had years to plan this, and this is the best he can come up with?'

'Sounds like a normal, reasonable plan to me,' said Shelley Carson.

'The problem is they are not a normal terrorist organisation because they are being led by someone who thinks at a higher level than most. He enjoys the strategy and the game that he knows will follow. This is too simple for him,' Tom continued.

'Perhaps he just thinks a simple plan is the best one? Perhaps he's not the supreme strategist that you were expecting him to be?' said Malik.

'But this plan just doesn't match his profile. He's left himself wide open. In chess, the only time you do that is when it helps you win the bigger game,' Tom said and then paused for a minute before looking at Mac.

'Does it really matter? We clearly have a golden opportunity,' Commander Malik interrupted. 'If we intercept the van on the way back down to London, this all comes to an end with potentially zero casualties. We can even add a bonus to that and capture one of the biggest and most wanted arms brokers in the world. We should hit them now. I have a specialist armed police unit ready to intercept the van.'

'I have a second SAS team that can be in Birmingham within the hour and deal with Benny,' added Captain Jax.

'I have to say,' said Mac, rubbing his hands together, 'that would be an incredible result.'

'Makes sense to me,' said Jax. 'At the same time, we can carry out our original plan to take the rest of them out at the business unit before Asif returns with the van.'

Everyone else around the table nodded in agreement, except Tom who was staring at the table again.

'This feels like we are being led by the nose and that this path has been sign posted for us to go down. Does that make sense? Maybe I'm wrong. Correct that... I hope I'm wrong,' said Tom with a worried look on his face.

'Sometimes, people just make mistakes,' said Malik shrugging his shoulders. 'I think that Baqri has made one. But if we don't move on this now, then we will be the ones who will make a much, much bigger one and go down in history for all the wrong reasons.'

'Well, unless you can think of a really good reason why not Tom, then Operation Volta is a go. We need to move quickly. How long till the van makes it back?' Mac asked.

'About two hours and forty-five minutes, sir,' came Malik's reply, after just a short pause.

'OK. So, we need to do this in order. We need to complete the mission on Unit 24 before anything else. We can't risk Baqri and the rest of the terrorists being alerted. Then, Commander Malik, your team following the van can intercept Asif Farooqi and the SAS second team can move on Benny Erickson and his group up in Birmingham,' said Mac. 'Tom, even though we now know that the EMP is not yet active, it still has a significant amount of explosives in it which pose a major threat to life. So, I need you to get yourself ready to move in the next half an hour.

CHAPTER THIRTEEN

The plan that had been described by Captain Jax the previous day seemed to start perfectly as an MI5 officer, disguised as a courier, dropped off the fake parcel addressed to Unit 24 on the London business park. Tom then started walking over to the terrorists' building with the parcel in both hands but still with a strong gut feeling that something was badly wrong.

'*The location of the unit is perfect,*' thought Tom, as he found himself having to squint to see the building due to the dazzling sunshine coming over the roof from the east. '*Baqri had been meticulous in his planning - there was no doubt about that,*' he thought. '*Perhaps this was all a trap, and the security forces were being drawn into a kill zone? Using the sun to blind your enemies was successfully used by Alexander the Great and Baqri was a keen scholar of military history. Perhaps that's it. But then again, Baqri's plan would never be to conduct a gun fight with the security forces, which he would ultimately lose. So what was it?*'

With that final thought, he was at the front door of the building. A steel door with a lock to the left-hand side and intercom located beside that on the wall. Tom pressed the intercom's button. No reply. He pressed it again after a minute wait and still no reply. Tom looked up and was now able to see between the first-floor window blinds. '*The lights were on but where the hell is the lookout?*' he thought. The building sounded eerily quiet - surely, he should be able to hear some sort of noise from inside or through the vehicle entrance shutters to the left of the front door?'

'Mac, there's no one answering the intercom and I can't see any look-out on the first floor,' Tom whispered into his covert microphone. 'I'm placing the lock-pick.'

Within seconds, the electronic pick had done its work and he heard a click from the door unlocking and walked in, still with the parcel in his hands.

'Hello?' Tom called out at a level that would only likely be heard from someone in the CCTV reception room by the front door and possibly on the stairs. He called out again as he moved into the empty room. After placing the jamming device on top of the CCTV control box, Tom removed the Glock pistol and quietly made his way up the stairs.

'Mac. First floor is empty as is the reception area. I reckon the whole place is empty,' said Tom, walking back down the stairs to open the door for Captain Jax and his team.

It felt like just seconds before the SAS team rushed into the building with Sergeant Lang behind and then after checking each room in turn, Captain Jax declared the whole building was clear of any hostiles. This was followed by an MI5 team who started combing the unit for evidence as Tom walked back to the meeting area upstairs and occupied one of the seats that Baqri and his terrorist cell had been sat in some five hours earlier around the table. The chair that Tom had chosen was slightly larger than the others with the addition of leather arm rests - Baqri's chair he guessed. As he settled into his seat and waited for Mac to arrive, he closed his eyes and immersed himself in his surroundings, almost in a state of meditation. Whatever plan Baqri had discussed with his group had been done at the very same table that he was now sat at. *'What were you planning? Where are you going to with the EMP, Mohammed?'* Tom wondered, almost trying to re-wind time to five hours before. His deep thoughts were abruptly interrupted.

'Jesus Christ!' Mac shouted as walked into the room with two MI5 officers, his Glaswegian accent now strongly apparent. What the hell just happened?' He sat down opposite Tom with a furious look on his face. As he did so, Captain Jax entered the room appearing solemn.

'Sir, we have just received an update. The armed police unit following Asif Farooqi, have intercepted and arrested him,' said Jax.

'Well, that's something ... isn't it? Well, isn't it? Do I take it from your face that it's not all good news?'

'The explosive lens in the van appears to be fake. In addition, my second SAS team have just reported back that the derelict industrial park in Birmingham was deserted - Benny Erickson had already escaped before they got there. Seemed like they left in a hurry,' Jax continued.

'Christ Almighty! To say that this is a complete disaster is the bloody understatement of the Millennium!' Mac shouted, almost frothing at the mouth. 'Let's just re-cap where we thought we were and where we actually are now. An hour ago, we thought we had a group of terrorists contained in a unit in

84

London with an EMP device which could not yet be set off. We had one of their group on his way back with the explosive lens device, which we could easily intercept and we had one of the world's biggest arms brokers in Birmingham ready to be captured or killed. Our current position is that we have let the globally wanted arms broker escape, we have one of the terrorists in custody whom we can't even charge with being in possession of an explosive as it's a bloody fake ... oh ... and we have no fucking idea where the EMP is that will send Britain back to the dark ages! Is that a fair assessment?'

Jax looked down at the floor and just said 'I think that's a fair summary, yes sir.'

'Well, Tom, you were right. But before you say that you told us so, we need to catch up on the terrorists and quick. Now more than ever, we really need your genius level IQ. Where is Baqri and how the hell did he and his cell get out of here without us realising?' asked Mac.

Tom was now staring at the plasterboard partition wall that separated the office area from the toilets, seemingly ambivalent to Mac's tirade.

'Tom!' Mac barked, annoyed by what appeared to be Tom's emotional detachment from the grave situation that they now found themselves in.

'A more important question, Mac, really should be this. What is their target location to set off the EMP?' he replied in a calm, serene voice. 'Am I right in saying that you tracked every movement in and out of this building?'

'We did, yes. Who left, when and where they went - all logged.' Mac replied, returning to his usual much more controlled tone of voice, having realised that Tom was actually ahead of him with the problem.

'Good. This should be quick then. I want to know if, at any time since they occupied the building, they visited a newsagents or stationers or anywhere else where they could have bought a map.' Tom stood up and walked around the table to the wall. 'If they did, I want a copy of every map of London that they sell,' he continued, as he examined four small holes in the plasterboard wall in the shape of a rectangle and then moved his finger to a slightly larger hole in the middle which seemed to have pen ink around it. 'And some drawing pins please.' he added.

Mac turned around and nodded at one of the MI5 officers stood behind him.

'Make it quick ... really quick!' ordered Mac.

As that officer left the room in some haste, Staff Sergeant Lang and Commander Malik walked in.

'Absolutely no clues on the EMP. This place has been cleaned from top to toe. They did leave a couple of things behind for you, though,' said Lang placing the objects on the table in front of where Tom was standing. 'A book and a packet of buttermints,' he continued.

Tom picked up the book and looked at its front cover. 'The Art of War,' Tom said with the faintest of smiles, as he then opened it to the inside cover. 'To Tom. Good luck! Mohammed.'

'How the hell does he know about you? You're an invisible agent for God's sake. No one knew about you until yesterday,' Mac said incredulously and now really feeling that the intelligence agencies were not the ones in control. 'He's toying with us! This guy has really got some ego!'

'How he knows about me is a good question and we can only conclude that Baqri has received inside information. He undoubtedly gets a buzz from this but, as always with him, there is a tactical reason for what he does. He knows that this will create mistrust between the different anti-terrorist agencies as we are now forced to search for the leak and that in turn means communication will be severely compromised between the security services. He also knows that we will have to divert some of our resources to investigate,' said Tom turning to a marked page of Sun Tzu's famous book, where he then saw a couple of lines which had been highlighted in yellow. 'If you are near the enemy, make him believe you are far from him. If you are far from the enemy, make him believe you are near,' Tom said reading aloud.

'Sorry?' said Sergeant Lang.

'Sun Tzu suggested that all war was based on deception,' Tom said looking at Mac who was now nodding.

'Our information that Asif was leaving this unit on his own to make an important collection in Birmingham and then return, was based on information that we received from our informant, Kalim Khan. Previously, we had received numerous bits of information from Khan regarding Baqri and his group which all proved to be correct and valid. This supported our thinking that we had a strong and undetected information source, but it seems that Baqri knew who Kalim really was and had been feeding him the information via Benny. For example, we received information of a small attack that was planned for Manchester and as a result we managed to prevent it. It seems this was all carefully managed by Mohammed Baqri,' said Mac.

'So, when Asif left in the van, apparently on his own, this fitted completely with the information that had been received from Khan and meant that the intelligence services had no reason to doubt it. As it happens, they had already loaded the EMP into the van and Baqri would have been in the back with rest of his group and out of view,' Tom continued.

'*Let your plans be as dark and as impenetrable as night, and when you move, fall like a thunderbolt,*' Jax said staring straight ahead and yet as if he was reading from the book.

Everyone in the room stopped what they were doing and looked at each other.

'I have a copy of that at home,' Jax explained.

'I am hoping that when your officer returns Mac, I might have a better idea of where, but the other question is <u>when</u> will they attack?' Tom said breaking the silence. 'Everything that Baqri does has a purpose. And everything in his plan is connected. So, let's start at the beginning. Why has he chosen today to make his attack? 6th of June - Why? What's the significance? Is there something in the Islamic calendar that is significant?' asked Tom looking at Commander Malik. 'Was there some terrible event in the past or perhaps it's an important religious date?'

'Not that I can think of,' said Malik.

'6th of June. 6th of the 6th. What's the connection?'

'Well, the only thing I can think of is 666. There are some Muslims who claim 66 is a holy number in Islam. Actually, the number of Allah – through cryptic numerology. But there's only the two 6's, so that doesn't make sense. Some Islamic scholars don't even believe it is a holy number anyway,' Malik continued.

'I don't think Baqri is particularly bothered about the thoughts of Islamic scholars. If it fits his purpose, then ...' Mac said shrugging his shoulders.

'I thought 666 was an evil number?' said Sergeant Lang.

'Well, that's a Christian belief. In Islam, there are some that think it was the devil that tricked Christians into believing it is an evil number when it is the number of the Quran and perhaps even the profit Mohammed. But most Islamic religious teachers don't accept that the use of numbers have any relation to the Quran,' said Malik.

'6 o'clock,' Tom whispered under his breath.

'Sorry? Did you say something Tom?' asked Mac.

'6 o'clock.' Tom repeated in a much louder voice so that everyone could hear. 'I think he means to set it off at 6 o'clock. 6pm on the 6th of the 6th. That's the date that Baqri wants to go down in history.'

'I don't see how that makes sense, Tom. Sorry to rain on your parade but why would you wait till 6pm to set off the EMP? Most of the working day is done then and if he wants to affect the British economy then wouldn't you do it at the start of the day?' said Mac.

'True. I could be wrong, but I think 6 o'clock ties in with his plan somehow. Admittedly, I don't know why yet.'

'I guess the number 666 would be quite ironic in Baqri's mind. The number of the beast in the bible and all of that,' said Staff Sergeant Lang.

'Actually, it's a bit deeper than just a number given to the anti-christ. There's another reason why I think we are onto something here. If you read the section in Book of Revelations from the Bible it says *Let him who has understanding calculate the number of the beast, for the number is that of a man; and his number is 666.* Now, that passage would originally have been written in Ancient Greek and a bit like in Roman, letters were also used as numbers,' Tom said as he started walking around the table.

'So, V is five and X is ten you mean?' said Jax.

'Exactly. Now the text says that the number is that of a man. As it happens, I read an article on this a few years ago and scholars of the time have worked out that the number 666 spells out Nero Caesar in Ancient Greek. The number of the beast is, therefore, that of the Emperor when Britain was occupied by the Romans. In fact, Londinium as it was known then, only consisted of what is now the square mile of the City of London where, of course, most of our financial institutions are now based. I reckon this is where Baqri intends to hit. During Nero's reign, Londinium suffered from huge violent clashes between the ancient Britons and the Romans and was at one point burnt to the ground. I think this is what Baqri hopes to replicate.'

'But Baqri's a Muslim, isn't he? Why would he want to relate to Christian text,' ask Jax.

'He's not really a practicing Muslim – just pretends to be mainly for the benefit of Sal Usman and others,' said Mac.

'More of a scholar than anything else,' added Tom, pulling out his seat again and sitting down. Silence filled the room as everyone considered Tom's theory, but it wasn't long before the MI5 officer tasked with finding the map of London burst back into the room, with something in his hand.

'Big stationers just outside the business park,' said the MI5 officer, panting slightly, having sprinted from his car and up the stairs. 'Good news is that they only sell the one map of London, sir, and the manager there remembers Brigid Doyle buying a copy. *Hard to forget her with those looks* was his exact words. He also remembers the knot tattoo at the base of her neck, when she turned around to leave his shop,' the officer said as he handed the map over to Tom with a box of drawing pins. Tom stood up again and walked around the table to the plasterboard wall where he pinned the map up using yellow pins, utilising the same four corner holes that were already there. Feeling around the centre he then found the slightly larger hole and inserted a red drawing pin.

'St Paul's Cathedral,' said Mac, slumping back into his seat. 'Jesus Christ, he's going to set it off outside St. Paul's Cathedral. Commander Malik, I need you to put a two-mile police cordon around that location.

'Straight away,' said Malik turning on his heels. 'I'll update Superintendent Carson, who is the Ground Commander. She'll take personal charge.'

CHAPTER FOURTEEN

Kalim Khan looked blankly at the man stood in front of him - the last person he expected to see.

'The Art of War?' said Baqri with a look of despair starting to appear on his face. 'Sun Tzu's book? No? Wow!' he exclaimed with a tone of incredulity. 'The education in this country just isn't what it used to be, Benny.' he continued, shaking his head at Benny Erickson. 'All warfare is based on deception, Kalim. In our case, the British secret service now think, thanks to you, that we are still in London with an inoperative EMP and that we have the explosive lens heading down the motorway. In fact, we had another vehicle already hidden here which now has the EMP on board and will shortly be fully operational after we have finished fitting the lens explosive.'

'So, Asif brought up the EMP from London? With you in the back?' said Khan.

'Correct. At some point, the security services will intercept the original van driven by Asif and find that the lens explosive inside it isn't even real. Oh, how I would love to be a fly on the wall at MI5 then,' Baqri said excitedly, rapidly clapping his hands. 'I can just see Deputy Director McGregor now - *'Jesus Christ! What the hell just happened? You're all bloody useless,'* he continued, trying to do his best Scottish accent. Baqri roared with laughter at his own joke.

Kalim's head dropped as he stared at the floor, now feeling a sense of terrible failure and deep guilt that the information he had supplied to MI5 would be instrumental in the disaster that was about to befall Britain's capital.

'But you're going to kill innocent people - including Muslims. You know that is forbidden in the Quran, don't you?' said Kalim, looking up and staring at Baqri.

'The Quran also requires us to protect the Islamic faith and punish those that commit sins against it. Those Muslims that die today will become martyrs, as we carry out the will of God.'

'The sins are going to be when *you* murder the innocent!' exclaimed Kalim.

'Innocent? I would hardly describe the British people as that. They are complicit in the crimes of their government.'

'Do you honestly …'

'Well, as much as I've enjoyed our little debate about the Islamic faith, we can't stand about chatting all day,' interrupted Baqri, as his face changed to a feigned look of sadness and with his mouth turned down in an exaggerated manner. 'So, thank you for the great service that you have done for us, but we have a holy calling to fulfill. Alas your part in this magnificent show has now come to an end.'

As he finished his last words, a slim figure dressed all in black, with a gaunt face and deep-set eyes appeared behind Kalim Khan and in one slow but precise action, pulled a knife across the throat of the MI5 operative from ear to ear. Kalim grabbed his throat with both hands and gasped for breath as blood gushed between his fingers. It took less than a minute for him to collapse to the ground and die, with his hands still around his throat and a wide-eyed look of shock on his face. A large pool of blood had surrounded his head on the concrete floor as Sal leant over the body and wiped the knife on Khan's shirt, with no sign of any emotion on his face.

'Sorry but I was getting bored,' said Baqri looking over at Benny Erickson and shrugging his shoulders.

'Alim is just finishing off fitting the EMP into the ambulance with the help of Brigid and Connor and it should be ready to leave in about five minutes,' said Sal. 'I don't understand why we are not going with them?'

'Ah, the ambulance. I bet that wasn't what you expected to see?' said Baqri. 'Specially adapted to conceal the EMP and to the layman will look no different from any other. We will be leaving well before the rest of them, by the way.'

Sal looked at him quizzically, clearly expecting a better explanation than the one he had just been given.

'My friend, we are not going with them because we have another target, which I felt Alim may not be entirely comfortable with. I wasn't sure that Connor would have been comfortable with it either. Anyway, I do, however, trust Connor to deliver the EMP to its target and Alim to ensure its successful detonation. Connor is, as you know, small in brain but big in heart and he will want to support Brigid in what she so desperately wants to do, which is to bring Britain to its knees. Once they have detonated the EMP, what I have then planned for us will inflict a wound so deep, that Britain will carry the images of it forever,' Baqri crowed.

This was like music to the ears for Sal, who allowed himself a rare, ever so slight, smile. The original plan, he felt, was impressive enough but it seemed that Mohammed Baqri was every bit the exceptional leader that he had hoped he would be, and that just crippling Britain for years was not enough for him.

'Waterloo train station sits within the one-mile immediate radius effect of the EMP,' Baqri continued. 'Britain's busiest railway station with an average of a quarter of a million travellers using it every day. At around 5.45pm, the ambulance will arrive near St Pauls Cathedral and at 6pm they will set off the EMP. Now, thanks to Benny, we also have a special Land Cruiser SUV which is both armoured and adapted to withstand the EMP blast. This has been packed out with Semtex. We will drive it down to Waterloo and park up outside the front of the station arriving just after the EMP has been set off. We then move to a safe distance and in the general direction of the river. As you know, it is only a five to ten minute walk from the train station to the bridge.'

Sal nodded.

'We detonate the explosives and escape via the river where a boat will be waiting,' Baqri said as if his plan should start making sense.

'No, I still don't get it,' said Sal. 'All those people will be inside the station. Even with an SUV packed out with explosives, that's not likely to kill many, if any, of them inside the station, is it?'

'You're quite right, Sal. Except, that you've forgotten one very important thing,' Baqri continued, holding a single finger up. There has just been a massive EMP detonation. The electrical interruption to the system at Waterloo will inevitably mean that the trains and control room will be rendered unoperational. So, what will the passengers do when they find that the trains aren't working, and neither is the underground?'

'They will start leaving the station to try and find taxis and buses, I guess,' replied Sal.

'Exactly,' said Baqri with more than just a hint of excitement in his voice. 'It's peak travel time - rush hour for all those passengers trying to get home. All those people will start assembling at the front of the station but will then find that even the buses and most of the taxis aren't working. Thousands of them all packed together right in front of the SUV. I will then use a remote device to explode the bomb in the Land Cruiser.'

Another faint smile now appeared over Sal's face as he appreciated the genius of his leader's plan.

'But the police will know we are coming. Or at least they know that the EMP attack is coming. Won't they have blocked off all the streets?'

'You should have more faith in me, Sal,' Baqri said with a broad grin on his face. 'Firstly, they don't know where the attack will be. They simply don't have the resources to block every street in London.' Baqri paused for a moment. 'Once the

EMP has arrived at its destination and then detonated, the security services will be left completely helpless. So, our first job is to ensure that Connor, Brigid and Alim reach their target.'

'You mean, by using the ambulance?' asked Sal trying to keep up with Baqri's plan. 'Are you sure the police won't stop it though, even if it is an ambulance?'

'Oh, I'm pretty sure that it will be ushered through without any problems. Brigid has a little collection to do on the way down to St Paul's Cathedral which will ensure that. Then, once the EMP has been detonated, we will be able to drive through the police roadblocks and there will be nothing that they can do about it.'

'Because their cars won't work, right?'

'Well done, Sal. But our Land Cruiser has been specially adapted. Don't forget, that the security services will also have their hands full with another issue. You may remember that at our briefing back on the business park, I mentioned that our brothers and sisters in *Adalah* will be on social media today, encouraging looting and rioting once the EMP has detonated? The police and security forces will be completely occupied just trying to maintain order. So, let ... anarchy ... reign!' said Baqri laughing and outstretching his arms to the side again.

Sal nodded his approval once again. 'But what about Alim though? He has always said that he is only doing this to cripple Britain for what they did to his family. I'm sure he would never have agreed to build the EMP if he thought that was also going to involve the deaths of civilians.'

'Well, yes. I think that is certainly true,' said Baqri, with a sheepish grin. 'He was one of only a few people in the world that could have built that EMP but he does have one little fault. I can confirm that, after much investigating, Doctor Farooqi is without a spine. So, I felt that it was probably best that the good doctor doesn't know what we are going to do. May Allah protect me from the wrath of an angry nerd, if he should ever find out,' continued Baqri mockingly.

'But he will though. Eventually, I mean. And if you want him to help you on more attacks in the future, he might not be so keen now.'

'Well, sometimes people just need the right motivation, Sal. Don't worry, we have secured the right motivation for Dr Farooqi to provide his skills for future targets,' Baqri continued with a smile.

Sal decided not to probe any further.

'Sal, there is one more thing that I would like you to do. When we detonate the bomb outside Waterloo train station, I want you to record the deaths of all those people, so that we can upload it later once we can get an internet connection. Their sacrifice that we have been forced to make, for the whole world to see. Let them all witness the justice that has been carried out on this day. Governments around the world will fear us and those that have committed crimes and thought that they had escaped justice will realise that they haven't, and their time of reckoning is near. The lives of these people will be forfeited for the crimes of their governments,' said Baqri fervidly, raising a fist in the air.

CHAPTER FIFTEEN

It was 4pm and the short journey back to MI5 headquarters had been both rapid and fairly uneventful. Like some ominous prediction of future events, the sky had now turned dark grey, and the first splatters of rain started to appear on the windscreen of the Secret Service's black Range Rover. As Mac made a succession of frantic calls on his mobile phone from the back of the car, Tom gazed out through the blacked-out glass at the reflection of the flashing blue lights from the windows of all the parked cars as their convoy of secret service, army and police vehicles sped past. At one point, the convoy briefly came to a halt while the heavy traffic attempted to move out of the way and Tom watched the swarms of people going about their normal daily lives and wondered how they would cope if everything that they were used to suddenly stopped. No electricity, no internet, no access to money, no means of travel and no work to go to, as their offices in the City would certainly be left as non-functional concrete monoliths. In fact, the City of London would become a desolate, deserted forest of buildings - like a scene out of an apocalyptic movie. Those same people now began running for cover as the splatters of rain started turning into a heavier downpour and amongst them Tom spotted a woman who was the spitting image of his wife, Luna.

Luna. Why had he not thought about her all day? It just didn't seem right. He reached into his right trouser pocket and took out his car keys again. Attached to it was the square brown leather fob which she had given to him the previous Christmas. Tom opened the popper and inside was a small photo of Tom and Luna in a group hug with their daughters, taken on one of their most favourite holidays at the shores of Lake Como in Italy. He gazed at the photo, remembering that special moment and was briefly, so very briefly, back there again. *God, he loved them.*

Tom's thoughts were snapped back to the current crisis as he became aware that Mac was now having a very uncomfortable call with MI5 Director, Sir Nicholas Meads, and was trying to explain how, with what appeared to be a straightforward plan, the mission had gone awry and, at the same time, the situation had become much more complicated. Tom contemplated his nemesis, Mohammed Baqri. It was clear that, for Baqri, it was more than just an attack on the British capital that he was looking for. The 'good luck' note in the copy of *The Art of War* that he had left for Tom suggested that he was looking forward to a battle of wits and the packet of buttermints was probably designed to side track the Secret Service by making it clear that he had detailed inside knowledge. The question still remained as to how exactly Baqri knew about him in the first place and who had been providing the information.

Now back at MI5 headquarters, Tom was again at the Operations Room table, with his black suit jacket hanging off his seat, and found himself staring in a meditative state at the bank of monitors, all of which were still displaying the MI5 logo.

'Sorry, Mac. What did you say again?' asked Tom.

'I said, where the hell is Baqri?' Mac repeated, bending forward and placing his hands on the table.

'Well, that was what I was trying to work out,' Tom said picking up the pen in front of him and then scribbling frantically on a pad of paper. 'I can only conclude that he was in the van with the rest of the cell and the EMP when Asif drove to Birmingham. It was the only time that they could all have left in one go.'

'But the SAS team that raided the industrial site in Birmingham found no one there and the only vehicle to leave the site was the van that Asif was driving back down to London, which we intercepted. We know he didn't stop anywhere on the way because our satellite was tracking every move that he made,' Mac said now shaking his head.

Tom continued scribbling on the pad, circling headings and drawing arrows down to the next box on his page.

'Well then, the only logical answer to that is that it wasn't the only vehicle to leave the Birmingham site. So, Baqri must have left after Asif and before the SAS team arrived. We know that Asif leaving in the van to go back down to London was a decoy and so they must be using a second vehicle,' said Tom.

'A second vehicle.' Mac repeated. 'A second vehicle which we have absolutely no idea what it looks like, you mean? Unfortunately, as I said, our satellite which was watching over the site was repositioned, since we believed that the van had the EMP on board.'

'Baqri hoped that we would. Worth sacrificing his pawn in the game - Asif I mean. He got us to waste valuable time raiding a business unit with no one in it and then reposition our main means of tracking them, leaving us completely clueless. You can't fault his strategy,' said Tom with a hint of admiration in his voice.

'Well, there's got to be some way of finding him,' Mac said and then paused briefly until the look on his face changed to a 'eureka moment.'

'The CIA, however ... I would be surprised if they hadn't also positioned a satellite over there as they are so desperate to get their hands on Benny Erickson.'

Tom stared at Mac and then slowly nodded. 'You're right. That would make sense.'

Mac reached for the telephone beside him on the meeting table, at the same time as Staff Sergeant Lang and Captain Jax walked into the room.

'Where's Commander Malik?' asked Tom.

'Detained,' said Mac as he replaced the phone on to its base, following a very brief conversation with his assistant. 'We have taken Commander Malik into custody on suspicion of giving away classified information. And before you say anything, Tom, it's not just because he's the only Muslim member of the team. Photographs have turned up of Malik with an associate of Mohammed Baqri.'

'How very convenient,' Tom said sarcastically. 'So, we now have the Head of Anti-Terrorism for the Metropolitan police locked up at the same time as the most devastating weapon ever used on Britain is heading straight into the capital.'

'Tom, we've got a leak. Fact. We can't risk word of our movements getting to Baqri. Malik's a risk. Anyway, Superintendent Carson has now taken charge and she's already there on the ground.' said an irritated Mac.

Mac didn't have to wait long before the phone rang.

'MacGregor.' he answered curtly. 'Oh, yes of course,' he continued in a more amenable tone and at the same time straightening his posture as if he was on parade.

'Good afternoon, Prime Minister,' Mac said after a slight pause. 'Yes, sir. As I said to Sir Nicholas earlier, we believe that St Paul's Cathedral is where they intend to set the EMP off. There's already a police cordon around central London and the army are now arriving to support them.'

As the Prime Minister spoke again, Mac's face changed and he pulled back a chair opposite Tom, slowly lowering himself into it. His eyes widened and Tom noticed him physically swallowing as he stared at the table. Mac then looked up, directly at Tom as if he would understand from his physical gestures exactly what the Prime Minister had just said.

'I see, Prime Minister. Yes, sir. I understand,' he continued before replacing the phone back on its base. 'The cabinet have decided that if this Iran sponsored act of terrorism is successful, then they will have no option but to respond militarily. They have decided that their first response will be for the Royal Navy to launch a massive missile attack on Tehran - effectively levelling the main part of the city. If Iran retaliates then the Navy will be instructed to up the ante.'

'How the hell to you up the ante on levelling a capital city?' asked Tom.

'Bigger and more powerful missiles. That includes the possibility of using nuclear weapons and he said that the probability of that happening is greater than we might think. You remember that the Prime Minister had a naval task force re-directed when we first got wind of this attack? Well, there's two nuclear subs in that group and they will shortly be within striking distance of Tehran.'

'Jes-us.' said Sergeant Lang in a particularly broad East London accent. 'Trouble is that he was elected by the people based on his hard man, take no crap attitude. I don't think there has been any other British Prime Minister in history more likely to authorise a nuclear strike than this guy. Do you know what? I reckon he'll do it.'

'I agree,' said Jax. 'Remember when he authorised HMS Daring to shoot down those Iranian fighter planes just for flying a bit too close to one of our oil tankers?'

'The thing is, he's not like most of the rest of his cabinet. He's not been educated at an elite private school, nor has he been to university. Instead, he has worked his way up from humble beginnings on a West Yorkshire council estate to becoming a world respected titan of British industry and

104

making his first million before the age of 21 - with a ruthless reputation thrown in,' said Tom.

Lang said, 'Well you don't get the nickname of Bob 'The Hatchet' Hatcher for no reason, do you?'

'Well, gentlemen,' said Mac rising to his feet again. 'I don't believe it is an exaggeration to say that millions of lives could be at stake if we fail to stop Baqri setting that EMP off.'

The brief silence that followed was abruptly interrupted by the phone ringing again. Mac picked it up swiftly - perhaps hoping that the Prime Minister had had a change of heart regarding Britain's response.

'Yes? Great!' exclaimed Mac reaching again for the remote control and lowering the overhead screen. 'Can you relay the images directly to the Operations Room please?'

'Some good news at last Mac?' said Tom.

'Well, something anyway. The CIA did have a satellite over the Birmingham site which continued surveillance after Asif left with the van. It was repositioned when Benny Erickson made his escape but apparently it was there long enough to capture the images of a second vehicle leaving about half an hour after Asif.'

Sure enough, as the anti terrorist team watched the screen, the video re-play showed a silver Land Cruiser SUV emerging from one of the buildings. The camera zoomed in, and the faces of Mohammed Baqri and Usman Salah were perfectly clear to the extent that Tom wondered whether they had either just been careless due to being arrogantly confident or their actions to be seen were deliberate. *If it was the latter, then for what purpose? At any rate it was them. They now knew exactly what vehicle the terrorists were driving and so surely their capture before they could set off the EMP was a certainty,* he concluded.

'Got ya!' shouted Mac. He sprung to his feet. 'Right then. Update Superintendent Shelley Carson on the details of the Land Cruiser and tell her to instruct all personnel to take no chances - shoot on site. That vehicle is not to get past the cordon,' Mac said looking round at his assistant standing behind him. 'I also want half hourly updates from her to include anything even remotely unusual. Plus, I want the London CCTV Control Centre to carefully monitor every road from the North of London heading towards St Paul's Cathedral. I want that vehicle found, and I want to know every move it makes. I'm going to update Sir Nicholas Meads and the Prime Minister. At last, it looks like we are on top.'

Tom looked at the large digital clock on the wall. It was now 4.30pm. According to the satellite footage, Baqri had left the site in Birmingham at 1.30pm. *Three hours had gone by since he left ... three whole hours. The terrorist cell could have made it to London in that time ... and probably have. God, that cordon around central London had better be tight. But Baqri would have surely predicted this response - wouldn't he?*

Tom felt his stomach churning and that horrible feeling now returned that things were not as positive as they first seemed.

CHAPTER SIXTEEN

The fourteen members of the government 'COBRA' committee sat in silence around the long rosewood table in the Cabinet Office briefing room at Number 10 Downing Street during the phone call between the Prime Minister and the Deputy Director of MI5, Iain McGregor. Nothing verbally was said but the nervous glances around the table when the matter of a nuclear response was mentioned meant no words were necessary.

'Prime Minister, with respect, we haven't actually agreed the use of nuclear weapons,' said the Defence Secretary, Tony Dawes, as the Prime Minister placed the phone back on to its base and realising that the rest of the cabinet were all now looking at him with alarmed looks on their faces.

'Do you think we should just take it then, Tony? Bend over for the Iranians and grit our teeth perhaps?' replied Prime Minister Bob Hatcher.

'Well, I'm not saying that we...'

'I'll tell you what, Tony. That's not happening on my watch. These types of countries respect only one thing. Strength. This country has become a soft touch. The British Empire was feared and respected throughout the world as a power not to be messed with. But now, we have become a timid nation with scared diplomats and politicians. If another country kills one of our citizens, then these days we just ask them very politely if they would mind not doing it again. Instead, we should be inflicting a degree of pain on them, such that they wouldn't dare think about doing it again and neither would any other country. Speak softly and carry a big stick the motto goes but what they should have added to that is you should be prepared to use that big stick,' interrupted Hatcher, clearly irritated but what he perceived to be the weakness of his Defence Secretary.

'This attack is coming from a terrorist organisation though, not Iran itself,' replied Dawes, trying to restore some degree of respect in front of his cabinet colleagues after his verbal mauling.

'Don't try and feed me that crap, Tony,' the Prime Minister swiftly retorted. 'We know Iran is behind this. They're as guilty as the terrorists. It might as well be Iran's Revolutionary Guard that's trying to detonate the EMP bomb in London. When we first discovered this plot, we warned the Iranian Government of the consequences, did we not?' said Hatcher looking at each person in turn at the table, who one by one nodded in agreement. 'What message does it send out if we don't back up our warnings with action? Look, I don't want to use nuclear weapons if I can help it but if they respond by attacking our navy task force after we hit Tehran, then they need to know that there is no scenario where this is going to give them a happy ending.'

Dawes sat back in his leather seat and stared at the one word scribbled on the pad in front of him which he had underlined multiple times - Nuclear. He now felt completely powerless, and it was clear that there was no turning the Prime Minister from his mind-set. Hatcher had always been a difficult man to manage and his reputation for belligerence was well founded. Often compared to a Yorkshire Terrier by the British press not just because of his county of origin, diminutive stature and centre parted brown hair but also because of his relentless and tenacious nature. After three years in power, Hatcher's hair was more grey now than brown but time had not blunted his sharp tongue. His relentless and aggressive yet patriotic style of leadership was though, at the end of the day, the main reason why the Conservative Party had won the last general election and why they were now in power.

'Geraldine, can we have an update on the evacuation of friendlies from Tehran and the American support please?' asked Hatcher, loosening his tie and adjusting his position in his seat so that he could look more directly at the Foreign Secretary.

'Most countries have managed to either evacuate all their nationals or are near to completing the process, Prime Minister. The American Fifth Fleet is expected to join the Royal Navy Carrier Group later this evening,' replied Geraldine Mathews.

'The US fleet includes the aircraft carrier USS Theodore Roosevelt, two missile cruisers, five missile destroyers and two nuclear submarines amongst others. They will be joining our carrier there, HMS Queen Elizabeth, three of our new type 45 destroyers and six frigates. Quite an Armada, which will be able to handle anything that Iran throws back at them. The Queen Elizabeth has thirty-six of the latest F35 fighter bombers and the Roosevelt has forty-nine various fighters on board,' added Dawes.

'See. I told you we would be using the *Big Stick!*' exclaimed Hatcher.

Both Hatcher and Dawes exchanged a rare smile before realising that everyone else around the table looked either confused or were providing a polite smile which still conveyed their lack of understanding of Hatcher's joke.

'Sorry.' said Dawes looking at his cabinet colleagues. 'For those that don't know, the USS Theodore Roosevelt is nicknamed *The Big Stick*. Not just because in military terms it is a big stick but because the quote *speak softly and carry a big stick* is attributed to President Roosevelt.'

Hatcher was fortunate to have a particularly strong friendship with President Monroe of the United States, which brought the 'special relationship' between America and Britain even closer. Monroe had also been a major figure in the business world, after inheriting a small family oil business and then taking it to become a major global corporation. Hatcher and Monroe had collaborated on several profitable ventures together during their time in business, which inevitably concluded with celebratory drinking sessions at various respectable and not so respectable venues. With Iran as the target, it was not a particularly difficult decision for President Monroe to agree to provide military support when asked.

'Prime Minister. Could I just ask what Russia's response is likely to be. It doesn't seem like we have discussed their reaction yet and I really think we should. I can't imagine that they will take the attack on their main ally in the Middle East particularly well,' said MI5 Director, Sir Nicholas Meads. Just like his understudy, Iain McGregor, Sir Nicholas Meads was dressed in what seemed to be the standard issue blue pin stripe suite with white shirt but with an Eton old school tie. A portly man with a slightly chubby face and bald head, save the closely trimmed patches of hair on either side. Looking over his half moon spectacles, Sir Nicholas looked almost Churchill like in appearance.

'Russia has indicated that it would regard the attack on Tehran to be an unacceptable hostile act - especially as it says that Britain has failed to provide irrefutable evidence that Iran is behind a planned bombing of London. They have concluded that this is just being used as an excuse to allow the US to cripple a country that they have always hated,' said Geraldine Mathews.

'I'm not sure what irrefutable proof looks like.' said Dawes. 'Even if we had the President of Iran on television admitting that they were behind the attack, the Russians would probably say that he was only doing so under duress.'

'Excuse me, Prime Minister. I have President Petrov on the line,' said the slightly built man sat to Hatcher's left.

Hatcher looked at the Cabinet Secretary, Sir Peter Hayward and nodded.

'Speak of the devil and he doth appear,' said Hatcher looking around the table before taking the phone. 'President

Petrov. How are you?' he continued, with the distinct air that he was not actually interested. 'I see. Yes, you have made yourself perfectly clear President Petrov. Now let me return the favour. I come from an area in England called Yorkshire. Oh, you've heard of it. Well, as a Yorkshireman, Mr President, you should know that we have a reputation for speaking very plainly. We call a spade, a spade - it helps save any confusion. So, I'm going to tell you straight. If that bomb goes off in London, I will level the government quarter of Tehran. If they then retaliate, I will level the whole city. So, I suggest rather than trying to use Russian citizens as a sort of human shield, you should evacuate them immediately. If you don't, then their deaths will be on you. You have been given plenty of warning and I am reiterating it to you again - get your people out. By the way, I've also put an exclusion zone around the fleet. Should any of your aircraft fly into that zone then our fleet has been authorised to shoot them down. President Monroe has also given the same instruction to the American Fifth Fleet.'

Prime Minister Hatcher leaned forwards in his leather seat, gripping the phone tightly.

'I'm not the one risking nuclear war, Mr President. You can help prevent any military conflict just by persuading the Iranians to stop the attack on London. I'm pretty sure you wouldn't let an attack on Moscow go unanswered, would you? So, please don't expect anything less from us. You seem to suggest that Iran may not be behind it and it's just a rogue terrorist group, but we know they are and so do you. I am not going to play that game, Mr President. If that bomb goes off, there will be a devastating response - make no mistake.'

CHAPTER SEVENTEEN

Tom's gut feeling was correct once again, as Baqri and Sal had already arrived some fifty minutes earlier at the safe house in London, having carefully avoided any town centres and CCTV cameras, thanks to a well researched map of their locations. The house itself was situated just outside the CCTV monitoring zone and Baqri had taken the precaution of getting Sal to park the SUV in the garage to avoid detection. Not being sure how many satellites would be monitoring the Birmingham meeting, Baqri had felt it prudent for the ambulance to leave the site last. By making himself visible in the SUV, he hoped that any focus from Secret Service surveillance would be on him and with blacked out windows in the rear, he was confident that the assumption would be made that all the remaining members of his unit would be with him - which in turn meant that the Security Services would not be looking for a third vehicle.

At the same time as Tom and the anti-terrorist team were speeding back to MI5 headquarters, the ambulance carrying the EMP had reached its destination in Camden, North London and parked up. The rain had now reached the point where it was so heavy that, from inside the ambulance, it sounded like a loud drum roll was being performed on the roof. Brigid looked across at Connor in the rear of the ambulance, having spent the last few minutes checking her bobbed red hair and make-up and ensuring her jeans and white buttoned top showed off her slim but curvaceous body to its maximum effect.

'How do I look?' she asked in a raised voice, trying to be heard over the noise of the rain.

'You're so beautiful,' replied Connor looking into her bright blue eyes. 'It's a good job that I'm not the jealous sort.'

'You know that it's you that I love. This is just an act. Something that I don't want to do but I must,' said Brigid leaning across and placing one of her hands in his. It seemed strange for her to see Connor in a paramedic's uniform and Brigid couldn't help but notice how uncomfortable he looked. Jeans and T-shirts were his usual preferred type of dress and suited his very large muscular physique better she thought. She ran her other hand around his square jaw line, up along the scar on the right side of his cheek and held it there.

'I know,' he replied and smiled at her.

The noise of the rain suddenly eased and the drum roll on the roof dropped to an occasional random beat. Brigid looked at her watch.

'Well, I reckon that's my cue. It's now 4.15. We should be on our way to St Pauls by say 5pm,' she continued and then gently stroked the side of Connor's face.

With that, Brigid opened the rear door of the ambulance, stepped out and walked around the corner into Cornwallis

Street - avoiding the large stream of water that was now running down the side of the road towards a gulley. The street was quite an attractive suburban residential road with generally well-kept Victorian housing and trees lining it on either side. Brigid approached the front door of number fifty-four. A typical mid terraced house of the period with solid red brick walls and bay windows which, like most of the properties in the street, had at some point been converted into flats. She walked up the three concrete steps to the black painted front door and turned to her right in order to press the top button on the intercom panel.

'Hello?' said the voice through the intercom.
'Laura. It's Rosie!' said Brigid in a perfect southern English accent, immediately recognising the voice coming from the speaker.
'Oh my God! Rosie! What are you doing here? Never mind, come on up,' replied the excited well-spoken voice.

The door buzzed open, and Brigid walked up to the top floor, where the front door for Flat 3 was promptly flung open and a thirty something, very attractive and petite blonde-haired female ran out and immediately flung her arms around her. After a long passionate kiss on the lips, Laura took Brigid's hand and led her into the living area of the apartment.

The flat was a sizeable three-bedroom property and absolutely immaculate inside with neutral decor and modern fittings and furniture, reflecting the occupiers desire for order and functionality. The spacious living room of some eighteen feet in length was somewhat minimalist in design with high quality oak engineered flooring throughout and just two white leather sofas, a chrome and glass coffee table in-between, and a flat screen television near the window. In the coves, on either side of the chimney breast were black open display units with various items including books and framed photographs. Even with this, the items were carefully, precisely and neatly arranged.

'Rosie, what are you doing here?' Laura said excitedly. 'I thought you were working today?'

'I was,' Brigid replied. 'The police have put some sort of cordon around central London, so my boss told me that I could go home early as it's killed the business today. But I thought I would pop in and see you instead. Hope that's ok? Sorry, I know that I should have waited for you to call me to let me know the coast was clear, but I've really missed you. Anyway, I assumed your girlfriend was working today with all the police goings-on.'

'Of course, it's OK. Shame you only have a few minutes,' said Laura with a suggestive smile. 'Yeah, you're right, she's working. She's always working ... or so it feels,' she continued, with a shake of her head. 'Married to her job, I reckon. Anyway, I'm so pleased you dropped in. Do you fancy a cup of tea or something?' she continued as she walked towards the kitchen.

'Thank you, gorgeous, that would be absolutely perfect,' replied Brigid, picking up a framed photograph off the top of the black wall unit to the right-hand side of the chimney breast. Taken at a wedding, Brigid guessed by the dresses and hats worn by the two subjects in the photo. On the left-hand side of the picture was Laura wearing a pretty floral dress and to her right was her partner, who looked decidedly less comfortable in a plain black dress. A very unremarkable looking woman who most people wouldn't have put down as being Laura's girlfriend had they not known. Brigid smiled at the photograph and then put it back before picking another one up beside it. This one was just of Laura's partner but this time she was in a uniform or, to be precise, the uniform of a Superintendent in the Metropolitan Police.

'So, where's Shelley working today then?' asked Brigid.

'Well, she's actually got a really busy day. She's in charge of the police cordon that you mentioned - like I said to you before, that's one of the roles she has when there's an emergency.' Laura walked through from the kitchen with two mugs of tea in her hands. 'There is something really strange going on today. She phoned me earlier to tell me that her boss had just been placed under arrest and that she was now acting Commander of the Met Police anti-terrorist unit.'

Laura placed the mugs of tea on the table and beckoned Brigid to sit down beside her on one of the sofas.

'Anyway, why are we talking about her? We should be talking about us. I don't want to be with her Rosie - I want to be with you. When can I tell her?' asked Laura excitedly.

'Soon gorgeous. Very soon,' said Brigid before picking up her mug of tea. 'Sorry darling but is there any chance that I could have a little more milk in mine?' she asked holding it out to her.

As Laura walked back out to the kitchen, Brigid removed a small glass vile from her jacket pocket, pulled out the cork from the top and poured the contents into the other tea. The quantity and type of poison used had been carefully measured so as not to immediately kill the victim but to produce a quick effect of bleeding and shortness of breath and which would then increase in effect over time.

Laura returned to the sofa and, in between her incessant jabbering, started taking sips of her tea. It wasn't long before she started feeling very unwell. Within minutes of that, she was coughing violently.

'Oh my God, Laura. Are you OK?' asked Brigid as if she was genuinely concerned by what she was seeing.

Laura coughed again into her hands and then to her horror notice that they were splattered with her blood. She looked up at Brigid and shook her head.

'I'll call an ambulance,' Brigid said taking her mobile phone out of her right pocket. 'Yes, ambulance please ... hello, yes I need an ambulance to flat three, fifty-four Cornwallis Street. Please hurry!'

Alim Farooqi pressed the 'end call' button on his mobile phone, placed it back in his pocket and nodded at Connor. After waiting for a few minutes, Connor switched on the blue lights and siren and drove around the corner. Alim stepped out from the ambulance in his paramedic's uniform and made his way quickly to the flat.

'We need to get you to St Bartholomew's hospital,' said Alim after a brief examination of Laura. 'Your heart is racing and you're clearly struggling to breath properly. I suspect that you are suffering from a Pulmonary Embolism. Time is of the essence. Unfortunately, there is a police cordon which we will have to go around.'

'Actually, Laura's partner is the police officer in charge of the cordon, so she could help get us through it quickly,' said Brigid.

Laura nodded as she coughed violently again into her hands and then looked to see even more blood than before. She grabbed her mobile phone from the coffee table and handed it to Alim after highlighting Shelley Carson's mobile number.

'OK. We'll call her from the ambulance,' said Alim.

Brigid and Alim helped Laura down the stairs to the waiting ambulance and on to a stretcher in the back before Connor accelerated away in the direction of the City of London.

'Hello. Is that Superintendent Shelley Carson?' asked Alim, having to raise his voice to be heard over the sirens.

'Yes, it is,' Shelley replied with a suspicious tone in her voice.

'My name is Paul Fernandez and I'm a paramedic with the London Ambulance Service. I need to advise you that I have your partner Laura with me who appears to be suffering from a Pulmonary Embolism. The nearest hospital to us that is set up to treat this sort of condition is St Bartholomew's, but it is inside your cordon. This condition is time critical, and Laura thought you might be able to assist us through it with minimal delay? As I say, we are up against the clock,' said Alim. 'Did you want to speak to her?'

'Oh my God! Yes ... yes please,' replied Shelley who, for someone usually totally unflappable, seemed completely stunned by the news.

'Shelley. I'm coughing up blood and ... can't breathe properly,' said Laura after a couple of pants for breath. 'Please help me - I'm really scared.'

'OK Laura. Try not to panic. I'll do whatever I can - you know that. Can you pass me back to the paramedic please?' said Carson.

Superintendent Carson placed her finger over the mouthpiece and beckoned over one of her officers whom she knew had received advanced first aid training.

'What do you know about Pulmonary Embolisms?' she asked.

'Symptoms are shortness of breath and a racing heartbeat. Quite often they will be coughing up blood too. Really dangerous Ma'am. Basically, if a blood clot breaks off and gets to the lung then the person will stop breathing. Brown bread. Sorry, I mean that they will most likely die, Ma'am. It's one where speed is of the essence,' replied the Sergeant in a broad London accent.

'Hello?' said Alim.

'Which road will you be coming in on?' said Shelley taking her finger off the mobile phone mouthpiece. 'If you tell me which road you'll be using, I will make sure you get straight through. I won't be able to leave my command post here, so please look after her for me.'

'We will do our best for her, of course. We have just left her flat and are now travelling up Eversholt Street. Then we will be crossing over the A501 Euston Road, which I believe is where your cordon is? From there it should be a quick straight run to the hospital. As long as we aren't held up then she has a very good chance of getting the treatment she needs in time,' said Alim, emphasising the need for the police roadblock to be lifted as they approached it. 'We will be there in a few minutes. I will stay on the phone if you want - just so you know it's us.'

The ambulance hurtled down Eversholt Street, flashing past the seemingly never-ending rows of shops, restaurants and cafes and only occasionally and very briefly slowing up to allow pockets of traffic to move out of the way. The perfectly straight road meant that Connor had a far-reaching view down the street from the ambulance's slightly elevated position and could see the police cordon across the ring road in the distance. He pressed his right foot down on the accelerator pedal as far as it would go.

'Just three and a half miles to get to St. Paul's ...' he whispered to himself, squeezing the steering wheel in a vice like grip as he felt a surge of adrenaline through his body - his huge arm muscles almost bursting through the paramedic's uniform. The mass of barricades, police cars and army vehicles that blocked their path loomed up quickly and as Connor took his foot off the accelerator pedal again, he noticed movement on the roof tops. He leaned forward slightly so as to be able to see up through the windscreen. Snipers.

'Oh my God,' Connor said quietly to himself, even though he was the only person who could have heard it. 'There's even a tank sat across the front.'

As he got closer, the flashing blue lights around the barricade became almost blinding off the still wet road and then to his horror, he noticed the tank's turret slowly starting to turn, until its main gun was pointing directly at the ambulance. Connor could feel his heart pounding.

'We're approaching the police cordon,' he shouted down the ambulance's intercom.

Suddenly, in what felt like a miracle, a plume of exhaust smoke appeared from the rear of the tank as it quickly reversed off to the side and was followed by a large group of police officers and soldiers clearing a section of the roadblock. Connor let out a loud sigh of relief as the ambulance sped through the cordon.

CHAPTER EIGHTEEN

'Still no sign of the Land Cruiser, Sir,' said Alice Andrews, the thirty-nine-year-old Head of International Counterterrorism at MI5.

'OK then. So, where the hell are they?' asked Mac, looking across the table at Tom and Sergeant Lang. The latter responded with a blank look and a shake of his head. 'Well, if you're right, Tom, about 6pm being their target time to set off the EMP, then Baqri's cutting it a bit fine. This is making me very nervous.'

'We're pretty confident that as soon as the Land Cruiser starts its run towards St Paul's Cathedral, we will spot him though. The cordon is an impenetrable ring of steel, sir. Police and army units including armoured vehicles are blocking off every road into the city,' Andrews replied.

'Again, Baqri knows this. He's planned for this. What I don't understand is how he intends to get through it. What am I missing?' Tom tapped his pen on the pad of paper in front of him.

'One thing I do need to make you aware of, Sir, is that I'm getting worrying reports through from the Cyber Team. Apparently, social media is going crazy. *Adallah* is telling everyone that they are about to break the system and that this is the time for the people to rise up and show those in power how they feel and to take what they are owed,' said Andrews.

'Great. Rioting and looting then. Any sign that people are listening to this?' asked Mac.

'I'm afraid so. Large crowds are starting to form on the streets - particularly in the more deprived areas of the city. They've been told to wait for the sign when all the lights go out and nothing will work. They've assured people that the police will be crippled at the same time. It's a very well thought out and prepared message that they're pushing,' Andrews replied.

'Of course, it is,' said Tom. 'The whole thing has been well thought out and planned.'

'Not much point in them nicking a TV when there's no power, is there?' said Sergeant Lang with a grin on his face - a grin that was not reciprocated by Mac who was now pacing up and down one side of the Operations Room table.

'Do you think that this is related to his plan to get through the cordon?' Mac asked, looking at Tom.

'Not really, no. They will only start rioting and looting when the EMP has been set off and they know the police can't respond. This may be just the icing on the cake for Baqri or perhaps something that we don't understand yet,' Tom replied, as Captain Jax walked into the room.

'Everything OK, Captain?' asked Mac.

'I think so, sir. No sign of the Land Cruiser and no breaches in the cordon. One vehicle has just been allowed through - an ambulance travelling from Camden Town which is on its way to St Bartholomew's hospital with a patient suffering from a Pulmonary Embolism. It was personally cleared by Superintendent Carson though,' said Jax.

'Oh, OK then. Good,' replied Mac with a relieved tone to his voice.

'Hang on,' said Tom after a short pause. 'Did you say that it was going from Camden to St Barts?'

Tom unwrapped another buttermint and popped it into his mouth. He slowly rose to his feet with a frown on his face, pushed his chair back and walked around the table to the wall which had the map of London retrieved from the terrorist's base pinned up in the centre - all the time looking at the floor.

'From what I remember, a pulmonary embolism is where a blood clot goes to your lungs and basically you can stop breathing - right?' Tom said looking around.

'That's correct. What are you getting at?' replied Andrews.

'Well, what I'm trying to say is that ... every minute counts doesn't it? So, why would the ambulance need to go to St Bartholomew's?' Tom continued with one finger placed on the centre of Camden and another on the hospital symbol of St Barts. 'The nearest hospital from Camden is St Pancras,' he continued, moving his finger up the map. 'In fact, it's just down the road - less than a mile from Camden.

'So, why did they need to go through the cordon then?' added Mac.

'Yes, quite. Can you contact your officer on the ground at that section of the cordon where the ambulance crossed through and ask him if there was anything strange about either the ambulance or the crew?' Tom asked, looking around at Captain Jax.

Tom was now very aware that everyone else in the room was staring at him, with a mixture of confusion and concern on their faces.

'OK. So, what I'm thinking is this. We are waiting for Baqri to appear in a Land Cruiser SUV. This is because we saw him on the satellite images getting out of the Land Cruiser and shutting the doors to the industrial unit up in Birmingham,' he continued looking around the room.

Everyone in turn nodded in reply as Tom walked over to a still photo shot of Baqri standing by the Land Cruiser and with his facial features clearly visible.

'Two points here. If the rest of his cell were in the SUV, why was *he* the one to get out. He's the boss at the end of the day. Secondly, why shut the door to the industrial unit at all? If they were the last ones out, why bother? Baqri is not stupid and must have known that there was a least a chance that a satellite would have been overhead,' Tom continued.

'Do you think he deliberately wanted us to see him then?' asked Mac.

'Yes, maybe. Baqri has so far shown that he has mastered the art of deception - I'm sure that Sun Tzu would have been proud. It's all been smoke and mirrors and nothing has been as straight forward as it first seemed. I'm not saying that he hasn't got something else planned as well but what if another vehicle like the ambulance is being used as a sort of Trojan horse to deliver its deadly contents to its target?' said Tom as Captain Jax caught his attention.

'Tom. The army Captain in charge of that section of the cordon says that the ambulance didn't appear to be anything peculiar, but he also said that the paramedic driving it was unusually large and muscular. He couldn't get a proper look at the driver's face because the ambulance was going so fast, but he remembers joking to another officer that it looked like the Hulk was driving it. He just seemed out of place,' said Jax.

There was a brief silence around the room as everyone absorbed what had just been said and one by one they all started looking at each other.

'Oh, Christ!' muttered Staff Sergeant Lang under his breath.

'Connor!' Mac said out loud what everyone else was thinking - his stomach now turning from the realisation that disaster had suddenly become much more likely.

'Give me the car keys,' said Tom to the MI5 officer who had driven them back to headquarters. 'I'm going to intercept them,' he continued looking round at Mac

'Tom ...' Mac started.

'Who else are you going to send, Mac?' Tom interrupted. 'Don't forget, I have the skill set for this. You can't tell Superintendent Carson what we know - we don't know to what degree she is involved in this. I think you may want to re-instate Commander Malik now though and consider detaining her until you've checked her out.'

'Agreed.' Mac said, nodding at the MI5 officer. 'Jax, take your team with Sergeant Laing in another vehicle and go with him. I better update the Prime Minister.'

At that, Tom grabbed his sat phone and the keys out of the MI5 officer's outstretched hands and sprinted from the Operations Room.

CHAPTER NINETEEN

'Well, they're through the cordon,' Baqri said, ending his call with Connor. He was now more excited than he could remember in a very long time and leapt out of his leather armchair. 'God is with us my friend and glory in His name awaits us.'

Baqri walked over to the living room window and looked out. A risk, he knew. He could be spotted by someone, but he had an over-whelming need to look upon all the people that he despised so much, going about their meaningless lives and then imagined how he was about to destroy them. How he loathed them all. The old lady in her tweed overcoat, slowly shuffling along the footpath, pushing her tartan covered walker towards the supermarket; the mother who had just pulled on to her drive after collecting her kids from after school club; the man from the gas company who had just started reading the meter at the house next door. They all disgusted him, and they would all suffer and rightly so, he thought to himself.

Baqri's thoughts then briefly turned to his old friend and mentor, Osama bin Laden. It was during his time with Al-

Qaeda that Osama had given him permission to develop his idea of an EMP attack. It was also Osama who had explained to him why the civilians of enemy countries were legitimate targets, and this included women and children. Baqri remembered precisely where he was when he received news that the Americans had killed him - locked up in a prison, courtesy of the CIA. Well America, your time will come. Then he would be feared across the world and others would flock to his cause when they saw what he could do. His great friend would have been proud of him now. And soon Waterloo would have a new meaning for Britain. Long remembered as the battle which saw the British defeat of Napoleon, it would soon also be remembered for something else. The bomb that he would shortly detonate outside Waterloo train station would kill thousands. *The Waterloo Bombing* it would be called and it would go down in history. '*He* would go down in history. The single biggest killing of civilians that Britain had ever known. His name would be remembered forever.

'They tortured me, you know,' Baqri said in a matter-of-fact way, still looking out of the window.

'Who? The British?' Sal looked up.

'The British. The Americans. Both,' said Baqri and then paused before continuing. 'We had just tested the prototype EMP out in East Africa with our brothers in Al-Shebaab. On the way back we were ambushed by an SAS unit. They killed everyone except me. I was handed over to the British Secret Service for interrogation. They put me in a white soundproof room with nothing else in it. Sensory deprivation they call it. No sound, no smell - nothing. The only time that I heard anything was when they blasted me with white noise if I tried falling asleep on the floor. I went for days without sleep, and they tried everything that they could to make me tell them what they wanted to know.'

'What *did* they want?'

'The location of Osama bin Laden. But I wouldn't tell them. The MI5 agents said that if I didn't tell them then they would hand me over to the CIA. You see, there had been a big incident a month before where the British press were making accusations that MI6 had been guilty of torture in Middle Eastern operations. So, they wanted to get out of the spotlight and disappear back into the shadows. Handing me over to the CIA was a simple answer to their problem if I didn't tell them where he was. They said that because of 9/11, the Americans did not care about human rights, and they would take me to a place where no rules applied, and they would literally do anything to me to get me to talk. They said that the pain would be anything beyond my imagination. But I still refused to tell them.'

'So, did they give you over to the Americans?'

'Yes. They were right in what they said too.' Baqri looked round at Sal.

He walked over to the centre of the room and slowly pulled up his T-shirt to show a tapestry of mutilated skin all over the back of his slim torso - like some sort of horrific ordinance survey map with large areas of burn induced patches of wrinkled skin, interspersed with deep and lengthy scars.

'My God!' said Sal, wide eyed. 'What did they do to you?'

'Whatever made them feel better. They didn't even ask me about Osama to start with. They just kept going on about 9/11 and then burnt me and cut me and beat me. This was almost ten years after 9/11 and yet they went on as if it had just happened.' Baqri then turned around and pointed to numerous small round burn marks all over his torso. 'My interrogator also enjoyed smoking - almost as much as putting his cigarettes out on me. Then they started asking me where Osama was, but I wouldn't tell them. They carried on where the British left off and started putting me in little boxes where you can't move or stretch you legs out. They would then turn the temperature down, so I was freezing or turn it up, so I felt like I was cooking. Every time I fell asleep, they woke me up again. I started hallucinating but even then, I wouldn't tell them.'

'But you did though, didn't you? In the end?'

'To my eternal shame, Sal, I did, Well, apparently I did. I don't even remember telling them.' Baqri's head dropped as he slowly pulled his T-shirt back down again. 'They broke me Sal and I failed him. But I will put that right today.'

Baqri walked back over to the window and looked out again. Yes, today he would have his revenge, he thought to himself. Britain, the attack dog of the Americans, would be muzzled. Then it would be the turn of America itself. Mighty America. Mighty America which he, Mohammed Baqri, would soon cripple. His Iranian backers would certainly be impressed by his demonstration on Britain. The 'Great Satan' they once called Britain but now that title had passed to America. Baqri had no doubt that Iran would then give him everything that he needed for his attack on the United States. He had fantasized about this day for so long that he couldn't remember a time when this wasn't the centre of his thoughts. Many, many years of meticulous planning, which would culminate in a single day of glory.

Sal couldn't help but be impressed by his leader's forethought. He had considered every detail and anticipated every action and reaction by the British secret service. For example, the safe house that he was now standing in, was carefully chosen for being so very average and unremarkable but provided them with the ability to come and go with the minimal chance of being seen. A standard 1970s semi-detached house with an integral garage and remote-control electric door, which allowed them to just drive in and out without having to step out of the Land Cruiser.

'We need to leave soon, Sal,' Baqri said, turning around to look at his faithful friend who had remained standing near the living room door for the last hour, almost motionless - as if on guard duty.

In many ways, Sal was *his* attack dog. Loyal, obedient and without fear. Baqri knew that this was someone he could always depend on and who would sacrifice himself without pausing for thought, if it became necessary. *Admittedly Sal was not exactly bursting with character and charisma*, Baqri thought to himself, *but then they were not the important qualities he needed from his right-hand man. What he did have, however, was a completely focussed efficiency and relentless determination to complete any task given to him.*

'Once they get to St Paul's Cathedral, Connor will call again,' Baqri continued. 'Then, by the time we reach London's first outer CCTV camera, the whole system will be down from the detonation of the EMP and they won't even see us coming. That gives us, say, twenty minutes to get to Waterloo, park up the SUV and make sure that we time it right to catch the thousands of commuters leaving the station.'

Sal nodded at him in an almost robotic manner, his deep-set eyes still dull and lacking any sort of emotion.

'Are you not surprised that this has all gone to plan, Sal?' asked Baqri with a slight grin.

'No. I have faith. In you and in Allah. You are carrying out His will, so how could you fail? But I must ask, how <u>did</u> you know that you could get the ambulance past the cordon?'

'*If you know your enemy and know yourself, you need not fear the result of a hundred battles.* Sun Tzu - *The Art of War,* my friend. I have, as you know, planned this over many years and I have got to know my enemy well. Very well. He is both predictable and stupid. Commander Malik would have been more of a challenge for us if he was still in charge of the police cordon. Such a principled and uncompromising man that I wasn't sure he would have allowed the ambulance through even it was carrying his daughter to hospital. Fortunately for us, Malik is a Muslim and so it didn't need much to cast doubt over his loyalties. This is why I call our enemy stupid. They say that there is no prejudice but all I had to do was have a photograph taken of Malik with one of my associates leaving a Mosque after prayers for him to be suspended. I knew that Superintendent Carson would replace him, and she was a much easier target. An efficient, competent and confident officer at work but in her personal life she is a <u>very</u> insecure person. I mean, have you seen her girlfriend, Laura? Wow!

OK, I know you haven't but take my word for it - she is gorgeous!' Baqri flamboyantly threw his hands up towards the ceiling. 'She is in a league so far above Superintendent Carson's and she knows it. So does Carson, of course, which makes her feel very vulnerable.

'So, then Brigid comes along. And this is where all the inside information has been coming from?'

'Exactly. So, I not only got to find out how the security services were likely to react in this situation, but I also got a means to deliver my EMP to its target,' Baqri said, throwing back his head laughing. 'The icing on the cake was the confusion and mistrust that it created between them. *Who's the leak? Oh, it's got to be the Muslim* I can hear them saying. The funny thing is that their 'leak' didn't even know that she was one.'

'Our victory is assured then.'

'You would think so, Sal. The only unknown element is this agent that they've defrosted. I can't believe they've got agents like this guy. Apparently, he didn't even know he was one. How the hell does that work? I don't have enough information on him which is the only thing that bothers me, and I can only assume that he has some qualities that they think will be useful. But then I think to myself, look he's just one guy.'

'None of them are a match for you, Mohammed.' replied Sal. You have already proven that. You will be revered throughout the Islamic world. The man who brought the West to its knees. Those countries that have sinned and those that have blasphemed and thought that there would be no divine retribution will be punished - *for God will punish them at your hands.* So says the Quran.'

Baqri stood up, walked over to the coat rack in the hallway and took his black jacket off the hook.

'We have a duty this day to carry out God's punishment of the infidels, my friend. Come, our time is nearly here,' Baqri said as he turned around again and then walked into the garage, stepping into the passenger seat of the Landcruiser. The menacing figure of Sal, dressed as usual all in black, settled into the driver's seat of the SUV, turned around and pressed the button on the remote control to raise the garage door. Baqri was also now uncharacteristically quiet, as he closed his eyes and pictured his dream coming true - the death and mutilation of British men, women and children and then the destruction of the Great Satan itself.

CHAPTER TWENTY

'I see,' said Hatcher after a long pause. 'So, how confident are you about this, Iain?'

Prime Minister Hatcher sat back into his chair and started rubbing and massaging his forehead with his left hand - his right hand tightly gripping the phone connecting him to the Deputy Director of MI5, Iain McGregor. As the closest civil servant to the Prime Minister, Sir Peter Hayward had become very adept in reading his boss's body language and there were clear signs of extreme anxiety, which he had only seen a few times before.

'I see,' Hatcher repeated again. 'Well, that's really bad news. Let's all hope and pray that your team manage to intercept them in time then. Please keep me updated, Iain,' he continued before replacing the phone gently and ever so slowly back on to its base.

'Shall I ask the others to come back in, Prime Minister?' asked Sir Peter.

'Yes please, Peter. Coffee break is definitely over. I think that they need to hear this straight away,' replied Hatcher.

The members of the government's COBRA committee filed back into the Cabinet Office briefing room, past the numerous scenic oil paintings on the walls and took their seats again at the table with a great sense of trepidation. Hatcher cleared his throat and took his time looking at each one of them in turn.

'Ladies and gentlemen. I have some news. I would like to say that it was good news but I'm afraid it isn't. It seems likely that the terrorists have managed to get through our cordon around central London and that they have the EMP device with them. They are believed to be on their way to St Paul's Cathedral where they intend to detonate it,' said Hatcher.

Audible gasps from around the table followed almost immediately and many committee members then put their heads in their hands.

'We do have a team trying to intercept them as we speak,' said MI5 Director Sir Nicholas Meads.

'We do. But we must be prepared for them not to be successful though. Tony, can you put the fleet on the highest level of readiness please for a strike on Tehran?' said Hatcher looking at the Defence Secretary. He then turned to Sir Peter Hayward. 'Can you get President Monroe on the phone? We need the Americans to be ready to strike too.'

It was less than five minutes before the phone in the Cabinet Office rang and Sir Peter handed the phone over to the Prime Minister once again.

President Jane Monroe may have had a similar career in business to Hatcher but physically the two could not have been more different. An intimidatingly large Texan woman of just over six feet in height and solidly built, Jane Monroe dominated every photograph taken with other world leaders. The difference in size between the American President and the British Prime Minister was a constant source of amusement and ridicule for the world's media who especially liked to mention that the person towering over the Prime Minister was a woman - in an attempt to antagonise and irritate Hatcher. If the truth be known, it did. One British tabloid commented that they couldn't see the President's lips move as both leaders sat beside each other one day and the Prime Minister explained their cooperative foreign policies - as if Hatcher was some sort of ventriloquist's dummy.

Personality wise, the two also appeared very different at first glance. Hatcher - belligerent and aggressive. Monroe - more easy going and relaxed. Deeper down, however, their core personalities were much more similar than they first appeared. Focussed, relentless, tenacious and with the same ethos that only strength would be respected by other countries. Though both adopted the policy of their own country first, they also knew that they were much better off together when it came to foreign policy.

'Good afternoon, Bob,' said Jane Monroe in her usual Texan drawl. After a long pause as Hatcher updated the American President, Monroe looked down the table in the White House Situation Room and then took a deep breath. 'OK. Right. Not such a good afternoon then. Well, that is, of course, really bad news. We'll be ready, don't worry. I had the same conversation with President Petrov. I told him to get his people out of Tehran because I intend to deal with the Iranian menace once and for all. I also told him not to test my resolve and that he should know by now that I am someone who makes good on their threats.'

After replacing the phone handset, Monroe cleared her throat and then stood up as she buttoned up the middle of her navy-blue suit jacket. Monroe's huge frame was still an imposing sight to everyone else in the room, as she placed her hands on the table and leaned forward to address her national security team.

'Ladies and gentlemen that was, as you probably gathered, the British Prime Minister. It seems that their efforts to keep the Adalah terrorist cell from entering central London has failed. So, I see no other option but to instruct our Fifth Fleet to prepare for a full missile launch against our targets in Tehran. We will co-ordinate this with the British carrier fleet. Admiral Womack, can you send out the orders please?' said Monroe looking at the silver haired Chairman of the Joint Chiefs of Staff, who simply nodded in reply.

'Excuse me, Madam President. Firstly, thank you for inviting me to join the meeting of your National Security Team at this time. I must ask though, why we are getting involved in this at all, when it is clearly a British problem,' said the Speaker of the House, Jennifer Wolff. A slim woman in her early 50's, with dark brown eyes and olive Mediterranean coloured skin, Wolff had a number of physical qualities that Monroe both admired and envied.

'Madam Speaker, I've decided to ask you to join us here today because the situation has the potential to turn nasty and when I say that, I mean it could turn nasty on a big scale but I hope you will give this operation your support in Congress,' replied Monroe. 'There are a number of reasons why we have no choice but to get involved. Firstly, Britain is not only our closest ally, but they are also a member of NATO. As you know, article five of the NATO treaty means that an attack on a member state is an attack on all NATO members. We are obliged to respond, if London is attacked. Secondly, if we don't support them on this, how can we expect them to support any action that we take when we are attacked? And thirdly ...'

'Sorry, Madam President. Am I missing something here? Why would *we* be attacked?' interrupted Wolff.

'Well, I was just about to get to that bit, Jen. We have received reliable intelligence that the attack on London is just a dry run for an attack on the United States. If this attack on Britain by *Adalah* is successful, then Iran intends to sponsor a much larger attack on us. The CIA tell me that there would be two targets - New York to take down our financial system and Washington to incapacitate us politically and administratively. The country will be crippled for years - many years, as every electrical circuit and microchip will get fried,' said Monroe.

'Dear God,' said Wolff after a brief silence. 'If that does happen, will we be affected militarily? If we're attacked by another country, for example, will we be able to respond?'

'We're not sure. All our systems are being assessed and upgraded where necessary, so hopefully we will be able to respond,' said Admiral Womack.

'Hopefully? God almighty!' said Wolff.

'So, you see why acting now is necessary. Iran is set on its path to try and damage our country and our way of life. We didn't start this Madam Speaker, but I can assure you, we will finish it. And one more thing I can tell you. I sure ain't going to let them get the first punch in,' said Monroe, finishing in a tone that every Texan would have been proud of.

'Madam President. We now have satellite positioning over the Fifth Fleet as it approaches the British Carrier Group,' said Admiral Womack, pointing at the monitors on the wall at the other end of the Situation Room.

There it was. The huge aircraft carrier USS Theodore Roosevelt surrounded by numerous Missile Destroyers and Cruisers, ploughing through the Persian Gulf. The satellite image then pulled back to include the British fleet in the picture - together an impressive site to behold. *Christ, we really are going to do this* thought Monroe but aware that her facial expressions were being watched by everyone else in the room - even if they did not appear to be looking directly at her. Monroe kept a stern face as she sat back down into her chair, continuing to watch the Fifth Fleet moving into position.

The door into the situation room opened and a senior aide walked over to the Secretary of State and whispered in his ear before turning on his heals and leaving as swiftly as he entered.

'Madam President,' said Secretary of State, Walter Houston. 'We have just heard back from both Iran and Russia.

It seems that they are now taking our threats seriously. Russia has informed us that it will retaliate if any of our attack results in the death of their citizens but at the same time stating that it is putting pressure on Iran to co-operate in getting the terrorists to call off the attack on London. Iran now sounds quite desperate to avert the strike on Tehran and, although it still denies that it was supporting the terrorist attack, they say that they will use all their resources to try and help prevent it. They are now putting this message out on their national tv and radio network and all over social media saying that their assistance demonstrates that Iran is not the evil country that America tries to make it out to be but a peaceful and gentle nation. Russia is putting out the same message.'

'Ha! Peaceful nation - my ass!' exclaimed Monroe. 'So basically, they are saying that they have been falsely accused but even so, they will still assist in trying to stop the terrorists. So, if we attack them now then they look like the victims and we're the bad guys. Clever. Do you think the Iranians will actually try and stop the attack on London?'

'Not clear, Madam President. They may do, under pressure from Russia. It would make them look like the saviours of the west. For Russia, it says to the world that they are the real global police and not the United States. All part of their long-term plan to shift influence away from us. President Petrov has been all over every news channel in every country,' replied Houston.

'I've just realised what this reminds me of. You know those Russian dolls?' said Monroe. 'Well, it's like that. You open the outer doll - being the terrorists - and there you find the Iranians. Open up that doll and you find the Russians.

Open that one up and at the heart of the whole thing you find Petrov.'

'Madam President, I have been informed that the Saudi Air Force has been put on stand-by to join our attack on Iran if necessary and Israel has also advised that it is ready for a strike. On the flip side, I have just been informed that the Russian Caspian Fleet has been put on high alert. As you know, Russia has been upgrading those ships for a couple of years now - for a moment like this I guess,' said Admiral Womack replacing the handset on the phone in front of him.

'Exactly for a moment like this. If I was a suspicious woman, then I might think that this has been many years in the planning by Russia,' replied Monroe.

'Madam President. Can I just add something?' asked Wolff. 'If that EMP device goes off in London and we continued with our attack on Tehran, the Russians could then attack us and just claim that they were protecting an innocent country from unwarranted imperial aggression. This PR that they are putting out is really making Iran look like a helpless, innocent little country and us the bully. Then if we strike back against Russia with our allies, where does it go from there? Russia can't be seen to be taking a beating can it. This is how world wars start. Surely this is a march down the path towards global nuclear war?'

The President leant forwards in her chair, clasped both hands together and then rested her elbows on the table in front of her - almost like she was praying. She then lowered her head and brought up her hands, holding them to her mouth - yet all the time looking at the monitors at the other end of the room.

Monroe changed her gaze to the Speaker of the House.

'Well, Jen. You better hope that the Iranians are good to their word and that terrorist cell is stopped then. We can't allow a country like Iran to attack us or one of our allies with impunity. It's their choice.'

'Admiral, please let me know when the fleet is ready to launch.'

CHAPTER TWENTY-ONE

The pain was now so excruciating that Laura was doubled over on the ambulance stretcher, her arms folded over her abdomen as she rocked backwards and forwards. Her screams were deafening and only interrupted by frequent violent bloody coughing fits.

'How much longer Rosie?' Laura whispered, squeezing Brigid's hand. 'I'm scared. I don't want to die. You won't let me die, will you?'

'Ah, well now,' Brigid replied in her natural strong Northern Irish accent. 'We've got a wee bit of a problem with that.'

Brigid looked down, smiled gently and stroked Laura's hand. Laura's face changed to a look of complete confusion.

'Oh, lovely Laura. Beautiful Laura. I am so sorry. Truly, I am.' Brigid said, sweeping back Laura's blond hair from her eyes - those beautiful blue eyes which were now streaming tears down her face from the pain. 'You seem like such a sweet girl. I'm sorry you're in so much pain,' she continued, wiping Laura's tears from both sides of her face.

'What's ... going ... on?' Laura panted, managing to get each word out between a shallow intake of breath.

'Look, why don't you just lie back and perhaps the paramedic can find something for the pain?' Brigid said looking at Farooqi and then pointing with her eyes at one of the overhead lockers.

Brigid gently pushed Laura's shoulder until she was lying down flat on the stretcher once again and continued stroking her hair.

'Rosie ... you sound ... different?' Laura managed to eventually whisper.

'Well, now. The thing is my name's not actually Rosie. Sounded like a good English name to me at the time. You know, English Rose and the like. I do like you, Laura. That's the truth. I also hate seeing you in pain and I'm afraid it will only get worse - if you can believe it. I don't want you to suffer - you don't deserve that,' said Brigid.

Farooqi opened the locker, took out a pillow and handed it to Brigid.

'Sleep well,' Brigid said quietly before placing the pillow over Laura's face. Brigid kept up a firm pressure with both hands, pushing the pillow down over Laura's face as she thrashed around. 'Shhhhh ... time to rest lovely Laura. Time for your pain to end.'

Laura screamed, muffled underneath the pillow, frantically grabbing at Brigid's hands. In less than a minute all movement had ceased, and her arms dropped limply down to her sides.

'Brigid,' Connor shouted through the intercom. 'There's a black Range Rover racing up behind us with blue lights flashing in its front grille.'

Connor had hardly finished his sentence before there was a massive bang to the right-hand rear corner of the ambulance followed by a jolt, knocking both Brigid and Alim off their feet and towards the front of the vehicle. Connor wrestled the steering wheel one way and then the other as the ambulance slid from side to side.

'He's trying to spin us,' Connor shouted through the intercom. 'Do something!'

'Must be Secret Service,' said Farooqi looking out the rear window.

'You think?' replied Brigid sarcastically, getting back to her feet. 'Right,' she muttered under her breath as she opened another locker and took out a Kalashnikov AK-47 assault rifle.

Pushing the safety lever fully down to the semi automatic position with her thumb, Brigid pulled the bolt back on the rifle with a satisfying clunk.

'Alim, the doors please,' said Brigid. 'See how he gets on with this then.'

Suddenly, the doors flung open, and Tom found himself looking at two people stood in the back of the ambulance. He then realised that those two people were Brigid Doyle and Dr Alim Farooqi. Brigid raised the rifle and proceeded to fire two shots into the windscreen of the Range Rover which, failing to actually penetrate the glass, just caused small shattered circles.

'Bullet proof glass,' Alim shouted at Brigid.

'Really? Are you sure your Doctorate isn't in the *Fucking Obvious,* Alim?' replied Brigid, scowling at Farooqi.

'OK, OK. Try shooting his tyres then.' Alim shrugged his shoulders.

'This isn't a particularly accurate weapon and I'm not that good a shot anyway. I haven't enough ammo to waste bullets. They're probably some special type of tyre anyway.'

Once more Tom accelerated hard towards the rear of the ambulance, crashing the SUV hard into its right-hand corner, in an attempt to spin it in a police pursuit style manoeuvre.

'Brigid!' Connor yelled again through the intercom, having wrestled the steering wheel again from side to side.

'I know. I know,' she shouted back still standing upright - having this time held on to a grab handle. She paused for a second while she thought. *His car might be armoured with bullet proof glass, but others aren't.* 'Connor, let me know when you reach the next major set of traffic lights. Turn the lights and sirens off and go through it when the traffic signal is red - see if you can cause some chaos,' she shouted.

'We'll actually be at the crossroads with the A40 in less than a minute,' Connor shouted back.

'OK, Alim give me a hand with the body. Let's see if we can slow him down,' said Brigid grabbing Laura's legs. 'There's one more favour I need to ask from you, Laura.'

Tom watched on, between the two bullet damaged areas of the windscreen, as the terrorists carried the body of what appeared to be a petite blond-haired girl over to the rear of the ambulance, and were now bent over the body, attempting to roll it out. He braked heavily in anticipation, the nose of the armoured Range Rover dipping sharply towards the road and the tyres screeching, as Laura's body was rolled unceremoniously out of the ambulance. Tom swerved the Range Rover around the rolling body, his previous training subconsciously kicking in, as he looked in his rear-view mirror to check that Jax and his SAS team, who were trying to keep up in their Land Rover, had also managed to avoid the body.

Connor looked in his wing mirror, relieved to see that the Secret Service SUV was now two hundred yards back - Brigid's actions having given them some valuable breathing space. As instructed, Connor drove the ambulance into the junction without alerting the crossing traffic but still managing to purposely knock over a motorcyclist and clip the ends of two cars which then started a domino effect with other vehicles crashing into one another. Brigid looked back at the chaos behind them - cars, vans, buses, HGVs, cyclists and motor cyclists now all blocking the junction. People started getting out of their vehicles to investigate the wreckage, and then a few of them started running over to the motorcyclist who was lying on the ground, barely moving and clearly injured.

Once again Brigid raised the AK-47 assault rifle. This time she moved the lever to the fully automatic position, depressed the trigger and continued to hold it down. The distinctive 'clack-clack' sound of the Kalashnikov rang out as Brigid sprayed bullets indiscriminately, sweeping from one side of the crowd to the other and then back again, until there was one final click telling her that the magazine was empty.

The result was complete carnage - a shocking, horrific massacre of men, women and even a young child who had made the fateful decision to get out of the car to look for her mother. Bodies, both wounded and dead, were strewn across the road. As the ambulance accelerated away from the junction, there was a brief pause of near silence. No one had expected the attack and it was so quick.

Then came the screams.

CHAPTER TWENTY-TWO

Brigid pulled the rear doors shut, placed the rifle on the stretcher bed and sat down beside it.

'Oh my God. What have you done?' said Alim. His face expressed a look of complete incredulity.

'I know, I know.'

'Those people did not deserve to die!' exclaimed Alim. 'What have you done?'

'What I have done is make sure that the bastard driving that Range Rover had no chance of catching up with us and stopping our mission.'

'But you even shot a child. These people are not my enemy. I didn't sign up to this,' said Alim angrily.

'These people are the enemy, Alim. They are part of the problem. They go on like timid little lambs and do nothing to change a failed system. My own father was blasted by a shotgun and then shot in the head - in broad daylight for God's sake. And what justice did we get? No justice, that's what. The bastards that killed him walked free.'

'And you think shooting a bunch of unarmed civilians will change things? What about the little child? Was she part of your failed system?'

'Of course, she wasn't. I didn't realise that she had got out of her car until it was too late. That was a terrible, I know. And it will probably haunt me till the end of my days. But you never know – she might survive. Hopefully.'

'So, was it worth it? Gunning down all those people?'

'OK, Alim. Would you prefer for us to have been caught? I did what I had to do and I'm not going to apologise. There are always sacrifices - Mohammed taught me that. Hopefully, there won't have to be any more casualties and we can just detonate the EMP, get the revenge that we are all so desperate for and then we disappear.'

Alim looked at Brigid and nodded.

'I understand why you did what you did but I want you to understand that I do not agree with it. It was bad enough that I helped you kill that young girl but shooting civilians … you went too far Brigid. Where did you learn how to use an AK-47, anyway?'

'Mohammed thought it was a good precaution to teach me - just in case we ran into trouble.'

Connor switched the blue lights and sirens back on and once more pushed the accelerator down towards the floor, racing along Fleet Street until St Paul's Cathedral loomed into view. Splatters of rain appeared again on the windscreen which then swiftly turned into another deluge, hammering down the roof of the ambulance.

'Alim, we're approaching St Paul's. You better get ready to start the timer,' Connor shouted through the intercom. 'I'm going to call Mohammed when you're done.'

Alim Farooqi unclipped the metal boxing which had been used to conceal the EMP. He looked down at his creation. Mixed feelings had now surfaced. Would his wife have wanted him to do this? He wasn't sure. But he simply couldn't allow her death and that of his precious daughter to go unanswered. He put his finger on the timer switch. He could see his wife in his head, and he could now feel her disapproval. She was such a pacifist, that the idea of potentially killing anyone would have horrified her. The fact that he had aided and abetted Brigid in the murder of Laura was terrible on its own. His wife would have been so disappointed with him. Justice had to prevail though. For his family. Anyway, his EMP device was not designed to kill – not directly anyway. Thanks to the rain, no one is likely to be anywhere near it when it explodes. The damage should be limited to Britain's infrastructure.

Brigid could see that Farooqi was wrestling with his conscience. He was still staring at the bomb.

'Are you alright, Alim? You're not getting cold feet now, are you? Just remember they murdered your family. Your family was everything. They took them from you. Make them pay, Alim.'

Alim nodded. He flicked the switch.

Farooqi shouted, 'Connor. It's activated. We have fifteen minutes.'

Connor pulled into the bus lane directly outside the Cathedral, then switched off the sirens but left the blue lights on. He picked up his sat phone. *People would assume that the ambulance crew were tending to someone inside the Cathedral. I mean, who interferes with an ambulance? Got to respect Baqri's planning. Mind you, this downpour is good timing too with people running to get under cover,* thought Connor, as he called Baqri's phone.

'We're here,' said Connor. 'We did have one issue with a Secret Service agent, but we lost him and it's all good. Alim has just set the timer and we're about to make our escape. I'll try and call you again once it's detonated, though Alim says he is not a hundred percent sure that our mobiles will work, even though he's tried adding extra protection to them. He thinks they will but says that as an EMP of this size has never been used before from a vehicle, then he can't guarantee it. When the lights all go off, then I guess you know it's worked.'

Connor looked down and placed his sat phone in the top pocket of his paramedic shirt. As he looked up again, he noticed in his door mirror that the traffic was urgently moving to either side of the road. Shortly, the headlights of something which had become a familiar sight emerged through the rain.

A black Range Rover.

CHAPTER TWENTY-THREE

Throughout the day, Tom felt his physical and mental strength continue to increase and his confidence with it. It was a strange feeling - a bit like he was evolving. Then, ever since he had taken the keys for the Secret Service Range Rover at MI5 Headquarters, he felt that a type of programmed automation had taken over him. His mind was now a combination of total serenity and single-minded focus. He had but one objective - the protection of his country and its people. A fear of death was now completely absent from his thoughts - a direct result of his psychological training many years before. The first stage of Dr Patel's mind conditioning was to accept that death was a certainty. Then once a person had accepted that - truly accepted that and agreed to it in their own mind - death was no longer something to be feared.

Still some fifty yards back, Tom turned the Secret Service SUV ninety degrees to the ambulance and stopped. Calmly, he opened the driver's door and walked to the rear of the Range Rover, opened the boot and removed a Heckler and Koch UMP 40 sub machine gun along with a magazine. As he stood in the rain unfolding the stock, inserting the magazine and flicking down the bolt, Tom felt like he had done this a thousand times before but, at the same time, knew that he couldn't have.

Connor had scrambled out of the driver's seat and was now standing at the rear of the ambulance with a pistol in his hands, shouting at the other two in the back to get out.

'Brigid, run for Christ's sake,' he shouted, as Tom walked back around the Range Rover.

This was the first time that Connor had got to see their nemesis properly. Older than he would have expected for a Secret Service officer and seemingly oblivious to the downpour of rain, with his white shirt already soaked through and with water dripping off his face - a face which looked completely emotionless. Connor could just make out his eyes as he continued towards them - a steely look of someone of complete focus. *Who is this guy?* he thought.

The rear doors of the ambulance flung open as Brigid and Alim jumped out and then sprinted past the front of the ambulance, like greyhounds released out of the traps. At the same time, Connor took cover behind the now opened rear door of the ambulance, only leaning out to take shots at the approaching Secret Service officer. A sudden, intense, searing pain surged up through his body from his left foot and was swiftly followed by the same from his other foot as Tom's first and second return shots had ripped through both of his boots - his feet being the only visible part of his body behind the door. A precise, almost surgical, action designed to incapacitate. Connor screamed out in pain as he fell to the ground like a sack of potatoes. His natural first reaction was to try grabbing at his boots, as he looked down at the profuse amount of blood that was now pouring out of them. Connor's feet now felt like useless weights but the incredible pain that he was feeling was mostly offset by the adrenaline that was coursing through his body as he saw the Secret Service officer still walking towards him without even a pause. He tried dragging himself across the ground on his side to where his pistol had landed, just outside of the protection of the ambulance doors, leaving a bloody trail in his wake.

'Don't do it, Connor. It's not worth it,' shouted Tom, raising his UMP 40 once again.

As Connor reached for the pistol, three more shots rang out from Tom's UMP, hitting Connor in the heart area of the chest in a grouping that any marksman would have been proud of. Connor's head slumped to the ground, his eyes open but lifeless.

'Connor!' shrieked Brigid, turning around to run back to him.

'No. Come on,' shouted Alim, grabbing her around the waist and pulling her back. 'He's dead. We've got to run … now!'

Brigid continued screaming as she thrashed around, trying to free herself from Alim's hold. Only when she saw the SAS Land Rover pull up and soldiers started running in their direction, did she stop struggling and accept the reality.

'Connor's got the keys to the old Toyota we're supposed to be using,' yelled Alim as they ran. 'Just keep running. Hopefully they'll be more interested in trying to deal with the bomb than with us.'

Having instructed his men to secure the area around the ambulance, Jax was now running toward Tom with his sat phone in hand. Bringing up the rear was the familiar sight of the ginger headed Staff Sergeant Lang, who arrived at the ambulance slightly out of breath.

'What?' said Lang in his east London accent, looking at Tom. 'We don't do a great deal of running in bomb disposal, you know,' he quipped, shrugging his shoulders.

'Yeah, I can see that.'

'Mac.' Jax mouthed as he held out the phone.

As Tom finished updating Iain McGregor, the rain started to ease, and he turned to Jax.

'Well, the good news is that Commander Malik is back in charge of the police operation and some units are on their way here to take over from your men. Superintendent Carson is being held for questioning. God knows where Baqri is though,' said Tom.

'Tom. I need Doctor Farooqi,' shouted Lang from inside the ambulance. 'This EMP is going to be way too complicated for me to deactivate in the eleven minutes or so that I have left. I don't think I can stop it going off. We need him alive.'

'I can help you with that one,' said Jax, with a finger over his earpiece. 'I'm getting a report through from an armed police unit that have caught them around the corner but apparently Brigid is holding a knife to Farooqi's throat.'

'She knows that we need him. C'mon,' said Tom as he started running, immediately followed by Captain Jax. As they rounded the corner, they found a line of armed police officers beside their cars, all pointing their guns at Brigid who was standing immediately behind Alim Farooqi.

'Put your guns down or I *will* kill him,' she shouted, pushing the blade slightly harder into Alim's neck and managing to draw blood, as if to prove her resolve.

'OK, OK,' said Tom. 'Put the knife down and let him go.'

'I want them all to step back from their cars - right back and then put their guns on the ground. First thing though, I want you to leave the key for that car on the seat. Start the engine first,' said Brigid pointing with her head at the nearest police car.

'Do as she says,' said Tom to the police officers.

As instructed, the armed officers started the car and started walking backwards away from their vehicles. Tom and Jax laid down their sub machine guns.

'Further!' Brigid shouted at the police. 'Now put your guns on the ground and take six paces back.'

Tom nodded at the officers who one by one laid their weapons on the ground and moved away from them. Brigid carefully walked towards the police car with its engine running, ensuring that she always had Alim between her and any possible threat, until she reached the open driver's door.

'What are you doing?' said Alim. 'Are you really going to kill me? Mohammed needs me.'

'Well, he needs you to not tell them how to stop the bomb, if that's what you mean,' said Brigid backing into the driver's seat. 'Who do you think told me to do this?' she whispered in his ear, before plunging the knife into his back.

Alim screamed out in pain as Brigid withdrew the knife and kicked him away from the car. He slumped to the ground, a large pool of blood quickly forming around him on the road.

Brigid wasted no time and pushed the police car's accelerator down hard, causing the tyres to squeal as she raced away and pulling her door shut at the same time. The police scrambled to pick up their weapons again, but the car was gone, screeching around the next corner before any of them could even try to get a decent shot in.

'Christ!' said Tom as he rushed over to Alim. 'Someone call an ambulance and you, get a first aid kit.' he continued, looking at the nearest police officer.

Tom lifted Alim Farooqi up by his shirt and then noticed that his eyes had started to roll.

'How do we stop this bomb?' said Tom, his face just inches from Farooqi's. 'How do we stop this bomb?' he repeated angrily, raising his voice and shaking Alim at the same time. 'This bomb of yours is going to kill thousands of innocent people. Is this what you wanted? What is wrong with you? You're a scientist not a terrorist. Tell me how to stop it. Tell me!'

'Tom, you're going to kill him!' said Jax, completely taken aback by the sudden change in Tom's temperament.

As the paramedics arrived, Tom stood up and stared at the ground – the frustration and anger that he was feeling was now very apparent to everyone else.

'He's alive but unconscious,' said one of the medics.

'I'll let Sergeant Lang know he won't be getting any help from Farooqi,' said Jax.

'We should update Commander Malik as well after you've spoken to Lang,' said Tom, surprising everyone again by his rapid return to being in full emotional control. 'See if they can find Brigid but more importantly find Baqri. I think there's a part two to his plan, Jax, or he would be here so that he could watch the fruits of his labour. As he's not here, then where the hell is he?'

CHAPTER TWENTY-FOUR

Staff Sergeant Lang looked down at the EMP device. The timer was relentlessly ticking down. 5.05 it said in bright red numbers. Much of the wiring seemed familiar but then there was so much more that wasn't. A tangled mass of multi-coloured spaghetti. *Five minutes. How the hell are you supposed to disarm a thing like this in just five minutes?* The news from Captain Jax that Farooqi had been incapacitated was bad news. Really bad news. He was on his own.

Andy Lang was the best of the best when it came to bomb disposal. The amount of medals that he had received in the nine years that he had been doing the job was, quite frankly, embarrassing. Even top brass used to stop and stare if Lang went past in formal uniform. Despite that, this EMP made him feel like an amateur. He had only ever seen one other EMP before and that was much smaller and less complex than the one he was now staring at. Despite reading up as much as he could on these devices before arriving at MI5 headquarters, it really didn't prepare him properly for seeing one of such scale in real life.

Normally confident in his abilities, this particular job felt like it might actually overwhelm him. Every time during his career that he had to defuse a bomb, it always started with a bout of nerves. The adrenaline would kick in and he would take a deep breath and remind himself that he was an expert. The question that his army colleagues always asked him was 'why would you do it?' He wasn't an idiot. He didn't want to die. He had a young family. But he didn't want others to die either and he had a talent for doing this. This bomb, however, made him feel strangely inadequate. It must have taken Dr. Alim Farooqi weeks to assemble, and he was expected to defuse it in minutes. No one knew the consequences of failing more than he did.

The normal course of action for a bomb would be to take it to a safe place and destroy it in a controlled explosion. Clearly, with this device, that was not going to be an option. *The good news*, thought Lang, *was that Farooqi didn't seem to have rigged it with any obvious anti-tamper devices. Probably didn't expect it to have been intercepted before detonation. Still need to be careful. Most of the components not being visible.*

The device was entirely encased in some sort of carbon fibre with the thickest area where he assumed the explosive lens was. Lang understood the need for this, as it kept the device stable during transportation. It had already taken him six minutes to find the thinnest area and carefully cut a section out with a hand-held circular saw followed by another section into the armature tube below that. He daren't try cutting into the thicker sections or risk detonation. There he was, staring at the spaghetti with just five minutes left. Despite what was depicted in Hollywood films, it was not always the red wire followed by the blue. It was whatever colours the bomb maker fancied at the time. One thing that did go through Lang's head though, was that the person who made this bomb was a scientist. *That surely meant a logical mind, didn't it?*

Lang picked up his set of wire snippers. His lucky snippers. *Never let me down before,* he thought and then immediately realised how ridiculous that sounded. *Of course, they haven't let you down before you muppet or you wouldn't be here.* He could feel himself starting to sweat. Very, very gently, Lang moved the wires around to see where they might be going. It was going to have to be guess. But an educated guess. He lifted up the yellow and green wire. Below that was the brown wire which he carefully pulled through to the top. *Right then. Here goes nothing.*

'Sergeant Lang,' shouted a voice behind him.

'Jesus Christ! Are you mental?' said Lang turning around. A fresh-faced policeman stood behind him.

'Sorry Sergeant. Captain Jax has been calling you. He's after an update as to whether you will be able to disarm it or not.'

'I switched my radio off. Just in case some pillock made me jump and I cut the wrong wire! You can tell him that this is definitely going to go off. Nothing can stop that. I might though be able to do something to improve the outcome though. Now get out of here.'

'Thanks Sergeant and sorry about making you jump,' said the police officer, looking a little sheepish.

'Oh, and tell him that he might lose most of the phones too.'

Lang pulled the wire through again and placed it in the jaws of the clipper. He could feel his heart racing.

One more deep breath.

Clip.

The digital display now said 2.35. *Time to go.* Lang jumped out of the ambulance and ran like he was back at school and doing the hundred metres.

'Everyone stay back,' he shouted, racing towards safety like a puffing steam train.

Meanwhile, Jax had returned to Tom with news.

'OK. I've spoken to Commander Malik. No sign of either Baqri or Brigid yet. As for Sergeant Lang, he said he will try his best to see if there is something that he can do.'

'What the hell does that mean exactly?' asked Tom.

'Well, I'm not entirely sure. From what I hear though, he is unmatched in his abilities. Fingers crossed then.'

'We could do with catching a break. Even if Laing pulls it off, we've still got Baqri running around. We need to find him, Jax. Will our phones still work? And what about our cars?'

'He's not sure. They may not. He did tell me previously though that the sat-phones should have enough protection and still work - so you're best using that. The device will be going off any minute and I understand that Sergeant Lang was moving to the perimeter to be at a safe distance for when it explodes.'

'I'll update Mac again then,' said Tom. 'Hopefully he'll be able to convince the PM that this doesn't warrant leveling Tehran.'

As Tom raised his satellite phone to his ear, the sudden and dramatic detonation of the EMP boomed out from nearby. The explosion sent out ripples of electromagnetic energy, like a pebble in a pond, shutting down all things electrical in its path. Tom looked on as every shop and office light around him went dark in quick succession, swiftly followed by the police cars. The incessant chatter from all their radios, which had been so frantic, just stopped. There was nothing but absolute silence and the silence was deafening. Tom, Jax and all the police officers stood motionless, temporarily paralysed by what had just happened.

Tom started to walk back in the direction of the ambulance. 'We better hope that Sergeant Lang was as successful as he had hoped.'

CHAPTER TWENTY-FIVE

'He's dead,' mumbled Brigid, her voice choked with emotion.

'Who? Alim?' replied Baqri, with his phone on speaker.

'Connor! Connor's dead!' Brigid shouted angrily, holding her sat phone in one hand and driving the police car with the other.

'Oh, right. I thought you meant that Alim was dead,' Baqri replied in a relieved tone.

Tom's clinical execution of Connor had resulted in a potent cocktail of emotions for Brigid – with the main ingredients being intense grief, unbridled anger and an all-consuming need for revenge. Just one minute talking to her mentor was, however, all that was needed for her anger to overtake all other feelings.

'Is that it? Is that all you can say? Connor's dead and all you can say is *oh, right*. He's just been gunned down by some bastard government agent and that's your reaction?' Brigid shouted, incensed by Baqri's nonchalance. 'How about something like, *oh my God, I'm so sorry Brigid* instead? I can't believe you just said *oh right!*'

Baqri looked at Sal beside him in the Toyota Land Cruiser, which was still sitting inside the garage of the safe house but now with its door open - ready for them to depart. He held his phone at arm's length as Brigid's tirade continued.

'I think she's a bit upset,' he whispered to Sal, as he covered the mouthpiece - Brigid's bellowing voice still audible.

'I'm sorry Brigid, of course I am,' said Baqri, trying to sound as sincere as he could. 'What did this government agent look like?'

'He was quite tall, well built with brown hair, which was greying at the sides, and wearing white shirt and black trousers. Must have been mid forties, I guess. Sounds like the guy that my contact Laura described - you know the one who was present at the MI5 meetings with her Police Superintendent girlfriend.'

'Ah yes, does sound like him. Must be this new type of agent that they've defrosted. I think they're referred to as *Invisible Sleeper Agents* because nobody knows who they are, and they've just been kept on ice for years. Oooh, think I'm going to call him *Frosty!*' said Baqri excitedly.

'Yeah, great Mohammed. You do that,' said Brigid, with a contemptuous tone in her voice. 'Well, I hate to break it to you but your new friend, *Frosty the Shitbag,* is murdering scum. He looked like the fucking Terminator walking towards Connor. It wasn't much of a gun fight – Connor didn't stand a chance. This bastard shot Connor once in each foot and then shot him three times in the chest. I tell you now Mohammed, I'm going to kill this guy,' said Brigid.

'Frosty the Shitbag, tra-la-la-la-la-laaa!' Baqri sang to the tune of *Frosty the Snowman.* 'Nope, that's never going to be a Christmas favourite.'

'Do you know what? You really are bat shit crazy,' said Brigid.

'*No great mind has ever existed without a touch of madness.* Aristotle said that you know.'

'Great. Thanks for that,' replied Brigid.

'What about Alim? Is he with you?' said Baqri, trying to re-focus the conversation.

'No. They caught up with us and we got surrounded by an armed police unit. I did what you told me to do, and I put a knife in his back,' replied Brigid.

'Well, hopefully if you put it in where I showed you, then he should survive but won't be in any condition to tell them how to stop the EMP going off.'

'I don't think he's going to want to do another attack with you after this, Mohammed,' said Brigid.

'Oh, I think Alim will join us again. I have an incentive, shall we call it, that will guarantee his co-operation. Assuming he lives, of course.'

Sal looked at Baqri with a confused expression on his face.

'I've taken out some insurance - we've now got his mother,' Baqri whispered again to Sal. 'If necessary, I'll send bits of her back to him until he agrees to what I want. Or I run out of mother parts.'

'Mohammed, there's probably only a couple of minutes left till the EMP explodes - maybe even less. I'm going to dump the car and then I'm going to leg it on foot. When all the city's CCTV goes down then I should be able to hide out somewhere. Then I'm going to ...'

Baqri looked over at Sal as the call with Brigid abruptly ended and the lights in the garage flicked off. The EMP had exploded.

'She's gone,' said Baqri looking at his sat phone.

'Is your phone still OK?'

'Yeah, mine still seems to be fine but then we're ten miles out and I had Alim upgrade the protection on it. Brigid must still be too close to the EMP. Well, anyway, I guess that's our cue to get going, Sal,' said Baqri.

'You're not worried by this agent that she described, are you?'

'Well, a little more than I did, I suppose. Anyway, all the CCTV will now be down as will their communications. Plus, none of their cars will work, so I can't see how he can stop us. Does feel a little like there is now a hound chasing the fox though,' admitted Baqri.

'Aren't we supposed to wait for our Iranian contact to call and confirm the attack?'

'If they didn't want this to go ahead then they should have said so earlier - they've left it too late now. Start her up then, Sal. Next stop, Waterloo train station. Departing Platform One for death and carnage!' Baqri said laughing excitedly like a little schoolboy.

Sal started the Land Cruiser and reversed it back into the road.

Baqri turned to Sal with a grin. 'My friend, I think that today is going to be a good day!'

As the Land Cruiser made its way down the suburban street in north London, Baqri looked out of his window and noticed that none of the houses had any lights on - not a single one. People were starting to come out of their houses to check with their neighbours to see if they had any power. Baqri then felt a great sense of accomplishment as they approached their first set of traffic lights, which appeared completely unoperational.

'Traffic's quiet today,' Baqri said with a sense of smugness.

Indeed, the only vehicles still moving on the road were either bicycles or older motor vehicles and even these were few and far between. As the Land Cruiser made its way on to the Hendon Way towards central London, Sal found himself having to weave his way between the lanes and around the more modern vehicles which had simply just stopped - including a police car. The officers were talking to other drivers who had all got out of their cars to investigate. As the Land Cruiser drove past them, Baqri saluted the policemen and laughed. Immediately the police officers recognised the vehicle and passenger from the numerous photos and messages that they had received throughout the day and instinctively tried using their radios to call it in, only to realise that they were as useful as their patrol car.

'The route that I've set out for us Sal, takes into account that some more urban areas might be enjoying a little bit of rioting and looting by now - as our brothers and sisters in *Adalah* will have updated social media about the EMP. So, as much as I would love to see people having a good time, I thought we should try and avoid those areas, where possible, as we have a timetable to stick to. I've also tried to select wide roads, having anticipated the high level of dead cars which you would have to navigate round,' said Baqri.

Sal nodded, remaining as ever, focussed on the job in hand.

'You will be glad to know, however, that I have managed to fit in some sight seeing, which I thought would be fun,' said Baqri. 'So, we will shortly be coming up to South Hampstead and then down to Lords cricket ground. Love a bit of cricket, don't you? A very dignified game, I've always felt. Then we'll be going past Marble Arch and on to Buckingham Palace. Wow, what a place! Did you know that Buckingham Palace has seven hundred and seventy-five rooms? It's about fifteen times the size of the White House. Amazing!'

Sal briefly looked at Baqri without any expression on his face. Geniuses are often eccentric, he thought to himself and there was no doubt in his mind that Baqri was a genius.

'Then, we'll go past Big Ben and the heart of the British Parliament - The Palace of Westminster. Did you know that Big Ben is actually the name of the bell and not the building? People often get that wrong. Named after a big Welshman called Sir Benjamin Hall who oversaw the re-building of the Houses of Parliament and the construction of the clock tower. Big Ben - get-it?'

Sal continued driving, showing little interest in the history lesson that he was being subjected to.

'Anyway, then once we are over Westminster Bridge, we will turn left where our final destination of Waterloo train station awaits. It's all programmed into your SatNav, Sal.'

As the Land Cruiser continued weaving its way into South Hampstead, Sal noticed in the distance that large crowds had formed outside some of the shops. As he got closer, he saw that looting was already in progress - particularly those shops selling electrical and high value items. In fact, there were so many looters that they were blocking the road by standing in the gaps between all the abandoned vehicles. Sal continued driving through the crowds as quickly as he could, trying to avoid running anyone over and sounding his horn every few seconds. At one point, however, the Land Cruiser came to a halt as a large, very over-weight middle aged man in a white T-shirt and jeans, with a similarly shaped girlfriend, decided that they objected to stepping out of the way and started kicking and banging their fists on the SUV's bonnet and doors.

'This is taking far too long,' said Baqri. 'Allow me,' he continued, as he lowered his window.
'Who the fu ...' was as far as the man managed to get before a shot rang out and he dropped backwards like a felled tree - now with the addition of a single hole to his forehead. There was a short pause of silence before the inevitable screaming began from his girlfriend.
'Shhhhhhhh!' said Baqri, with the forefinger of his other hand held in front of his lips.
Her hysterical screaming continued for only a few seconds more before a second shot rang out and she too received a

bullet hole to the head - her face frozen in time as she slumped to the ground.

Shouts and more screaming immediately came from parts of the crowd as they started fleeing from the proximity of the Land Cruiser to the safety of the shops. Baqri continued the occasional shot into the air as Sal navigated his way through the congestion and out the other side to a much quieter section of road.

'Well, I didn't want to shoot many more of them,' said Baqri as Sal looked over at him. 'After all they're doing a very worthwhile job. Having said that, many of them really need to loot some fashion shops for new clothes. The number of times in the past that I've said people should be shot for what they're wearing. Well, at last, that's another tick off my list.'

Lords cricket ground was now just half a mile away when Baqri's sat phone rang.

'Yes, General. Good afternoon,' said Baqri.

For the next few minutes, Baqri said nothing but stared straight ahead as he, unusually, just listened. Sal could see out of the corner of his eye anger gradually start to appear on Baqri's face as the phone conversation continued.

'I see, General. So, what you are saying is that the fearsome Iranian Revolutionary Guard have discovered that they have no backbone. Is that what you are saying? You are on the verge of greatness, General, and now you want to call it off. It's too late for that. I have already sacrificed pawns in this game - this game which I intend to win. When this bomb goes off, you will now get none of the glory, but you will still get the blame. Good luck with the British and American fleets by the way,' Baqri said as he pressed the 'end call' button.

'British and American fleets?' asked Sal.

'Yes, apparently a large allied naval task force has arrived in the Persian Gulf and parked itself off the Iranian coast. They have told the Iranian Supreme Leader that if we manage to successfully damage London then they are going to wipe Tehran off the face of the map. The General tells me that they believe British Intelligence still doesn't know about the bomb in this car, but they are sure that if this kills thousands of British citizens outside Waterloo train station then they will definitely retaliate against Iran.'

'Are we really going to continue?'

'Of course we are, Sal. Once we have demonstrated what we can do to Britain, I can assure you that we will have countries queueing around the block to back our attack on America.'

CHAPTER TWENTY-SIX

'Thank you for the update, Iain,' said Prime Minister Hatcher. 'We're operating on the back-up generator for our general electrical needs, but the phone line came back online pretty quickly - as you can probably tell. Good work, Iain. Your country owes you and your team a debt of gratitude,' he continued before replacing the phone back on to its base.

'That sounded positive, Prime Minister,' said Foreign Secretary, Geraldine Mathews.

'Yes, it was. Much better than I was expecting, bearing in mind that only a few minutes ago we were plunged into darkness,' replied Hatcher. 'First thing, could you arrange to get President Monroe on the phone, please Peter?' asked Hatcher looking at the Cabinet Secretary, Sir Peter Haywood.

As Sir Peter picked up the phone to his more junior staff, Prime Minister Hatcher cleared his throat.

'Can I have everyone's attention please?' said Hatcher in a raised voice, pulling his leather chair up closer to the table in the Cabinet Office briefing room and straightening his back. 'That was Deputy Director Iain McGregor on the phone, by the way. So, as I'm sure you all realise, the EMP device did detonate, and we were unable to stop it. The good news, however, is that our special MI5 lead team have done an incredible job and managed to do enough to limit its impact. The financial sector remains unaffected and the disruption in the power supply should only be temporary. There will still be some things that have been permanently damaged and will need repair or replacement such as some car electrics, phones and domestic appliances - but much of that depends on how close they were to the blast. The bottom line is, though, that the country has not been completely crippled by this attack and disruption to our economy should be minimal.'

Around the table there were audible sighs of relief and many members of the COBRA committee simply muttered *Thank God*.

'I'm afraid, it's not all good news. On the way to delivering their bomb to St Pauls, the terrorists opened fire on a crowd of civilians. Five people were killed, including a five-year-old girl, and a further six were injured - two of which are in a critical condition at St Thomas's hospital,' said Hatcher.

'Did all the terrorists escape, Prime Minister?' asked MI5 Director Sir Nicholas Meads, breaking the short period of silence in the room.

'Well, one of our agents shot and killed a member of the group outside St Paul's. He was actually the driver of the ambulance carrying the EMP. Another one of the group, Doctor Alim Farooqi, was stabbed in the back by the female terrorist, who then escaped the scene,' continued Hatcher.

'Nice,' said Geraldine Mathews sarcastically. 'So, she stabbed one of her own group just so that she could get away?'

'Well yes, but she also ensured that he didn't give our team any information as to how to stop the device going off. Doctor Farooqi was the man who designed and built the EMP. He is still alive and in a serious but stable condition at St Thomas's as well - and under armed guard, of course,' said Hatcher.

'So, what's our response to this?' asked Dawes.

'I think there still needs to be some repercussions for the attack on us. The fact that the EMP didn't send this country back to the dark ages is no thanks to the efforts of Iran. At the end of the day, they are still responsible for it and must be punished,' replied Hatcher.

'The entire destruction of Tehran might be perceived by the rest of the world as disproportionate though, Prime Minister,' said Mathews.

'Agreed. So, when I speak to President Monroe, I will be proposing that we focus our attack on non-residential targets - such as military bases and isolated government buildings. I imagine that the Russians will probably go along with that rather than risk full out war?' Hatcher looked over at Foreign Secretary Mathews, who nodded back in reply.

'Prime Minister. I'm sorry to interrupt but we have just received some news which you may want to consider before you speak to President Monroe and make your final decision,' said Sir Peter Hayward, who had picked up the phone expecting to find the White House on the other end.

'Sir Peter, the expression on your face is giving me grave cause for concern. OK. Let's hear it.'

Sir Peter replaced the phone handset back on its base and slowly raised his head, as he tried to process the information that he had just received.

'Spit it out!' said Hatcher in his usual blunt Yorkshire manner.

'The Iranians claim that the terrorists have another vehicle which is, at this very moment, on its way to Waterloo train station. The leader of the terrorist cell, Mohammed Baqri and his right-hand man Usman Salah are going to set off a large conventional bomb outside,' said Sir Peter, which was quickly followed by more gasps from around the table. 'Because of the EMP detonation, none of the trains are currently operating as all the signal and communication equipment is temporarily offline. They're hoping to catch all the commuters as they leave the station. Of course, it's rush hour, so we are talking about thousands of people.'

'Just when I thought that this nightmare was over,' muttered Hatcher.

'I've taken the liberty of already advising Iain McGregor at MI5, Prime Minister,' said Sir Peter. 'He's dispatching his team to try and intercept them, but they do have the issue that somehow they have to locate some transport which will actually work. The EMP detonation means that very few of our police or military vehicles which were located nearby will be operational and communications will also be hit and miss.'

Hatcher leaned back in his chair and rubbed his forehead again, hating the feeling of not being in control.

'We also have both the Iranian Ambassador and the Russian Ambassador waiting in the lobby and asking to be able to address you, Prime Minister,' said Sir Peter.

'Why the hell are they here? Well, you better show them in. Let's see what they have to say.'

The vocal noise level in the Cabinet Office room had risen to an almost deafening pitch as the various members of the committee furiously discussed the latest new development for a threat that they had thought was behind them. As the Ambassadors were swiftly ushered in, the room fell silent.

The Iranian Ambassador, Ali Javadi, was a small man of around sixty-six years of age with a short, yet slightly receding grey hairline, and neatly kept short grey beard. Small round spectacles sat very high up on his prominent roman nose, so that they were as close to his dark green eyes as possible. The thick lenses of his glasses along with their location on his nose made his eyes look huge - like a 'Mr Magoo' type caricature. His attire was impeccable, however, with a dark blue tailored suit and fine white cotton collarless shirt.

'Mr Ambassador and Madam Ambassador. It's unusual to see two ambassadors at the same time. Why are you here?' said Hatcher, as direct as ever.

'Prime Minister and members of the committee. Iran is not your enemy,' said Javadi, looking at the Prime Minister and then around the table. 'We are a compassionate, peaceful nation and despite the false allegations that you have made about us, claiming that we are behind today's attack on your country, we have been working tirelessly for your benefit and using every resource we have to find the terrorists. As you know, our efforts *have* proved successful, and we have managed to uncover a second part to the terrorist attack which we advised you of immediately. I have also recently been told that one of your Frigates has attacked and destroyed a gun boat of the Revolutionary Guard. Even under this extreme provocation, Iran does not retaliate but offers you the hand of friendship. Hopefully, this will show you that we have only good intentions towards Britain and America.'

'And you managed to say all of that with a straight face,' said Hatcher mockingly. 'That gun boat had breached the exclusion zone and had been told several times to turn back. And as for your hand of friendship ...'

'I'm not sure what you are implying Prime Minister? You surely don't think that we have anything to do with this despicable act against Britain?'

'I'm not particularly good at the subtleties of politics Mr Ambassador, so I won't even try. We *know* that your country is behind it.'

'Excuse me, Prime Minister, but what actual proof do you have of this?' asked Maria Antonov, the Russian Ambassador.

'We have confirmed intelligence reports, Madam Ambassador. This has been corroborated by several other countries' intelligence agencies,' said the Director of MI5, Sir Nicholas Meads.

'With respect, Sir Nicholas, this is not hard proof. The source of this *information* is probably the same for all the intelligence agencies. What if it is wrong? What if it has been fabricated?' replied Antonov.

'Iran is behind this attack, Madam Ambassador. You know it and we know it. I'm not going to play this game and you both need to be aware that there will be consequences. What those are exactly, will depend on whether that bomb goes off outside Waterloo station or not,' said Hatcher.

'Prime Minister, I must formally protest on behalf of the Russian Federation and to warn *you* that there will also be consequences if you attack Iran, and this results in the loss of Russian lives. We do not feel that an attack on a weaker country without irrefutable evidence should be allowed to go unchallenged. The Russian Federation will protect innocent countries from the bullying of Western powers,' said Antonov.

'Madam Ambassador. I would strongly advise that Russia stays out of this. We have already asked all other countries to ensure that their people are evacuated - including yours,' said Hatcher. 'None of us want to see this escalate any more than it has to, but there will be a reckoning. You better pray, Mr Ambassador,' said Hatcher looking at Ali Javadi, 'that we manage to stop that bomb in time because otherwise Tehran *will* follow the fate of Sodom and Gomorrah. I can promise you two things, Mr Ambassador - fire and brimstone.'

Once the ambassadors had left the Cabinet Office briefing room, Hatcher turned to the Foreign Secretary.

'What do you think, Geraldine?'

'Well, I certainly think that you left little room for misinterpretation there, Prime Minister,' said Mathews, who was still sometimes taken aback by the directness of her boss. 'My thoughts are that, at the moment, both the Iranians and the Russians will let some form of retribution happen for the detonation of the EMP, so long as they can sell it at home as being very minor. The problem will come if that bomb does go off outside Waterloo and it kills hundreds or even thousands of people. You will have to follow through with your threat about attacking Tehran. If you don't, we will never be taken seriously again and will appear weak and soft to other organisations and other countries.'

I have never relented to bullies and I've never backed down to them. I'm certainly not going to start now, thought Hatcher. *All my life, people thought that I was going to be any easy target because of my size And at every point, I have proved to them that my bark isn't worse than my bite. Try picking on me and I will bite you so hard that you'll be begging for a rabies vaccination.*

'And I bloody will. That wasn't just bluster,' said Hatcher banging his fist down on the table, startling everyone else.

The room went silent, and many members of the COBRA committee sat bolt upright in their seats, transfixed by the sight of their Prime Minister focussed and passionate.

'I won't let this proud and great nation be humiliated on the world stage,' Hatcher said banging his fist on the table again. 'This small but mighty island which controlled the biggest empire that the world has ever known - that defeated the Spanish Armada and Napoleon Bonaparte - a country that stood alone against the Nazi war machine in 1940 and whose 'few' beat the Nazi Luftwaffe in the skies over Britain - that won two world wars. This country is no-one's whipping boy. The British people expect us to strike back and strike back hard. We will not let them down!' he shouted over the sound of cheers and table pounding.

CHAPTER TWENTY-SEVEN

'Madam President, I have just received word that we have destroyed a Russian S70 Hunter which had entered the exclusion zone around the fifth fleet,' said Admiral Womack, replacing the phone back on to its base and then reaching for the remote control for the wall monitors.

'Just remind me, Ted, what sort of aircraft that is?' asked President Monroe.

'It's an unmanned drone, Ma'am,' said Womack. 'But you shouldn't imagine it as one those little drones that you may have seen before - more like one of our Stealth Fighters. This aircraft flies supersonic, weighs about twenty tons, with a huge wingspan and has a two-ton payload of missiles. I'm afraid that's not the only infraction. If you would please look at the screen, Madam President. This is a Russian MiG 29 fighter which has just entered the exclusion zone, even though we warned the pilot to turn around. It is still proceeding towards the naval task force, and we have warned it twice more.'

Jane Monroe rose from her chair, walked down to the bottom of the Situation Room and sat down on the end of the table, directly in front of the monitor, and crossed her arms.

'This is the Russian aircraft, and these are two of our FA18 Super Hornets following it,' said Admiral Womack, pointing at the coloured triangles on the screen - each of which had an identification box over them. 'And this is the US and British naval task force. As you can see, the Russian aircraft is heading directly at it,' he continued as he identified the cluster of white dots in the middle of the map, labelled as the Persian Gulf.

'Shoot it down, Admiral,' said Monroe in a decisive but sombre tone, as the rest of the National Security team started assembling around him to watch the screen.

Monroe watched on for a minute, as the icon for the MiG along with its identification box suddenly disappeared from the screen. Everyone in the room continued staring at the screen until the President stood up, buttoned the jacket of her navy-blue suit up again and, in her trademark relaxed style, sauntered back to her chair.

'Well, everybody,' said Monroe in her slow Texan manner. 'I'm sure ya'll know that this won't go down too well with Russia. They tend to get a little bit ... shall we say, tetchy ... when we blow up one of their aircraft. I believe, however, that this was a deliberate attempt to test our resolve and we have now shown them that we are good to our word. There should be little doubt in the mind of President Petrov about the seriousness of our intentions if the attack on the UK is successful.'

There was silence in the room as Jane Monroe leaned back in her chair. *What will Russia's response be? She could expect a call from President Petrov that was for sure, but would they really risk escalating the whole thing? At the end of the day, the choice of where and how far this situation went was up to Russia and Iran. America would stay strong and prepared.*

'Admiral Womack. Please ensure that we remain on the highest state of alert. I think we can expect to be tested a number of times in the near future,' said Monroe.

'Yes, Ma'am,' said Womack. 'Our aircraft are doing non-stop reconnaissance missions around the perimeter of the exclusion zone, Madam President. As are the British, of course.'

'Madam President, talking of the British,' said James McInnis, the President's fresh-faced 35-year-old Chief of Staff. 'We have just notified them about the MiG and S70 Hunter incidents, and they tell us that they have just had an incident of their own. Apparently, an Iranian Revolutionary Guard gun boat breached the exclusion zone, so the British sent a small boat out to tell it to turn around. The Iranians instead then tried to capture it but it escaped. A British frigate was forced to destroy the gunboat when it started firing on them.'

'Seems like they're trying to test both of us,' said Monroe.

'Madam President, I have also just been made aware that the Russian fleet, which left the Syrian port of Tartus this morning, has just entered the Suez Canal. This will then take it through to the Red Sea and we believe their final destination is the Persian Gulf,' said Admiral Womack, turning to another monitor showing satellite images of the Russian fleet. 'You might be confused by thinking that Russia had planned for a confrontation, bearing mind that their fleet had already set sail before we downed the S70 Hunter drone.'

'It seems that the Russian bear is still trying to prove its strength on the world stage and consolidate its position in the Middle East. What exactly does the Russian fleet consist of Admiral?' asked Secretary of State, Walter Houston.

'It's a carrier group with the Aircraft Carrier *Admiral Kuznetsov* at the heart of it. Other vessels include the Guided Missile Ship *Veliky Ustyug*, the Missile Cruiser *Marshal Ustinov*, two Varshavyanka class submarines and ten other ships,' said Womack.

The President looked over at her Chief of Staff. Her respect for James McInnis wasn't purely down to the fact that he was a workaholic who slept just five hours a night but that he always seemed to manage her Presidential matters with such apparent effortless and efficient ease. With a master's degree in mathematics from Harvard as well as an early career as a corporate analyst, McInnis was also highly respected through the government for his ability to evaluate and dissect any issue down into its core components.

'Can we have your comparison of how the fleets compare, Admiral?' asked McInnis.

'Well, the British fleet is very high tech. Their aircraft carrier and destroyers are the newest ships out there and state of the art. I would put them up against the Russian fleet on their own. Our fleet is also technologically superior to the Russians and, of course, we have the numbers. The Russian fleet might be a little bit more dated but it's still effective and, of course, technology isn't everything when it comes to a battle. A surprise and co-ordinated attack by their naval task force as well as fighter aircraft from their bases in the Middle East would still be devastating,' replied Womack.

'OK, so this is how I see it,' Monroe said slowly. 'We are the greatest military power on the planet - are we not?' she continued, looking around the table and observing the nodding heads. 'I think we need to remind Russia of that fact. I think that we need to show them that they're playing in the wrong league and that we don't appreciate them pissing in our pool. I think that we need to stick a gun right up against the Russian nose and tell them to back off or we're gonna blow their goddamn head clean off.'

The hardening of the President's tone was now starting to alarm the more pacifist members of the National Security Team and the Speaker of the House, Jennifer Wolff. Wolff started fidgeting in her seat as she looked around the table to see if she could work out from their body language who else was getting uncomfortable.

'Madam President. As Supreme Commander of our armed forces, you obviously have the power to make military decisions as you feel fit. But if you want my support with Congress, then I would really urge restraint and not fan the flames of conflict. Have you ever known the Russians to back off? They will never allow themselves to be humiliated in front of the world, so we really need to make sure that a political escape route is left so that they can save face. Otherwise, this could escalate to a nuclear conflict,' said Wolff.

'The one thing that I have learnt about the Russian bear, Madam Speaker, is that they only respect strength. If they pull out a pistol, we pull out a shotgun. If they pull out a shotgun, we pull out a goddamn bazooka. I intend to put them in a position that makes Petrov back down or he <u>will</u> face the humiliation of the destruction of his entire fleet. Admiral, have we another fleet that we can send as well, so that it arrives on the other side of the Russians and effectively boxes them in?' asked Monroe.

'We could send the sixth fleet from the Mediterranean, Madam President. The Russians will see it following their fleet up the Suez Canal. Should make them nervous,' replied Womack.

'OK, good - do it. Also, put our nuclear deterrent up a notch - DEFCON 3. And make sure the Russians know that we've done it. If they're gonna sit at the poker table with me then they need to know that I <u>will</u> call their bluff. I'm a Texan, after all, and one thing we do know a bit about and that's poker,' said Monroe leaning back again in her chair.

Speaker Wolff had now moved from being alarmed and uncomfortable with the President's rhetoric to simply being terrified - her mouth physically dropping open at her latest move.

'Madam President - I must formally protest at this decision. Have you never heard the expression *don't poke the bear*? If you corner the Russians, then how do think this is going to pan out?' said Wolff.

'Jen, the previous administration were weak with Russia,' interrupted Secretary Houston. 'I'll give you some examples. We pulled our troops out of areas where we had been helping our allies defeat terrorist organisations. So, what happened?

190

Russia stepped in as if they were the saviours of the planet and gained global praise. We did nothing when Russia annexed territories from other weaker countries around them - those countries which were our natural allies. When there had been a humanitarian crisis somewhere in the world, it was Russia who was the first to step in with aid. We allowed them to create and promote dissent within our own country and we allowed them to increase their own global influence at the same time as diminishing ours. Now they are supporting a rogue country which is helping terrorists cripple our closest ally - with the aim of moving on to us next. It's clear to me that this has been a long campaign by Russia against us.'

'And one which I have no intention of allowing to succeed,' continued President Monroe.

'Madam President, sorry to interrupt you but I have the British Prime Minister on the phone. The EMP has partially detonated in London and worse still, there is a huge conventional fragmentation bomb on its way to Waterloo train station,' said Chief of Staff, James McInnis.

President Monroe took a moment to absorb the information from her Chief of Staff before picking up the phone in front of her.

'Bob? Jesus, what the hell happened?' asked Monroe.

For the next few minutes, Jane Monroe sat quietly - only occasionally nodding her head, as Prime Minister Hatcher updated her on the situation in London.

'I agree. I'll get Admiral Womack to co-ordinate our response,' said Monroe before replacing the phone receiver and then looking around the table.

'So, as James just mentioned, the EMP did go off in London. But before y'all get too worked up, the good news is that a special MI5 team managed to minimise its effectiveness before it detonated. All their financial and government sectors are already back to normal, and they expect everything else to be fully up and running by tomorrow,' said Monroe to audible sounds of relief and a 'Thank Goodness' from Speaker Wolff, who slumped back into her chair, now feeling that the conflict may have just de-escalated a notch or two.

'The MI5 team will now try and intercept the leader of the terrorist cell and his right-hand man before they get to Waterloo. Apparently, their leader, Mohammed Baqri, had another part to his plan and that was to set off a bomb at the train station once commuters discovered that none of the trains were operating due to the EMP and they then all assembled by the road. In case y'all don't know, Waterloo is Britain's busiest train station and so it would be fair to say thousands of people would be killed if they were successful. What the terrorists don't know is that the EMP didn't detonate fully, and the police are moving to cordon off the station anyway. In fact, the Prime Minister has been told that the city's extensive CCTV system should be coming back online soon, so there is a good chance that they will capture or kill the terrorists,' Monroe continued.

'That all sounds very positive, Madam President, but I assume we're not just going to let Iran off this?' asked Secretary Houston.

'The Prime Minister feels that Iran should still be punished for the EMP attack but that a limited military response is more appropriate rather than a full-on attack on

Tehran. He's thinking that perhaps we hit some of their military bases and airfields to show the world that there are consequences. Sounds fair to me and I doubt the Russians will be inclined to retaliate. If this pans out, then it seems that we may even see a de-scaling of military activities - but not yet. I'm sure you'll be pleased to see that, Jen,' Monroe said, smiling at Speaker Wolff. 'Admiral, could you liaise with the British on our response?'

'What are we going to do if that other bomb does go off at Waterloo station or somewhere else, Madam President and kills hundreds or even thousands of people?' asked Houston.

Jennifer Wolff slowly sat upright in her chair again - her stomach now churning in anticipation of the President's response. President Monroe stood up and, once more, slowly walked down the table to the bank of monitors and stood staring at the map of the Persian Gulf.

'Well, Walt.' Monroe raised her hand and then tapped on the satellite image of Tehran.

'Then this will be our next target.'

CHAPTER TWENTY-EIGHT

'We've got the location of Baqri.' Jax's voice was barely audible over the sound of all the sirens from the numerous police and emergency services vehicles which had now arrived at the scene outside St. Pauls Cathedral.

Tom was standing with Staff Sergeant Lang, staring at the wreckage of the ambulance, which had been ripped apart like a tin can by the blast of the EMP and with little more than its chassis still recognisable.

'Well, I don't think that's a bad result, really,' said Lang scratching his head. 'OK, the ambulance may need to go to the body shop for a small paint job and that hole in the road underneath could do with being filled in. But apart from that, it's all good,' he continued with a grin on his face.

Tom looked at the smouldering wreck and smiled back at him.

Tom said, 'Staff Sergeant Lang, I must say that I think you are nothing short of a genius. Well, for a ginger Cockney that is.'

'Oi!' said Lang with a look of feigned offence.

'Tom, we know where Baqri is. We've got to go,' shouted Jax again, as he ran over to the other two. 'Staff Sergeant Lang, you're with us too. Think we're going to need you again.'

Tom looked at Jax quizzically.

'I'll update you once we're on our way - this isn't over yet. We're going to need to borrow one of these police vehicles which have just arrived from outside the area - ours are dead,' said Jax.

At the same time as the MI5 team were requisitioning a marked BMW X5 police car, Baqri's Land Cruiser SUV had just passed Marble Arch when he received an unexpected call on his sat phone.

'Benny the Bomb! Lovely to hear from you but your congratulations are a little premature. Still got to blow up a train station yet!' exclaimed Baqri laughing.

Even though he was aware that the nickname given to him by MI5 was meant to be disparaging, Benny Erickson nevertheless used it as a sort of trademark - a brand that made him famous throughout the world for the services that he offered. At some point, he always felt, he should really thank Iain McGregor at MI5 for coming up with it.

Baqri's laughter abruptly stopped. His facial expression changed to a look of disappointment and annoyance.

'That's very, very irritating. How confident are you about the reliability of your contact's information?'

'Everything OK?' asked Sal, as Baqri ended his call.

Baqri looked out of the window in silence, with a face like a little boy in a sulk because he had just been deprived of his favourite toy. A few moments later, his face changed as he looked at Sal with a smile.

'Well, I'm a glass half-full sort of person, Sal,' said Baqri, clapping his hands together. 'Change of plan. Apparently, thanks to *Frosty* and his team, or *Frosty the Shitbag* as Brigid prefers to call him, the EMP only partially detonated and they're now on their way to intercept us before we get to Waterloo - which by the way is expected to return to being fully functional very shortly. So, you need to turn around and head to this destination,' he continued, tapping a destination into the SatNav.

'How the hell do they know where we are going?' asked Sal, as he performed a U-turn in the road.

'The Iranians have ratted us out. They're now so scared that their capital city is going to be wiped off the map, they basically told the British everything about our plan. Well, the plan as far as they know it. There is, of course, a Plan B. As Sun Tzu said, *'a plan that cannot be changed is not a good plan.'*

'What about the Russians? asked Sal.

'Well, the Russians have cooled a bit on the whole thing. They seem to be concerned about the likely actions of President Jane Monroe or Calamity Jane, I think I'll call her.'

'Calamity Jane?' asked Sal, frowning at Baqri - often finding it difficult to keep up with his random phrases.

'You know - *'Oh, the Deadwood Stage is a-rolling on over the plains.'* Or how about *'Just flew in from the Windy City?'* Baqri sang, as if he was in the famous film.

Sal briefly looked over at Baqri with a blank look on his face.

'You know the fabulous western musical with Doris Day? No? Wow, Sal - are you telling me that you've never seen it? OK, I'll try and phrase it a different way. Apparently, the Russians mentioned something about a humongous, gun toting, female redneck who currently occupies the White House. Their concern is that the problems in the Gulf are going to escalate as President Monroe seems to be set on a military conflict. Iran was supposed to be their fall guy but now they've just folded.'

'So, we are...I mean, *Adalah* is on its own then,' said Sal as a statement of fact.

'Oh no, Sal. We're certainly not on our own.'

Sal glanced over at Baqri with a confused expression on his face.

'Eyes on the road, Sal. And you need to step on it. I gather that London's ridiculous all-seeing CCTV system is due to come back online very shortly and then it won't take them long to track us down - so time is short. Chop chop.'

Sal increased the speed slightly of the Land Cruiser but not so fast that it compromised his ability to weave around the occasional abandoned vehicle.

'No, I don't get it. If the Iranians have pulled out and the Russians are starting to get cold feet, then where is Benny getting his information from?'

Baqri thought for a moment as how best to phrase his answer, scratching his goatee as he did so.

'OK, so the best way to think of this is like you were at one of those tables in a casino. Players come and go. Some leave the game, perhaps feeling their luck is about to run out and others, like Iran, realise that they didn't have the backbone to be in the game to start with. Other players join the game when others leave, and the game continues.'

'So, who has joined the game?' asked Sal.

'An organisation called *The Collective*. Benny described it as probably the most powerful organisation that we've never heard of. Financiers, business leaders, politicians, bankers - even some world leaders apparently. No one knows who their members are - they don't even know. Decisions are done electronically and are encrypted - highly sophisticated, so that if one of them is discovered they cannot disclose the names of anyone else in the organisation because they simply don't know. The decisions that this organisation makes affects the world but very few people have ever heard of it.'

'I don't understand why they would want to help us though?' said Sal.

'From what Benny was just saying, they were expecting our attack to be successful and that a conflict between America, Britain and Russia would follow. Perhaps a few of their members had shorted shares in some major British companies, perhaps it's all about the oil price and maybe others had political motives. I don't know Sal, but what I do know is that if we manage to detonate this bomb successfully, then there will be a major military conflict in the Gulf or maybe even on a global level - and that's what they want. *The Collective* were suitably impressed with our EMP apparently and that it actually detonated - albeit with reduced effect. They're the ones who provided Benny with the intel on the MI5 team.'

'OK, but why should we want to be with them? *Adalah* is based on carrying out God's justice - not capitalism which is all these people seem to care about,' said Sal.

It was unusual for Sal to question his leader and for a moment Baqri was quite taken aback. Sal had a point though. He truly believed that he was a soldier of God and that he was carrying out *his* will. Baqri thought for a moment as to how he could square the circle in Sal's mind so that he would find the situation to be acceptable.

'Sal, when Allah decides to help us, it is not for us to question the way that he provides it,' Baqri said, almost like an Imam speaking to his congregation.

Sal nodded, now realising that despite the initial disappointment of the EMP device failing to fully detonate, there were still grounds for great optimism in the form of their new ally. Baqri was right too - it did not matter where divine support came from because clearly this was God's work.

'One more thing that's very exciting,' said Baqri. 'They have pledged to support us both financially and operationally in our attack on America. Do you realise how big this is, Sal? These people have powerful contacts everywhere.'

'Mohammed,' said Sal, pointing at the now active traffic lights on the approaching crossroads.

'I think we can assume that their CCTV is now also operational. We are on borrowed time, Sal. *Frosty* will soon come looking for us along with the whole of the Metropolitan police force.'

Sal looked at the Sat Nav but having to squint slightly as the sun emerged from behind a cloud.

'We will be arriving at Wembley Stadium in approximately fifteen to twenty minutes,' said Sal pushing down on the accelerator.

CHAPTER TWENTY-NINE

The police BMW X5 raced away from the incident scene outside St Paul's Cathedral with Tom, once again, at the wheel. Beside him sat Captain Jax who had now developed a great deal of respect for the more mature MI5 officer and a close bond was starting to form between the two. As the police car hurtled around the London streets, Jax found himself staring at Tom.

'What?' Tom said in a raised voice over the sound of the car's engine, seeing Jax out of the corner of his eye. 'Are you wondering whether you're going to look this good when you're my age?'

'Ha!' said Jax smirking. 'Actually, I was thinking what an amazing program MI5 had developed with this ISA thing. When I first met you, I have to admit that I wondered what the hell they were playing at. Middle aged guy whose job was an architect. I thought '*Are you kidding me? We're putting the fate of a mission to save thousands of lives and our nation's economy in some Invisible Sleeper Agent who hasn't shot a gun in years?*'

'Yeah, I have to admit I thought something similar,' said Lang from the back seat.

'That's nice. Thank you, guys,' said Tom sarcastically. 'I have to admit, I wondered about you as well, Jax.'

'You did? In what way?' asked Jax.

'Well, the first thing I wondered was how the hell does a guy so small and skinny have such a deep voice.'

Jax smiled at Tom and nodded - clearly not the first time he had heard that. Lang laughed.

'Is there something amusing you, Staff Sergeant?' asked Jax.

'No, Sir. Just remembering a really funny programme I watched on TV the other day,' Lang replied tongue-in-cheek.

'But you've done well for yourself, Jax. Captain in the SAS. Bet your family are proud,' said Tom.

'Well, they are, yes. Mostly, anyway. Except my granddad. He's Jamaican and when he heard the news that I had made it into the SAS, he just said *'that's ok but it would have been better if he had become a great cricketer instead!'* said Jax, trying to do his best West Indian accent.

The laughter in the car was abruptly interrupted by the ringing of Jax's sat phone and the group was quickly brought back to the reality of their current on-going situation.

'You won't believe this,' said Jax, as he ended the phone call. 'All the CCTV has now come back online, and they've located Baqri's SUV.'

'Hey, hey,' said Lang. 'Everything coming back online already. Not a bad job Staff Sergeant Lang - even if I do say so myself.'

'So, that's good news, isn't it?' asked Tom.

Jax said, 'The thing is, their Land Cruiser has just turned around. It's now going in completely the wrong direction if

201

they wanted to go to Waterloo. It's just turned north - back up the A5. What the hell is going on?'

'Someone's tipped them off, that's what's going on,' said Tom, turning the police car west and accelerating hard.

Tom thought for a moment.

'When we raided the unit on the Sovereign Business Park in London this morning, they were already gone. When your men arrived at the disused warehouse in Birmingham, they were already gone. I think you said at the time that your unit had reported back that Benny Erickson and his men *seemed to have left in a hurry?*' And now, Baqri does a U-turn as soon as we discover his intended target. We thought that it was all down to information given out by Superintendent Carson but there are also other forces at work here, gentlemen. I'm not sure that we can trust anyone but ourselves.'

The silence in the car was broken again by the ringing of Jax's sat phone. It was Mac.

'Deputy Director McGregor wanted to let us know that the British and American fleets have just attacked key military targets within Iran in retaliation for the EMP detonation outside St Pauls,' said Jax ending his call. 'So far, the Russians have just condemned the action but not taken it any further. He also wanted to advise us that Prime Minister Hatcher and President Monroe have resolved to launch a full-scale missile attack on Tehran should this second bomb explode with the loss of considerable lives. They didn't put a figure on what 'considerable' meant apparently. Intelligence reports from MI6 have concluded that Russia will then almost certainly feel forced to retaliate.'

'Jesus,' said Lang. 'And then where does it go?'

'Well, bearing in mind that Monroe has apparently sent the US sixth fleet from the Mediterranean to join their fifth fleet and the British task force in the Persian Gulf, their most likely scenario is the attack and decimation of all Russian ships,' replied Jax.

Tom said, 'This is how world wars start. The difference being that this time around, everyone has nuclear weapons pointed at each other.'

'Well, no pressure then. We better work out where the hell Baqri is heading. Somewhere where they can inflict maximum casualties, I guess. Any ideas?' asked Jax.

'It has to be a place where a large number of people gather. At the end of the day, Baqri wants to go down in history. Killing a few people just doesn't cut it. That's why he chose Waterloo. So, where else would he go, assuming he keeps heading Northwest?' asked Tom.

Tom turned the BMW on to Southampton Row, heading north towards the A501 - just two and a half miles from Baqri's Land Cruiser and floored the accelerator in the X5.

'A large gathering? What about a concert? Or maybe a big sports event or something?' said Jax.

'You mean something like a big football match? Bit like the Euro Finals today at Wembley Stadium, do you mean?' said Lang.

Tom and Captain Jax in unison, looked at each other.

'Ninety thousand football supporters from little children to old pensioners,' Lang continued.

At the same time as the police BMW X5 was racing towards the T-junction with the A501, Baqri was just approaching the turning for the Westway towards Wembley. Tom had successfully closed the gap between them to less than two miles but then, as he turned left at the junction, the team found themselves facing an impenetrable wall of police cars blocking the road. A sea of blue flashing lights and a dozen armed police officers positioned behind their cars - all aiming their semi automatic weapons at the X5. The BMW screeched to a halt as Tom slammed on the brakes and then looked in his rear-view mirror. Behind him - on the other side of the T-junction - was another row of police cars with armed officers stood behind.

'What the hell's this?' said Lang from the rear of the car.

Jax said, 'The *other forces* at work, I would say.'

Tom briefly considered turning around and driving back down the way that they had come until two more police SUV's pulled up immediately behind him. They were now trapped.

'Put your weapons down,' shouted the police inspector in the middle of the barricade, as Tom, Jax and Lang stepped out of the BMW with their hands raised in the air.

'Inspector, I'm an MI5 officer and, as you can see, these guys are British army,' Tom shouted back.

'I repeat. Lay your weapons down,' yelled the Police Inspector.

Tom looked behind them. The doors of the other two police SUVs opened.

'My team,' Jax said smiling, as the SAS unit exited their vehicles and levelled their weapons at the police.

'Inspector, as you can see, these are SAS soldiers. Do we look like the two terrorists that are supposed to be running around London to you? Do you really want to engage in a shoot out with the SAS? We currently have a lunatic on his way to Wembley stadium with a four-thousand-pound bomb and, by stopping us, you are going to be responsible for allowing them to kill thousands of people and probably start a war. Do you want that, or should I just call Commander Malik?' shouted Tom.

Jax looked at Tom, surprised by his offer.

'We're up against the clock, Jax. It's the quickest way to get us moving again - assuming I'm right, of course, and that Malik is one of the good guys.'

The intervention by Commander Malik was swift and within minutes the Police Inspector had stood up from behind the blockade, instructed his men to lower their weapons and move their cars, and then started walking towards the MI5 team.

'I'm sorry but we were told that you were colluding with the terrorists. We were ordered to stop you at any cost,' said the Inspector.

'Who told you?' asked Jax.

'I don't know where it originated from by our instructions were relayed by our Control in the normal manner,' Inspector Harris replied.

'It doesn't matter at the moment. It's *us* that need to slow *them* down now,' said Jax, returning to the front passenger seat.

'We reckon that they will take the Westway onto the A40 and then north up the A406 and past Brent Park. Inspector, would you be able to get your men to block off the surrounding roads? I'm hoping that we can not only stop them just before Wembley but capture them as well. Probably best to liaise with Commander Malik,' said Tom, as he also climbed back into the police SUV.

'Do you think they're trying to time the explosion for when all the football supporters leave the stadium?' Tom asked, looking around at Staff Sergeant Lang in the rear.

'Well, if that is the plan, then I need to tell you that with a bomb this big, the carnage will be like nothing you could have ever imagined. It's not just the immediate casualties who are near the explosion but, of course, there will lethal flying debris from other things nearby - like the parked cars,' said Lang. 'Actually, thinking about it, if they were to get <u>under</u> the stadium and set off the bomb when people are still watching the match then ...'

'Go on,' said Jax.

'It's just a thought but ... if he managed to drive through say one of the service gates and get underneath Wembley stadium, then the intensity of the blast from a four-thousand-pound high yield bomb could actually damage the integrity of the building's structure and probably enough to affect the stadium above it,' replied Lang.

'Are you saying that Wembley could collapse as a result?' asked Jax.

'Well, it's unlikely that the whole stadium will but parts of it might if you detonated it in the right place,' said Lang.

'And one thing I can guarantee is that Baqri will have done his homework on this. He will know exactly where to put the van,' replied Tom, as he once again pushed his right foot hard down on the accelerator and raced away from the roadblock.

'Yeah, but surely Wembley would have some measures in place to prevent this sort of attack. You know, like barriers and security and stuff,' said Lang.

Tom replied, 'Except you're forgetting one important thing. Baqri now has new powerful friends helping him. I reckon they could make all that disappear for him if they wanted to.'

CHAPTER THIRTY

The engine of the X5 was now screaming, as Tom pushed the Police SUV harder and harder along the A501, weaving in and out of obstacles and going at speeds that, at times, seemed to resemble a video game. Shops and abandoned vehicles went by in just a blur and the rest of Jax's SAS team were now a considerable way behind - being highly trained for combat but less so for high speed driving. Jax and Lang sat there feeling that they should at least be a little bit nervous by the speed that Tom was driving at, but instead somehow feeling completely confident is his abilities.

'Yes, sir,' said Jax, answering his phone in a slightly raised voice to be heard over the engine noise. 'Well, we're catching up on them quickly now - after our little delay courtesy of the Metropolitan Police. Yes, sir, we reached the same conclusion. Any idea who is behind it? I see. I'll pass that all on to Tom.'

The stand-off with the police had indeed cost the MI5 team considerable time, as they were now some five miles behind Baqri's Land Cruiser. Tom's exceptional driving, however, meant that the gap was now closing again - and fast.

'According to Iain McGregor, MI5 have discovered that a group called *The Collective* are the ones who have intervened on behalf of the terrorists. They may have been helping them from the very start but trying to stay out of the spotlight. He said that from now on we should only communicate with him and Commander Malik,' said Jax.

'Who the bloody hell is *The Collective?*' asked Lang.

'He didn't want to go into it. Mind you, it didn't sound like he could give us much detail on them even if he wanted to. He just said that the challenge has now moved to another level and that, ironically, we are now dealing with a powerful organisation of *invisibles*. Not like you, Tom. He said they are a group of influential and powerful but anonymous individuals from around the globe. I don't know how we are supposed to deal with that. I mean we'll fight anyone in the world, but we can't fight them if we don't know who they are.'

'OK and the other question is who are the people in this *Collective*? I mean I've never heard anyone even mention them before today,' said Lang. 'Now we find out that there is a group of unknown individuals out there who are somehow able to mobilise two police armed response units against us without anyone knowing who gave the order. Who the hell do we trust? I mean this group makes the frigging Illuminati sound like they were an open and transparent organisation by comparison.'

'As Mac has said, Staff Sergeant, our circle of trust is limited to the five of us. We need to concentrate on stopping that bomb because, at the moment, that's all we can do. I can't help but feel though that this will be the easy bit. Whatever master plan *The Collective* have for the world, I'm pretty sure that us stopping Baqri will be just a mild inconvenience for them,' said Tom ominously as the Police X5 raced along the A40 overpass and on to the Westway.

Tom empathised completely with Staff Sergeant Lang's anguish over their situation. They were no longer just trying to stop a terrorist group supported by a rogue state. This had now become much bigger - in fact it always had been, but they just didn't know it at the time. It had seemed so simple and straight forward to start with. Everything was black and white. But now a large area of grey sat in the middle - an area occupied by *The Collective*.

'Tom. I have good news and bad news,' said Jax, pressing the end call button on his phone. 'The good news is that we are just a few miles behind Baqri now, thanks to your mad driving. The bad news is that MI5 have now lost sight of them.'

'Sorry Sir but what do you mean by *they've lost sight of them*? How have they lost them? Does the CCTV not go that far out or something?' asked Lang.

'It does but the whole of London's CCTV system has just gone down,' replied Jax, raising his eyebrows.

Lang said, 'No prizes for guessing who's behind that. Sort of feels like we're playing against someone who keeps cheating to make sure his team wins.'

'I'm not going to let them win - whatever they do. Can you call Mac back and ask him if we can get satellite surveillance instead - if he's not already got it?' said Tom before he paused for thought. 'Also, find out where they were when the CCTV went down.'

The Police X5 had now passed North Acton, travelling along the triple lane carriageway at speeds of up to one hundred and twenty miles an hour at times. The road had now become noticeably busier due to the presence of traffic which had been far enough away not to be affected by the blast of the EMP. Tom was forced to leave the sirens and lights on, even though he knew it risked alerting the terrorists.

'Mac said that, as if by incredible coincidence, they lost the CCTV link at the same time as Commander Malik was trying to organise police roadblocks,' said Jax, putting his sat-phone down again. 'So, it looks like they were trying to blind Malik - which they've done of course. Anyway, Mac says that they are still following the Land Cruiser by satellite and we're just under a mile and a half behind them now.'

Tom had expected further intervention by *The Collective* in favour of the terrorists, so the loss of the cctv system really didn't come as any big surprise. At least with satellite surveillance still operational, he felt confident that they would catch Baqri well before he made it anywhere near Wembley stadium. With a skilled piece of driving, the X5 dodged its way around and through the traffic, up the slip road and on to the A406 North Circular Road.

'Keep your eyes peeled gentlemen. We should be on them very shortly,' said Tom, pushing the X5 hard again.

'You're kidding me, right? ... Really? ... How? ... Jesus!' said Jax, ending another call with Deputy Director McGregor. With

211

a clear look of irritation on his face, he turned to Tom. 'Get this. Although they *were* also tracking them by satellite, the satellite has now suddenly been re-directed by persons unknown. So, we really are now completely blind.'

The news that contact had been lost with the Landcruiser now forced Tom to reduce his speed, as he considered his next move.

'You're having a giraffe!' exclaimed Sergeant Lang from the back seat in his finest Cockney rhyming slang. 'Who the hell has the clout to re-direct a satellite as well as disable the capital's cctv network?'

Tom considered Lang's last question. And it was a good question. Whichever member or members of *The Collective* were responsible for this had really stuck their necks out. Surely it couldn't be too difficult to track them down - not many people had the authority to do what they had done. They must be getting pretty desperate. *Better make sure that we serve them up a big portion of disappointment* Tom thought to himself.

'What are you thinking?' asked Jax, noticing that Tom had a slight smirk on his face.

'I'm thinking this. We know that Baqri plans everything to the Nth degree. We forced him to change targets from Waterloo to Wembley Stadium. He will have laid out a plan for that as well. The satellite and cctv surveillance will have gone down at the times that they did for a good reason. So, what doesn't he want us to see? Also, put yourself in his boots. Your biggest risk right now is being visually identified by police units. So, what would you have planned if you were him?'

'I would try to avoid main roads where you are more likely to get spotted by the police, I suppose,' said Lang.

'I'd probably want to get rid of that Land Cruiser as well. It's not exactly subtle, is it?' Jax added.

'Problem is it's carrying a four-thousand-pound bomb. So how do you move a bomb that big?' Tom replied and then paused for thought again. 'Jax, can you have a look at a map? They don't want us to see something or somewhere. What is there in the area immediately after the point where we lost the satellite?'

'Well, there's a slip road about half a mile ahead of them and off that is the Northfields industrial estate with various light units such as a car part suppliers, builders merchants and a tyre centre,' replied Jax looking at his phone. 'Behind that are some waterways. Looks like the River Brent and the Grand Union Canal. Not sure that's going help them get their bomb to Wembley though,' replied Jax.

'Mmmm,' said Tom. 'How many ways are there in and out of that industrial estate?'

Jax replied, 'It looks like there is only one way in from the North Circular slip road but there are a few roads that lead out on the other side. Having said that, if they were trying to get to Wembley Stadium then all those roads join up with just two main roads - the Ealing Road being the most direct or the longer Bridgewater Road. If they have gone that way rather than sticking to the North Circular, then they could keep a much lower profile and ... hang on a minute ... are you thinking what I'm thinking?'

'I am. If they want to swap vehicles, then that's an ideal location. Drive into an industrial unit, transfer the bomb over to another vehicle and then out the other side. Jax, can you get some police units there quickly? Get them to block off the access road and also the two main roads on the other side,' said Tom. 'I bet Baqri intends to take the Ealing Road.'

It was only a matter of minutes before the MI5 team had driven through the industrial estate and on to the Ealing Road. Tom knew that even though Baqri would have been well prepared, moving a four-thousand-pound bomb would still have taken a little time. This meant that if he had correctly guessed the right road that they had taken, Baqri and Sal had to be very close by. The BMW X5 raced down the road and just before the Wembley Mosque, the police roadblock came into view. Tom drove down the side of the queuing traffic at a much slower speed, so that Jax could take a good look at each of the drivers.

There was no sign of the terrorists though and Tom now felt concerned that had chosen the wrong road. The other alternative, he thought, was that perhaps the loading of the bomb had taken a little longer - in which case he would be ready for them. He drove the X5 up to one of the officers at the roadblock and opened his window.

'Have you let anyone through so far?' asked Tom.

'Just two vehicles,' replied the policeman. 'An MX5 convertible and we've just let a large van through from the local builders' merchants on the industrial estate. We searched both of them thoroughly.'

'Tell me about the van,' said Tom.

'It looked like a standard Grant and Sons delivery van - a big Mercedes Vanio in grey. It was full of boxes of screws and nails. They were delivering to a new housing development just north of Wembley. He showed me the delivery note. As I said, we searched it thoroughly before letting it through,' replied the police officer.

'Tell me about the occupants,' said Tom.

'Only the one, actually. Looked like he was an Indian Sikh - you know with a turban. He showed me his company I.D. and I questioned him about his workplace - which all seemed to check out,' replied the officer.

'I see. Thank you,' said Tom as he started putting his window back up again.

'Scary looking bloke,' said the police officer as he started to turn around.

Tom stopped his window and paused for a second.

'What do you mean?'

'Well, he wasn't exactly a barrel of laughs. Serious bloke. Gaunt face. Black beard. And he had these really intense deep-set eyes. He's how I imagine death would look if it was a person,' replied the officer.

Tom and Jax looked at each other. No further words were needed. Tom accelerated away, causing the tyres to screech as the BMW catapulted through the police roadblock and narrowly missed one of the other police officers.

'How the hell did they manage to move that bomb over so quickly?' asked Jax.

'Specialist equipment and a well-trained team, I guess. The van must have been specially adapted to conceal the bomb near the front section I reckon, and then boxes of nails stacked high at the rear to conceal it,' shouted Lang over the deafening combined noise of the engine and siren. 'Just in case a two-ton bomb wasn't going to kill and maim enough people on its own!'

The police SUV hurtled down the middle of the road, Tom now also sounding the car's horn in an effort to stress the urgency to other road users.

'OK, so if that's Usman Salah driving the van, where the hell is Baqri?' asked Lang.

'Good question but one that's going to have to wait. I can see the van in front - Grant and Sons, builders' merchants,' replied Tom.

'Yeah, and there's Wembley stadium,' said Lang pointing straight ahead at the iconic landmark that was quickly looming up.

The sight of a police BMW X5 in his mirrors complete with flashing lights and wailing siren had, unsurprisingly, not escaped Sal's notice - causing him to pull out into the middle of the road, increase his speed and weave his way along the Wembley High Road. At one point the van seemed blocked in by a bus and a line of static traffic beside it - all waiting for the traffic lights to turn green. Sal pulled the van on to the long paved pedestrianised area outside a parade of shops and continued accelerating. Most people managed to jump out of the way of the vehicle careering along the path, except for one elderly man who had not even heard it behind him and was clipped by the wing mirror. The traffic had parted for the police vehicle, however, and so when the van re-entered the road, the MI5 team were directly behind it. Again, Sal weaved the van through the traffic at surprisingly high speeds but with Tom managing to keep the BMW within centimetres of its rear bumper.

Jax said, 'Tom, I hate to tell you this but if you don't stop him now, then once he turns round the next corner, he will have a straight run at the West Service Gate under Wembley Stadium.'

Tom just nodded in reply - his mind in a zone of single concentrated focus. Once again, he pushed hard down on the accelerator, drawing the police SUV alongside the rear of the van and turning it into the rear right wing - this time managing to spin the pursued vehicle immediately. Sal tried in vain to regain control of the heavily laden van by wrenching the steering wheel one way and then the other but ultimately failing as it continued to spin several times before eventually coming to a stop - facing the police X5.

Before the MI5 team had even opened their doors, Sal was already leaning out of his window and firing shots at the police vehicle from an MP9 machine pistol, which had been hidden in a secret compartment under his seat. Pedestrians who had been bystanders were now screaming and running for cover, as were some drivers and passengers who had been in the surrounding vehicles. Others were simply trying to hide in the footwells of their cars.

'Shit!' shouted Sergeant Lang ducking behind the front seats, as the seemingly endless stream of bullets smashed through the windscreen, showering the inside with glass. 'Good job the police searched that van properly,' he sarcastically muttered under his breath.

A single bullet struck Tom in the shoulder, causing him to very briefly grimace with pain before he continued to exit the BMW and take up a crouched position behind his door. Jax had now also taken cover behind his door and had started to return fire with short but precise bursts from his Heckler and Koch G36, forcing Sal to duck below the dashboard of the van. Suddenly, the tyres of the van screeched as it lunged backwards into another pedestrianised area and continued reversing at high speed in the direction of an open-air shopping precinct - which was now teeming with people who had cautiously stepped outside the shops when they had heard the gunfire.

Seemingly oblivious to the bullet wound to his shoulder, Tom opened fire at the van with his UMP40, deliberately shooting the tyres while Jax re-directed his fire towards the engine area. The hail of bullets from Jax and Tom's sub machine guns riddled the front of the van with so many holes that by the time they stopped firing, it looked more like a colander than a vehicle. A loud bang followed by a plume of smoke from the engine compartment confirmed that the van had been neutralised, as it came to a full stop.

'Get away! Get back inside!' shouted Sergeant Lang frantically running towards the numerous civilians who were now pooling together in the middle of the precinct in the belief that the incident was now over and were gradually moving closer to the rear of the van as their curiosity got the better of them.

As Lang ran past, the driver's door of the Grant and Sons van slowly opened, and a bloody hand emerged. Sal fell out and on to the ground, bleeding profusely from the numerous bullet wounds to his body. In his left hand, however, was a device which Jax immediately recognised as a remote-control bomb detonator switch. Sal pushed himself up on to his knees and looked up at Jax and Tom who both had their sub machine guns trained on him. He smiled at them - a rare thing for him - and then just kept nodding as he moved his thumb over the button on the device whilst raising it into the air.

'I die a martyr. But these people will now all die for the sins of your country. It is God's will. Allah Akbar!' shouted Sal.

Sal then noticed something out of the corner of his eye. A red laser dot had now appeared on his hand. His eyes widened. Before he could react, an intense pain seared through his arm as a bullet from Jax's rifle ripped through his wrist causing him to drop the detonator switch, which then in turn fell to the ground and bounced a couple of feet away. He cried out in pain. Gripping his wrist with his other hand he sat back on his ankles, which were now surrounded by an ever-increasing pool of blood.

'Don't kill him,' shouted Tom to Jax as he started walking towards the detonator switch. 'I need to know where Baqri is.'

Sal said, 'As if I'm going to tell you.'

He lunged at the switch.

Jax's reactions were quick and his shooting precise, firing a further four rounds into the body of Usman Salah.

But it was too late. His momentum carried him forward just enough.

'Tom!' screamed Jax.

Tom was fifty yards from the van when it exploded, only just having had time to turn around and dive to the ground with his arms covering his head. The detonation was devastating, as nails and screws together with fragments from the van and the bomb itself, ripped into everything around it. Shop windows had been blown in for hundreds of yards and many of the nearby buildings themselves showed structural damage including nails stuck in the walls. In total, eight civilians had been killed including a mother and her young daughter with many more seriously injured. The scene was graphic, horrific and shocking. Bodies of the dead, dying and injured lay where they fell - many mutilated by the flying shrapnel. Lang was now running between those who were wounded but still alive, in an effort to assess the most urgent cases for first aid as Jax sprinted over to Tom. Now just arriving at the scene, the remainder of Jax's SAS unit started establishing a cordon around the area and in the distance the strangely comforting sound of the sirens from emergency vehicles were getting closer.

'Tom ... Tom! Speak to me!' said Jax, attempting to roll Tom over.

Jax then noticed two fairly large holes in Tom's side, which were undoubtedly caused by bomb fragments, as well as two nails which were embedded in his right arm that had been covering his head.

'Are you OK?' said Jax, immediately realising how stupid his question sounded.

'I've felt better,' replied Tom quietly.

'Look. You're losing a lot of blood, so I'm going to have to put pressure on your wounds. There are ambulances on their way though and they'll be here in a few minutes - so just hang in there and keep talking to me,' he said, rolling Tom back on to his side.

'I've just realised something, Jax. Your first name is Aaron, so your initial would be 'A'. That makes you 'Ajax'. You're an ancient greek hero. Did you get much of a ribbing from your school mates?' whispered Tom, trying to stop his eyes closing.

Jax said, 'Not for long, I didn't, no! And *you*, keep those eyes open. Do you hear me?' He pushed down on Tom's wounds in an attempt to stem the bleeding.

As the sun broke through the clouds behind the SAS team, an ethereal aura surrounded Jax's head.

'Actually, you look more like you're God or Jesus now with that light behind you,' whispered Tom with a faint smile.

'That would be a shocker, wouldn't it? Jesus turns out to be a black man!'

Tom briefly laughed before being swiftly stopped by a coughing fit.

Tom said, 'Wouldn't that be great? That's going to upset a few people and a whole lot of paintings are going to have to be changed. Please tell me you're Jesus and I can die laughing.'

'I wish I was, my friend. But you're not going to die because I'm not going to let you - do you hear me?' said Jax sounding more like an army drill instructor. 'I'll tell you what I *do* want you to do though. I want you to start thinking about something important in your life. Like your family. You need to live to be there for them. Don't let them down, Tom.'

'Luna and the girls,' whispered Tom. His mind wandered back to the last time he saw his wife. He remembered how he kissed Luna before leaving their house to go to what he thought was to be a conference in London. Their small argument the night before not mentioned again. He remembered how he then stroked her nose before gently placing his hands on either side of her face and then kissing her forehead. Yes, his gorgeous wife. His beautiful daughters. He could see them all in his mind. He loved them so much. But he just felt so tired. So very tired. He just wanted to sleep.

'Jax, my keys ... my keys,' Tom panted, his breathing now much shallower.

Jax searched his pockets and handed the keys to Tom, who managed to open the leather fob to reveal the photo of his family once again.

Tom felt the light fading and his eyes starting to close.

'I'm sorry, sweetheart,' Tom whispered stroking the picture of Luna's face. 'Please forgive me.'

CHAPTER THIRTY-ONE

Five days had gone past since the terrorist attack on London and Britain's capital was still trying to get itself back to some sense of normality, as the public, government and media tried making sense of what had just happened. Iain McGregor was now standing outside his boss's door at MI5. *Sir Nicholas Meads - Director MI5* read the highly polished stainless-steel plaque. Mac briefly checked his slicked-back black hair in the reflection.

'Well, this is going to be an interesting conversation,' Mac thought to himself before he let out a sigh and knocked on the door in front of him.

'Come,' was the abrupt but well-spoken response.

Sir Nicholas Meads's office could best be described as old-school opulence. Intimidatingly spacious and with half of the entire left hand side wall consisting of shelves filled with rows of beautiful leather-bound books - in either red or green but never a mix of the two on any one shelf. On the right-hand side of his office was a large rosewood cabinet filled with more technical based books - mainly on law - and on the wall a group of photographs, including one of him receiving his knighthood from the Queen. Covering the floor was the finest Axminster carpet - in crimson. All this lead down to a large and very impressive 19th Century mahogany desk complete with a high back Chesterfield executive chair in red leather and behind that a large window, overlooking the river Thames. The balding and slightly overweight Churchillian looking figure of Sir Nicholas Meads, dressed in his usual pin stripe blue suit, was sat at the desk - frantically scribbling on a piece of paper.

'Have a seat, Mac,' said Sir Nicholas, in an accent typical of a wealthy middle-class Old Etonian - pointing at one of the two much smaller black leather chairs opposite him. As Sir Nicholas looked back down at his desk and continued to write, Mac noted how this posture emphasised his double chin. 'Well done on the terrorist attack, Mac. I understand that Prime Minister Hatcher and President Monroe have subsequently decided against launching a full-scale missile attack on Tehran itself and instead went for another military base as a symbolic gesture - after giving the Iranians due warning to evacuate, of course. Apparently, the Russians felt that was a reasonable and proportionate response and so a full-scale war has been averted. All thanks to your team. Sorry about your Sleeper, by the way. He really was quite impressive,' said Sir Nicholas, putting the lid on his fountain pen and placing it on his desk.

'Yes, he was,' said Mac, deliberately lowering himself very slowly into his seat before looking up and just staring at Sir Nicholas Meads, hatred filling his eyes.

'Oh, I see,' said Sir Nicholas after a short period of silence, peering over his half moon glasses. 'I get the feeling you want to ask me something?'

'I do, yes. It's a simple, one word question ... Why?' said Mac.

'Why?' repeated Sir Nicholas, taking off his glasses and placing them on the desk beside his pen. 'Well, I could bore you with tales of my dis-functional family - such as how my son has such a terrible gambling addiction that he is hundreds of thousands of pounds in debt and has tried to kill himself twice. How this has driven my wife to become a raging alcoholic. Apparently, I'm the source of our family woes, according to her, for never being there when our son needed me. Anyway, however you want to cut it, the bottom line is it all comes down to money.'

'But you must have realised that we would track it all back to you? The re-positioning of the satellite. The sudden loss of the capital's CCTV system?'

'The thing is, Mac, when you're in so deep sometimes, you have no option but to keep going,' said Sir Nicholas rising from his seat and walking over to his drinks cabinet. 'Can I offer you a whisky?'

Mac shook his head. Sir Nicholas proceeded to pull the stop out of his Edinburgh crystal decanter and pour a very large measure of his favourite Glenlivet 25-year-old single malt into one of the matching crystal glasses.

'You see, if the EMP had detonated properly, then I would have made a fortune - and I needed to make a fortune. All my life's savings - every penny of it - was used supporting and helping my problematic family. I even managed to raise a big chunk of money against the house with one of those equity release mortgages.'

Sir Nicholas sauntered back to his seat, placing his glass on a sterling silver coaster which was on the top right of his desk. 'So, I ended up as poor as a church mouse. But I had a fantastic government pension and a few other retirement products. Then an American contact of mine happened to mention an organisation who had a reputation for bringing extraordinary wealth to its members. People who had influence, power or wealth. People like me. So, I joined them and used all the spare money that I could get my hands on to short the shares in a number of major British companies, in the belief that Britain would suffer a huge economic shock and the stock market would crash.'

'When you refer to *an organisation,* you mean *The Collective?*' said Mac.

'Yes, indeed. A group of similarly minded people who would act for the mutual benefit. The collective good, if you will. That's how it was sold to me anyway. Never imagined that it would go as far as it did though.'

'So, you decided that the loss of your savings due to your *dysfunctional family*, as you call it, was more important than loyalty to your country?'

'Oh Mac. Come on,' said Sir Nicholas, downing almost half of his whisky in one swig. 'If the EMP had gone off as planned, there probably wouldn't have been any casualties. Do you think I would have wanted the death of innocent civilians on my hands? I've spent my entire adult life in the civil service and most of it in MI5 with the sole aim of protecting these people. I'm no traitor - I've dedicated my life to looking after others. But I don't deserve to die penniless and neither does my family.'

'God, you're a bloody hypocrite!' said Mac. 'Of course there would have been casualties. Even if there were no physical casualties, there certainly would have been financial ones when the stock market crashed - other people whose pensions and savings would have been destroyed as you sent them all straight to the poor house. That very same place that *you* wanted to avoid. We would have tens of millions unemployed and the whole country would have been sent back to the dark ages. But that's ok because you would have been a rich man.'

'Britain would have eventually recovered, Mac. Probably stronger than it was before.'

'And the risk of war? You know how close we came to a full-scale war with Iran and Russia? This had every chance in turning into a World War or even nuclear Armageddon!'

'Oh, don't be so dramatic, Mac. It was never going to get that far. *The Collective* would never have let it,' replied Sir Nicholas in a dismissive tone.

'Don't try and justify yourself. People have died today and it's down to you.'

'That was never meant to happen. At any rate, they only died because your team were much better at their job than anyone had anticipated. There weren't supposed to be any casualties. The plan was that the EMP exploded, and the stock market crashed and that's it. You need to understand that initially, I didn't know anything about the second bomb. But as

I said, once I was in, then there was no way out. Funny thing is that I never thought when I signed off your *Invisible Sleeper Agent* development program all those years ago that it would be quite so successful. Quite ironic, really, that one of them ends up being the cause of my downfall. I imagine you have more of them?' asked Sir Nicholas.

Mac nodded.

'Well, I've just written my resignation letter to the Prime Minister,' said Sir Nicholas, pointing at the piece of paper on his desk that he had been scribbling on earlier. 'I'm sure he won't want the embarrassment of this going public. I was due to step down early anyway, so he could always just say that it was due to health concerns or something,'

'I need to know what you know about *The Collective*,' said Mac, folding his arms and looking distinctly irritated by his boss's apparent nonchalance. 'The trouble is, we believe that although the EMP was not entirely successful on this occasion, Baqri and his terrorist cell have sufficiently demonstrated that the destruction of a major economy like Britain's is possible. We believe that an attack on the United States is now on the cards.'

'Sorry Mac, I can't go discussing *The Collective* with you. Are you mad?' said Sir Nicholas, frowning. 'You don't seem to understand how powerful this group is. I doubt I would even make it home this evening before I suffer an untimely accident.'

'And you don't seem to understand that you're finished either way. I've already met with the Prime Minister, who has no intention of letting you enjoy a nice comfortable retirement

- he would prefer to take world ridicule before he lets you do that.'

'Ah, Prime Minister Hatcher. Or should I say, *'The Hatchet'* - living up to his reputation as the world's most belligerent leader,' quipped Sir Nicholas.

'So, you have been given two choices,' said Mac, all but ignoring Sir Nicholas's side swipe about the Prime Minister. 'The first one is that you are arrested and charged with treason and other serious offences. You and your family will face public humiliation, followed by the loss of everything else in this world that you have left. Assuming *The Collective* haven't already killed you and your family by this stage, you'll be sent to prison where you will die, of course, and probably much quicker than you might reasonably expect. Prison is <u>such</u> a violent place and I imagine that it will be a very tricky job trying to keep safe the ex-Director of MI5. Especially when you consider just how many prisoners think of themselves as committed patriots. What they would do to someone who has been convicted of treason - well, I dread to think. The Prime Minister's thoughts are that your demise will serve as a good deterrent.'

'Not sounding particularly tempting so far. And the other choice?'

'The alternative is that you unexpectedly and painlessly pass away here at your desk from what will be found to be natural causes. You will be honoured and remembered as the head of the country's Secret Service when it defeated potentially the biggest terrorist attack the world has ever seen. You will be buried with full honours and the country will recognise your contribution by not only ensuring that your family's money worries simply disappear but that they are given full protection and are set financially for life. The condition for this, however, is that you tell me what you know about *The Collective* first.'

Sir Nicholas rose from his chair, picked up his glass of whisky and strolled over to the window.

'So this, as they say, is the end of the road,' he said, staring directly out over the river. 'Rather a disappointing finale to my life, I can't help but feel. I have to say, I was looking forward to my retirement - you know playing a bit more golf, taking my sailboat out whenever I could and generally just having a bit of quality me time. I know your opinion of me is pretty low at the moment, but I want you to know that I'm not a traitor - I'm really not.'

'Sir Nicholas,' said Mac, trying to re-focus the conversation. 'Tell me about *The Collective*'.

'To be honest, Mac, there really isn't much I can tell you about them except that they won't appreciate their current raised profile. Much prefer to stay in the shadows, pulling strings,' replied Sir Nicholas, as he threw the rest of his whisky down his throat.

'When you say *pulling strings*, does this include Iran? And Russia?'

'Iran, Russia - it doesn't matter. They're all just puppets to these people. Most countries don't even realise that they're being manipulated and those that do are powerless to do anything about it.'

'Are you saying that Iran was manipulated into supporting the terrorists because it served the need of *The Collective*?'

'Of course!' replied Sir Nicholas. 'And Russia was manipulated into supporting Iran and Britain and America were manipulated into reacting to it all. As I said before, there was never a risk of a full-blown war but for the participating members of the organisation to make money, the stock markets had to believe that there was.'

Sir Nicholas walked back over to his drink cabinet, poured himself an even larger scotch than the first one and then turned to face Mac.

'Cheers!' he said, raising his glass. 'My doctor always said it would be the booze that would kill me one day. Well, at least I got to prove him wrong.'

Mac raised a faint smile and nodded in reply.

'I can't believe you don't drink the stuff, Mac. Surprised that your fellow countrymen haven't disowned you.'

'Well, it's not something that I will publicly admit to whenever I pop back to Glasgow.' His faced then changed to a much more serious expression. 'Tell me, Sir Nicholas, who runs *The Collective?* Who are we after?'

'I don't think anyone actually does run it, Mac. You're treating them like a normal criminal organisation and they're not. As the word implies, they're a collective. We're so used to everything being black and white - we identify an organisation and then we identify the people associated with it. But the problem you have is two-fold. Firstly, no-one knows who anyone else is in *The Collective*. Everyone is compartmentalised - like being in your own little cell. You don't get to verbally talk to anyone else, you never get to meet them, and you don't know their real names. Everyone is randomly provided the name of a mythological character - mine is Apollo. So, the point is that if one member is discovered they cannot disclose the details of anyone else.'

'But what about your American contact who introduced you to them in the first place? Was he not one of them?'

'No, he would only have been a paid messenger. They obviously wanted to get me on board and probably discovered my money issues. So, he would have been sent to try and hook me. He would never have met or spoken to anyone in the organisation. It would all have been done electronically - you know an electronic instruction followed by an electronic payment, probably from an offshore private bank.'

'There must surely be some way to find out who's in this organisation?' said Mac, thinking out loud. 'OK, so what's the other problem?'

Sir Nicholas said, 'Well, the other problem is that there doesn't appear to be any form of leadership. The normal way to dismantle a crime organisation is to cut off the head. But what if there isn't one? All the decisions taken by *The Collective* seem to be taken by a consensus between participating members.'

'Sorry. I'm trying to understand this. So, for the London attack, how did it work then? From the beginning, please.'

Sir Nicholas Meads sat down behind his desk once again, took a large gulp of whisky and placed his glass back on to its coaster.

'Right then, here we go,' said Sir Nicholas. 'So, this is my understanding of how it works. It starts when a member of *The Collective* puts forward a proposal that resembles a business plan. In this case, the member was called Cerberus and he or she had learnt of Baqri's plan for an EMP attack on London. So, they put together a document which analyses the risks and rewards for *The Collective* to provide its support if needed. The plan then initially goes electronically to a number of other members who have been identified by the system as being suitable analysts for that proposal and they in turn then provide their opinions and recommendations.'

'Hang on. What's this system that you're referring to?'

'They have some very advanced Artificial Intelligence system. It's amazing. The system is the link between members and also the link between the members and outside third parties.'

'Like Mohammed Baqri and Benny Erickson, you mean?'

'Exactly. But remember that *The Collective's* preference is always to stay in the shadows and manipulate if possible, rather than having to contact other groups directly. At any rate, the system uses a sort of filter to ensure that all messages leaving *The Collective* cannot help identify any of its members. The same applies for internal messages. But it's also much more than that. So, once the plan for the EMP attack on London was agreed and approved, the system then identified which members were required to fulfil the plan and a summary, but non-specific brief is sent out. Once those members agree to be involved then they are effectively locked in - like signing a contract.'

'Like you were, you mean?'

'Indeed. When *The Collective* found out that the EMP had failed but that the terrorists had a second bomb, they moved to support them as it would still be in their interest. I had no option but to help. Breaching a *Collective* contract would have been detrimental to my health.'

'So, what sort of people are in *The Collective?* All we have been able to discover is that they are a group of rich, powerful and influential people,' said Mac 'but what are we talking here? Politicians? Police Officers?'

'I really don't know Mac, but I just get the impression that they are top of the food chain. So, expect some senior politicians - world leaders even, plus military and police chiefs and business tycoons all in the mix.'

'Well, there has to be a way of discovering who they are. Someone must have created this A.I. at their centre and if we can get to that or the person that created it then we can surely find out the names of everyone involved. What about if we were to get access to the messaging system that you mentioned?'

'The messaging system is via an app. It's actually a weather app - you may even use it,' said Sir Nicholas, showing Mac his phone.

'Yes, I do,' said Mac in a slightly perplexed tone. 'How the hell do you send messages through that?'

'Well, if you are a *Collective* member involved in a particular project - that's what they are called by the way – *projects* - then you get re-directed to a secret encrypted messaging area when you log in. I guess that different projects are accessed via different apps, and I believe the apps are temporarily hi-jacked by a sub-routine which the *The Collective* inserts. The developers of the app won't even be aware of it, and it is then removed when a project has been completed. As I said before, the system will automatically filter out any messages that may give away the identities of the members.'

'Sir Nicholas, you could help us breach this organisation. We could set something up by using the messaging system. We'd protect you, of course, and get a new life for you and your family,' said Mac unconvincingly.

'Oh Mac. Good try and that line might have worked on someone else. And yes, if it was just a conventional terrorist organisation that you were dealing with then I might have been tempted. But you can't protect me from them. No one can. If I start actively helping you to get to them, then I'll be putting my family's lives at risk. I may have already said too much.'

Mac nodded in reply.

'I was going to say good luck opening Pandora's box but I'm not sure they will let you get anywhere near it. Anyway Mac, that's all I can tell you really - so perhaps you would be good enough to leave me whatever little present you want me to take,' said Sir Nicholas.

Mac leant across the desk and, with a 'plink', dropped a white tablet into the whisky glass of Sir Nicholas Meads.

'Don't worry, it's completely painless and undetectable. You'll just drift off into a deep sleep. Goodbye, Sir. I'll wait outside.'

CHAPTER THIRTY-TWO

'I don't get it,' Luna Rivers mumbled, staring at the oak floor of her sitting room. She leaned backwards on the sofa and looked up once again at the man who was now occupying her husband's favourite leather Chesterfield armchair. 'I ... don't ... understand.'

Luna could feel her eyes starting to well-up but somehow she managed to compose herself and continue speaking with a little more fortitude. 'Mr McGregor, we are an ordinary, normal family. This is completely mad ... totally ridiculous. There must be some mistake.'

'There's no mistake Mrs Rivers, I can assure you.'

'First, I get reporters turning up on my doorstep, wanting me to tell them my story. When I tell them I hadn't got a clue what they were talking about, they decided to camp outside my doorstep. They've been there for weeks by the way and I'm not sure where <u>you</u> have been? One of them asked me whether I knew that Tom had been pursuing terrorists at high speed through the streets of London, having shootouts with them outside St. Paul's Cathedral and then helping to prevent a bomb from killing thousands of people. I thought it was some sort of practical joke and expected a TV camera crew to jump out of the bushes. And then … then you turn up and tell me …yeah by the way, he <u>was</u> a member of MI5.'

'I completely understand why this is difficult to come to terms with. I really do. We were aware that the press had landed on your doorstep, so one of the main reasons that I'm here is quite simply to tell you the truth about your husband and what happened to him,' said Mac.

'Difficult to come to terms with? That's the understatement of the century. I'm trying to get my head around how a guy in his forties can possibly be this amazing agent that everyone is going on about. My husband is … I mean was, just an average guy and you are trying to tell me that he was some sort of secret agent? He was hardly James Bond, was he?'

The man sat opposite was, however, exactly what she expected the Director of Britain's secret service MI5 to look like. Slicked-back black hair, intense dark brown eyes and a sharp pin-stripe suit. Luna's father, who was a senior officer in the American Diplomatic Corps, always told her that the best way to assess a man was to look at his shoes. It was difficult to find fault with this man's plain black laced Oxfords which were perfectly polished (but not overly so) with not even a spec of dust to be seen.

Mac raised a very light smile and then one eyebrow at Luna's remark but was also aware that he needed to appear sensitive.

'Sorry Mrs Rivers. It's just that your husband had made a similar comment,' Mac said in a gruff Glaswegian accent. 'But not all of our agents look like James Bond, you know.' He smiled again in a hope to make some further emotional connection. 'And <u>actually</u>, we have a range of different types of agents to fit the needs of the job. Interesting, though, that you would say your husband was just an average man.'

'I would, yes.'

'That's good. Perhaps if we described him as superficially average that would be more precise - he appeared to someone looking in that he was just an average, ordinary guy. Consider this for a moment. Have you ever wondered how some people can be fit and healthy even in old age and others look old before their time or suffer from a range of illnesses?'

'I have, actually.' Luna frowned. 'I was talking about this with Tom a couple of months ago. His Dad is ninety years old, and we were saying how amazing he is. He looks fifteen years younger and is as fit as a fiddle.' Luna paused. 'I'm not sure, though, where you are going with this, Mr McGregor?'

'Let me ask you a few questions about Tom and we'll see if this will make things a little clearer,' continued Mac. 'Let's start with Tom's physical attributes. How was his health? Did he see the doctor often?'

'No, he didn't really. Yeah, I would describe his health as being good.'

'Alright but how many times in the last year did Tom visit the doctor? How many times was he ill?'

'Well, he wasn't. The only time that he saw the doctor was for an annual check-up.'

Luna paused for a second and then her frown intensified as she stared at the floor again.

'Apart from those checks ... there's nothing else, thinking about it. I can't even remember the last time that he saw the doctor because he was ill. If he ever has been.'

'And the result of those tests?' continued Mac.

'It was always all clear - perfect health.'

'Interesting, don't you think? Especially when you consider that the average person visits the doctor over five times a year.'

'Now you mention his health, I have just thought of something else. We were talking about a friend of ours the other day who had broken their leg skiing. Tom told me that he had never broken a bone in his life and he couldn't even remember the last time he even got bruised. He's not the best skier either - always falling over!'

'Mmmm,' said Mac, nodding. 'What about his sight and hearing?'

'I did insist that he saw the optician a few months ago just for a check - he was forty-five years old you know. His vision was three levels above 20/20, which the Optician told him was fighter pilot level. Good hearing too, as far as I know,' Luna said with more of an understanding tone in her voice.

'Good teeth as well? I ask this as it is linked to general health and particularly cardiac issues,' said Mac.

'He saw the dentist last year. Apparently, he was stunned at how good Tom's teeth were, considering he hadn't been for years. He had a such a sweet tooth as well and incredibly, he still didn't have any fillings.'

'Yes, I *had* noticed his sweet tooth. He rather liked his Buttermints, I found.'

'Yeah, what was it with him and those Buttermints? He used to always have a pack in his car and just crunched his way through them. The dentist said the state of his teeth didn't make any sense but just put it down to his superior genes.'

'Indeed.' Mac nodded again. 'Genetically superior. And would you say that he was above average for intelligence and physical strength?'

'His intelligence was one of the things that attracted me to him in the first place. As for the physical side, he always used to brag that he could run longer and lift heavier weights at the gym than men half his age.' Luna paused for a second. 'But then I can run for longer than many much younger than me - probably because I don't fill my face full of junk food like the younger generation. I can speak from experience Mr McGregor, having two teenage daughters.'

Mac smiled at her again. 'He was, I think it is fair to say, slightly larger than the average man though? Well built?'

'I suppose he was, yes. Tall and quite muscular but not some sort of mountain.' Luna paused again. 'So that adds up to him being a secret agent? Well, how stupid of me not to have spotted that,' she said sarcastically. 'Anyone who has ever met him would think he's just a really nice normal family guy. He was a middle-aged architect for God's sake!' Luna exclaimed and then quickly calmed down. 'Sorry, it's just so painful for me at the moment - and this is completely blowing my mind.'

'No need to apologise. I completely get it,' said Mac, with a sympathetic look. 'A *nice normal guy*, as you put it, is exactly what people should think. You see, it's all down to genes, Luna. What I mean is, there are some people with weak genes and others with strong genes. With each generation there is, shall we say, a throw of the dice. Now, imagine that over a number of generations you have been able to mix more strong genes together and less weaker ones. You then get a sort of super-human. Not like a comic book character, I mean, but someone who is naturally tougher and more resilient. Someone whose genes allows him or her to age at a much slower physical rate. They will often still look their age - facial lines and greying hair for example - but their core elements deteriorate much slower and, of course, they start at a higher level to begin with. Tom was an incredible genetic mix really. Don't get me wrong, he wasn't Superman - if you cut him, he'd still bleed.'

'Oh, I know that! The trouble was that most the time he didn't even realise he *was* bleeding when he'd accidentally cut himself. I would point out to him that he was bleeding and he would look at the cut completely mystified and say to me '*how did I do that* ?' said Luna rolling her eyes.

'Yes, I'm not sure if that particular genetic trait is a benefit or a defect. He had, shall we say, a de-sensitised nervous system. His brain didn't register low level pain damage at all and higher-level damage wouldn't be registered to the level that most people would find incapacitating. On the flip side, it meant that there was the risk that he could just 'bleed out' without even realising it. For us, however, the physical attributes on there own were not enough. They have to have the right mental attributes. So, how would you describe his temperament?'

241

'Always very calm and controlled - I guess you would describe him as being long fused. I think I only saw him lose his temper twice in all the years that I had known him. Even then, he quickly regained control as he felt that to lose your temper was a personality fault. You could almost see the *error* message running through his head.

'He also had one more trait which we found very appealing. He was very good at relating to people and in particular what they were thinking. He could get inside their heads, so-to-speak. For us, this was particularly useful in trying to work out what the terrorists were planning and what their next moves might be.'

'Well, he was very good at ruining every plot of every TV programme we had ever seen,' she said raising her eyes to the ceiling followed by brief smile. 'I think I need a drink,' said Luna, standing up. 'Would you like some wine or something stronger like a brandy or a whisky, Mr McGregor?' she asked.

'No, thank you Mrs Rivers. Surprisingly for a Scot, I don't touch the stuff. Well, not anymore anyway.'

Luna felt completely dazed by her conversation with the MI5 chief and decided that she needed alcohol like never before in her life. 11am was not a time that she would have normally regarded as acceptable to start drinking but this was not a normal day. After walking into her kitchen and pouring herself a large glass of her favourite Sauvignon Blanc, she then realised that she was dressed in her scruffy 'stay at home' jeans and an old striped cotton top and then thought to herself that, in fact, she could not care less. She wasn't expecting the Director of MI5 to visit her after being told four weeks earlier by the police that her husband had unfortunately been killed by terrorists in a bomb blast in London. She stared out of the window and down the garden with a cauldron of thoughts swirling around in her head. She then became aware of her own reflection in the glass.

Oh God, she thought. Weeks of what seemed liked never-ending tears had taken its toll and her face looked pale and puffy. Her usually bright green eyes looked lifeless and blood shot.

'I think you can call me Luna now, Mr McGregor. As this is now the most surreal day of my life, I think we can drop the formalities,' she said in a more friendly tone, walking back into the living room.

'Thank you, Luna, and please call me Mac or Iain if you wish.' He smiled gently at her again. 'How are the girls dealing with the death of their father by the way? Must be incredibly difficult for them too.'

'Not surprisingly, they're absolutely devastated - as we all are. They're now back at university after we decided that the best thing to do was for them to try and return to some sense of normality. Their campus security is on high alert and should stop the reporters getting to them as well.'

'And you? How are you coping? Any plans to return to Washington? Might help you as well to get some normality back in your life or at least distract you a little.'

'Well, I would be lying if I said that I hadn't thought about returning to America but at the moment I'm a complete wreck to be honest. God, I miss him. One moment I think that I'm getting better and then I completely fall apart again. This may sound a bit odd but before we cremated him, I could have done with seeing him and touching his face again - for the last time. I think it would have helped me. But the bomb blast ...' She burst into tears.

'Luna. I think the counsellors, who have been helping you through this, were right. Would you really have wanted to have seen Tom like that - the last image you have of him? Better you have good memories of how he was.'

Luna nodded and walked over to a large oak sideboard and picked up a photograph of them on their last family holiday. 'Actually, there is one thing Iain that I really need to know. Was my husband always an agent? I mean, when I married him was he already an agent? Because if he was then basically, he lied to me throughout our entire married life.'

'I'm sorry, Luna. Yes, he was, but you have to understand that it wouldn't have helped anyone for you to know. Can you imagine if you had to try and keep a secret like that for your whole life? Never being able to speak about it to anyone and then if your husband went away, you would be worrying whether he was on a mission and whether he would come back. Not something that anyone should have to live with, I am sure you will agree? There is also a security issue. These special types of agents need to be completely indistinguishable from the general public, so they not only look like your average person, but they have normal jobs and lead normal lives. In fact, they are known as *invisibles* at MI5. The only people who know their identities are me and the head of our Special Science Projects Team. Even our former Director, Sir Nicholas Meads, who tragically passed away very recently, didn't know their full identities and didn't feel the need to either. You see the idea of a secret agent is somewhat of a misnomer - our normal agents are not secret at all. The intelligence services in other countries know who they are, and we know who theirs are.'

'I still can't believe we're talking about Tom,' said Luna, retaking her place on the sofa.

'The thing is Luna, we are living in an age of extremism. The people we face are completely dedicated to the killing of our citizens and the destruction of our way of life and we need an equally dedicated defence. And it's not just a question of dealing with the extremists, as many of these groups are what we call *state sponsored* - other countries who would benefit from any damage caused to us are supporting them. This would include passing on the identities of our agents. The *invisible* agents are not only unknown to these people but are genetically superior and have the right psychological profile as well. They are as committed to protecting innocent people as the extremists are to killing them. Where the extremists say that they are willing to sacrifice their own lives to achieve their goals, ours are willing to do the same to prevent them. Your husband had the perfect profile that we were looking for - loyal, protective, courageous and relentless.'

'Isn't all this top secret? Should you really be telling me all this?'

'The answer to your question is that it's not really a huge secret in the intelligence community. Some of our closest allies are doing the same as us, with the same objective that these agents stay completely anonymous until they are needed. The big advantage with these types of agents is that with their superior genes, we have a much larger time window to use them and so we can use the right person for the right situation - there's no rush.'

'Sorry, did you say there are more like Tom out there? Around the world?'

'They have been equally effective in countries like the United States for example. Your next-door neighbour whom you see every day, does a nine-to-five job and is happily married with kids could be one.' Mac realised that he was getting too close to the boundary of 'need to know' information. 'Anyway, we were keen to try and give you some answers in the hope that you can get some normality back in your life. We thought it was only fair that you knew that Tom was an incredibly brave man whose sacrifice saved many lives. As I hope you understand, I can't though go into the details of his mission.'

Mac became aware that his attempts to explain and excuse her husband's actions were not being completely successful as Luna was now looking at all her framed photos on the table beside the sofa. She picked up a black and white photo of her being lovingly held by her husband on their wedding day. A very arty picture she always felt but now it was clear that he was a man that she really did not know at all. Tears started rolling down her face once again, as she turned her gaze to the MI5 chief.

'I'm sure this is all great for the secret service and I know I should be proud of what he has done but I can't get away from the fact that he lied to me for the last twenty-one years that I have known him. For me, keeping that secret is the same as lying. He married me knowing that I did not know the real Tom.'

Luna put her hand over her mouth and wept.

CHAPTER THIRTY-THREE

'I don't believe it!' Brigid shouted down her mobile phone. 'You know that bastard that killed Connor - your friend, *Frosty the Shitbag*? Well, he's still alive! How the hell is he still alive? When you called me four weeks ago, you told me that Sal had shot him and also blown him up as well. So, I repeat, how the hell is this guy still alive?'

'Well, that is quite impressive, I have to say,' replied Baqri.

'Impressive! Is that what you think?' Brigid continued yelling down the phone. 'He killed Connor. Do you not get that? I loved Connor and he just gunned him down. I'm going to finish the job. This guy is going to die. I'm going to kill him in his hospital bed.'

Baqri rubbed his small black goatee before deliberately exhaling loudly. Now dressed more like a tourist in a blue floral-design short sleeve shirt and blue jeans, he not only appeared quite relaxed, despite the apparent failure of his mission, but even slightly excited.

'Brigid, I'm sorry about Connor. I really am. But ...'

'But you're now going to come out with one of your stupid quotes, aren't you?' Brigid said, the anger in her voice really bringing out her Northern Irish accent.

'Confucius said that when you embark on a journey of revenge, dig two graves,' said Baqri undeterred by Brigid's dismissive remark. 'That was all I was going to say, and I don't think that's stupid. I don't want to see you get killed and you're not going to get near him. They're going to have his room guarded - you know that don't you?'

'I'll find a way - don't worry about that. And that Confusious, or whatever his name is, was right. There will be a second grave. Because I'm going to kill his wife as well. I don't just do an eye for eye when the man that I love is killed,' she raged down the phone.

'You want revenge. I get that. But bide your time. You can't avenge Connor from the grave, can you? So, come and join me here. What we will do next will be beyond anything anyone has ever seen before - our enemy's worst nightmares on an epic scale,' said Baqri, starting to sound excited again.

Brigid said, 'Where are you exactly?'

'Pyongyang.'

'That's North Korea, isn't it? What the hell are you doing there?'

'Well, I'm sitting at a table outside a quaint little cafe, enjoying the warmth of the lovely sunshine and hoping to get a cup of coffee.'

'You know what I meant,' said Brigid.

'Yes, I did - of course. I'm working on something very special. You can be part of it, Brigid. Don't waste your life on a futile effort to kill this guy - you're the last one left of my team.'

'Last one?'

'Well, as you know, Asif has been locked up for *being a member of a terrorist organisation,* I think they put it ... oh and some other stuff as well. Who cares? He was weak. But even such a pitiful excuse for a human being like Asif has uses. He made a good decoy and allowed the rest of us to get into London undetected - so at least he had some purpose. Then Sal, as you know, died setting off the second bomb and Alim is, apparently, in an induced coma in hospital after you stuck a knife in his back. So, I guess that just leaves you.'

'Hang on. Sticking a knife in his back? Which is exactly what you told me to do.'

'Well, yes, I did. Fair point. You may, perhaps, have done too good a job. I was sort of hoping to have retrieved him by now so that we could start work on my next plan. Not have him turned into some sort of drooling vegetable - if that's a thing. But hey, I'm getting used to disappointment.'

'Yeah, I guess Sal must have been a big disappointment for you too. You know dying and all that,' said Brigid sarcastically.

'Sal fulfilled his purpose. That was his destiny. He knew it was going to be a one-way trip.'

'Oh, that's lovely. Such a touching tribute to your loyal friend. I can only hope that, one day, I too will receive such heartfelt words when I die.'

Baqri rolled his eyes and let out an even louder sigh.

'How the hell did you manage to escape anyway?' asked Brigid.

'Well, as Publilius Syrus said *it is a bad plan that admits of no modification.*

'What the hell are you talking about?' said Brigid.

Baqri waved at a waitress who was serving another table in an attempt to get her attention. Just five small black round metal tables and chairs sat on the paved area outside the Ujeong Cafe, ideally located overlooking the River Taedong in Pyongyang. He gazed out over the river, squinting slightly from the bright reflection off its waters and recounted his fortunate escape.

'The plan needed changing, Brigid. MI5's faithful bloodhound, or *Frosty* as we call him, just didn't seem to understand the idea of quitting. So, when we got to the Industrial Estate in Wembley, Sal dropped me off by the Grand Union Canal where there was a boat waiting for me. It took me all the way round to near Heathrow airport and from there a private jet was waiting to get me out. The British secret service would have had no idea where I was. Sal continued with his mission because, as I said, that was his destiny. My destiny is to change the world and inflict punishment on our enemies, not die in a bomb blast.'

'So, was it all worth it? You know all the scheming and the plotting? Two of our team dead, one nearly dead and one stuck in prison for the rest of his life. All so that you can kill eight civilians with a bomb,' Brigid said mockingly.

'You shouldn't understate your own contribution though, Brigid. You managed to gun down ten people, if I remember correctly. Two more have since died in hospital, so you now have a tally of seven dead - including a child. And don't forget that girl you poisoned. What was her name? Laura? So, well done to you, I say. In fact, you managed to almost achieve the same number of kills with an AK-47 as Sal did with a four thousand pound bomb. Just a shame I wasn't there to see it. You've got quite a talent there, Brigid' said Baqri laughing.

'You're a sick bastard. I didn't intend to kill that little child either. I'm not proud of that.'

Baqri looked up as the petite Korean waitress approached his table, dressed in black trousers, crisp white shirt and a multi-coloured scarf around her neck.

'Annyounghaseyo!' she said with a smile followed by a small bow.

'Good morning to you too. Could I just have a coffee please?' Baqri replied with a grin and performing the hand gesture of someone sipping from a coffee cup.

'Ye mullon!' replied the waitress, bowing again and then disappearing back into the cafe.

Baqri removed his thumb which had been covering the mouthpiece. 'Sorry, Brigid. Lovely little waitress serving me. What a country this is. Anyway, coming back to your question, yes it was worth it. And I'll tell you why. OK, I'll admit that I would have preferred to have turned Britain into an insignificant third world country and then topped it off by blowing a few thousand of their ridiculous and pointless people into teeny weeny little bits,' said Baqri, indicating with his thumb and forefinger what a very small bit looked like, even though he knew Brigid couldn't see his gesture. 'But there were still a few positives to come out of this.'

'Such as?' asked Brigid.

'Well, we've proved that we have the potential to cripple a country like Britain which has supposedly one of the finest intelligence services in the world. We've also managed to expose MI5's secret program of *Invisible Sleeper Agents* and so we'll be better prepared next time. And not forgetting that we have discovered that we have a powerful backer which we didn't realise we even had.'

'You mean this group that you mentioned before - *The Collective?*

'Yep, that's them. And can I just say - Wow! Do you know how major that organisation is?' Baqri said excitedly. 'I had never even heard of them before, but they are awesome.

They shut down London's CCTV system and managed to get MI5's tracking satellite re-directed away from Sal. They even had a number of armed Metropolitan police units re-directed to block the MI5 team when they were getting too close to us. Incredible.'

'And yet Frosty still managed to screw things up for you.'

'Yes, he really was a worthy adversary. Shame I never got to meet him. I would like to have played a game of chess against him.'

'Well, now he's going to die. So, I'm afraid you're never going to know. Try not to miss him too much,' said Brigid dryly.

Baqri rolled his eyes again and then looked towards the sky. Though Brigid had always been a slightly difficult member of his team to manage, due to her typically fiery Gaelic nature, she had certainly proved her worth recently - adaptable, intelligent and with a natural ability to manipulate others by using her indisputable good looks and extrovert personality. She was, however, also headstrong and he always felt that this would be her undoing. Baqri's thoughts were interrupted as he realised that the Korean waitress had returned, carrying a tray in one hand. After placing a cup of white coffee with a milk jug and sugar on the table in front of him, the waitress smiled, bowed again slightly and walked back into the cafe.

'Clearly I'm not going to persuade you that this is a futile and suicidal mission Brigid, so instead I will just wish you good luck,' said Baqri.

'One thing I don't understand, Mo. If Alim is critically ill in hospital, how the hell are you going to make another EMP for your next target?'

'Well, we'll see. The latest information that I have received, indicates that Alim's condition has stabilised. We may need to arrange to recover him soon though.'

'So, you do need him then?'

'Yes, we do really. But I think we can do a whole lot better than just a small EMP attack for our next lucky winner. I'm shortly meeting with someone whose network can help us develop something so completely devastating, that America will think that it's facing the '*End of Days*.' Quite poetic when you think of it - we've always thought of ourselves as being the instrument of God's justice and even called our group *Adallah*. Soon we will be in a position to carry out God's wrath on *His* enemies and it will be glorious. For it says in the Quran, '*Indeed, We shall wreak vengeance on the guilty,*' said Baqri before pressing the red button on his phone to end the call.

The waitress returned once again and as she placed the empty cup and milk jug back on the tray, she inserted a small folded over piece of paper between the sugar sachets. Baqri opened the note and smiled.

CHAPTER THIRTY-FOUR

Unusually for Brigid, her planning had been absolutely meticulous. Now with her hair coloured blonde, skin self tanned and adopting her previous persona of 'Rosie', she was preparing for her revenge. Keeping a lid on her impulsive nature was far from easy though, but she knew that the reward at the end would be worth it - the death of the man who killed Connor. Baqri had already told her in a phone call after the bomb explosion, that Tom had been taken to Northwick Park Hospital in Harrow and that his condition was described as critical. Not expected to survive the day, was how they described it. Yet ten weeks later he was still alive.

'So how the hell was he still alive? He was right there when a four-thousand-pound bomb exploded. No normal human being should have survived that. Perhaps he isn't actually a human being after all. Perhaps he is a Terminator like she originally described to Baqri when he gunned down Connor,' mused Brigid. *'Actually, I don't really care what you are - today you're going to die.'*

Over the previous few days, Brigid had laid down the groundwork to gain access into Tom's hospital room which she knew was under armed police guard. Her next step was a

Friday evening visit to a late-night bar located near to the hospital. *Le Chic* was a large and very contemporary venue - flush with glass and chrome fittings along with faux leather seating and was, due to its policy of discounted drinks for health workers, also extremely popular with staff from the Northwick Park Hospital - particularly after their shift had finished. Opposite the top corner of the bar was a small DJ's box from where all the cheesiest party anthems were played at the weekends and giving the bar its local nickname - *'Le Grande Fromage.'*

As she entered the bar, Brigid noticed a solitary female figure sat at a high table halfway down the bar. The girl looked to be approximately twenty-five years old, with shoulder length brown hair tied into a pony tail and was just slightly larger than medium build. She was in Brigid's opinion though, above average in looks with a tanned complexion, large round dark brown eyes and an attractive face which benefited from pronounced cheek bones. Brigid watched her for several minutes before concluding that she was on her own and then approaching her.

Having befriended general ward nurse, Donna Jefferies, and ensuring that she was completely intoxicated, Brigid proceeded to steal her staff identification card from her handbag while Donna was relieving herself in the ladies toilet. Brigid had then explained to her new 'friend' that her name was Rosie and that she was due to start work at the hospital in the Intensive Care Unit, as she was transferring from another hospital in Sussex - confident that the nurse would not remember the exact details of their conversation the following day but would probably still recognise her and remember that

Brigid was a nurse if she was to run into her. Some independent corroboration of her identity may prove useful, she thought, should she be challenged at the hospital.

'I don't suppose there are any good-looking doctors in here that work in the ICU are there, Donna?' said Brigid in her best English accent, placing her vodka and orange back on the high table that they were sat at.

As best as she could, Donna pointed towards the general area that was the end of the bar. 'Not sure about good looking but as it happens,' said Donna slurring, 'Duncan over there is an ICU Doctor. Can you see him? Near the toilets - wearing blue jeans and a really boring brown check shirt. The short dumpy one with the mousey blond hair. He's a Kiwi by the way.'

Even in her drunken state, Donna's summary of Doctor Duncan Bradley could not be faulted. *'He was, however, perfect,'* thought Brigid. *'She was in a league so far above his that he will think he's hit the jackpot.'* If there was one thing that Brigid had mastered through her life, it was how to manipulate men.

'Dangerous thing,' Donna slurred, wagging her finger and nearly falling off her stool. 'You know, mixing business and pleasure. I've done that before with a doctor working in that hospital. Didn't end well.'

'Oh, I'm pretty sure that this will end exactly as I want it. Right then,' said Brigid hopping off her seat and adjusting her low-cut pink crop top to ensure that she was revealing much more of her ample yet pert breasts than just the usual cleavage. She stood up straight and checked her tight-fittings blue jeans and then looked at Donna. 'Think I'm gonna see if I can get his attention. How do I look?'

'Well, I would!' Donna slurred and then letting out a giggle. 'You go girl!'

The toilets were located just past the end of the bar, where Dr. Bradley and a colleague were sat, and Brigid made a point of 'accidentally' tripping as she walked past as if she was drunk and then grabbing Duncan Bradley's arm.

'Whoops!' She exclaimed laughing and then looking into his eyes a little longer than someone normally would for just a casual glance. 'Sorry about that handsome,' she continued before smiling and then turning to walk into the toilets.

'Oh my God!' said Doctor Miko Kawalski, nudging his friend and colleague. 'She is gorgeous. Did you see those beautiful blue eyes? I had a Polish girlfriend who had eyes like those. OK, you were probably looking at something else - right?'

'Yes, stunning,' said Duncan - his New Zealand accent still very pronounced. 'But I don't think she would be interested in me, somehow. She sounded very posh, didn't she? Probably just her usual extrovert personality - don't look too deep into it, Miko.'

'Hey, I saw the way she looked at you. She's definitely interested. '*Whoops - sorry, handsome,*' said Kawalski mockingly, grabbing Bradley's arm and winking at him.

'God, you're a juvenile delinquent! How did they ever let you out of Med School?'

As Brigid made her way back from the toilets to her table, she briefly stroked the back of Duncan's hair before turning around and grinning at him again. By now, it was not just the two doctors whose eyes were following her back to her table but most of the men in that part of the bar.

'That girl is hot - smoking hot. Bet she's amazing in the sack. I mean look at her. She is sex on two legs,' said Kawalski. 'Go on, Duncan. Give her some of your best lines.'

'Are you crazy? I really don't need my self-esteem to take another nose-dive.'

Brigid returned to the table, hopped back up on to her stool and then beckoned Duncan over with her finger. 'Hook, line and sinker,' said Brigid, turning to Donna, as Duncan pointed at himself and mouthed the word 'me' back to her.

'I'm not surprised. Reckon he thinks Christmas has arrived early,' said Donna, still slurring and now propping her head up with her hands.

Brigid nodded very slowly and deliberately - grinning at Duncan as she did it.

'And the lights are all green!' exclaimed Kawalski. 'Actually, her mate's not bad. Sure I've seen her before at the hospital. She's a nurse on one of the wards, I think. So, now I'm free and single ... see if you can get us in there, will you?'

'You're like a dog on heat, you are,' said Duncan.

As it happened, the first thing Brigid suggested to Duncan as he arrived at her table was that he invited his friend over as well and Miko Kawalski didn't need to be asked twice. As he engaged in his best chat with Donna, Brigid turned to Duncan.

'Sorry, Duncan, isn't it? My name's Rosie. I thought it would be better if you came over here - bit too loud down the other end to be able hear anything,' she said laughing. 'My friend Donna here tells me that you're a Kiwi,' said Brigid trying to make small talk and having noticed his nervous body language.

'Yeah, that right,' replied Duncan, looking a bit like a rabbit stuck in the headlights. 'I come from the wop-wops, outside Wellington.'

'Wop-wops?' asked Brigid, never having heard that expression before.

'Oh, sorry. It's Kiwi slang for the sticks - you know the middle of nowhere.'

'Got it,' said Brigid laughing, 'And you're a doctor, right?' Duncan nodded in reply.

'Is that something you always wanted to be?'

'Ummm, yes,' was Duncan's very short, closed reply, still finding Brigid's looks very intimidating.

'So, was there anything in particular that made you want to be a doctor? Were your parents both doctors?'

'Actually, they weren't. My Mum was a district nurse and my Dad died when I was really young. So, she basically brought me up on her own from the age of five - along with my little brother. She's always been my hero and I guess the caring for others bit probably rubbed off. You know looking after us in the evenings and others during the day with the job she was doing,' said Duncan and then realising that he may have spilled too much personal information far too quickly and then thinking that this had now probably killed his chances with this stunning blonde.

'So, what happened to your Dad - if you don't mind me asking?' said Brigid.

'Killed in a car crash. He was only twenty-five. Drunk driver on the wrong side of the road.'

'Oh my God! That's terrible. I'm so sorry,' said Brigid touching his hand.

'Thank you,' he replied, feeling slightly more comfortable in Brigid's presence. 'Dad's death did leave the family really poor though and we just sort of scraped by. Then I managed to win a scholarship over here in England, which paid for all my medical training. And now I can afford to send something back to Mum every month - sort of making up for all those years that she sacrificed for me.'

'That's an amazing story. Bet your Mum is proud of you. You're a great son, aren't you?' Brigid said, staring straight into his eyes and stroking the side of his face.

Duncan smiled back and then took a large drink of his pint of lager. 'Brave juice' he thought to himself. He wasn't used to being chatted up by really attractive girls but now he had the best-looking girl in the bar flirting with him. Sure, some of the other female doctors and nurses at the hospital were nice and friendly but he could never remember a girl like that flirting with him - really flirting with him. *For Christ's sake, don't blow it, Duncan,* he kept saying to himself.

'So, I noticed the tattoo at the base of your neck - looks like some sort of knot. Does that have a meaning?' asked Duncan, awkwardly trying to make small talk.

'It's called a *Serch Bythol*. It's a Celtic symbol for everlasting love.'

'Oh, right,' replied Duncan, not sure whether he should pry any further.

'I had this boyfriend once whom I was completely in love with. So much so that I got the tattoo. Together forever, I thought. But then one day everything changed.'

'I'm sorry. I didn't mean to be nosey,' said Duncan.

'Don't worry,' replied Brigid, touching his arm. 'Oh, I love this tune. Come on, have a dance with me,' said Brigid jumping off her seat, pointing at Duncan and singing the words to *can't get you out of my head* by Kylie Minogue, directly at him.

Brigid grabbed Duncan by the hand and pulled him in the direction of the small dance floor.

'What are you doing? I can't dance!' he said, grinning at her like a besotted schoolboy.

Brigid danced with Duncan for the next hour, touching him both regularly and provocatively. She then moved closer to him, pressing her body up against his and kissed him full on the lips and when his mouth opened, she used her tongue to play with his. Her lips were full and yet soft, her kiss passionate and yet somehow sensitive.

'Oh my God,' whispered Duncan in Brigid's ear as she slowly rubbed the front of his jeans at the same time as erotically biting and licking his ear.

'Excuse me lovers,' interrupted Donna. 'I'm on duty tomorrow and really need to get home.'

'I need to get home too,' said Brigid, feigning a sad face.

'Rosie, you can always come back to mine for a coffee,' said Duncan enthusiastically, now completely aroused and desperate for the night not to finish.

'I don't think we would make it as far as boiling a kettle if I came back to yours,' said Brigid, kissing him on the lips again. 'And you told me a few minutes ago that you're on duty tomorrow at the hospital. You've got an important job and you need to get some sleep. But don't worry - you'll see me really soon. I promise.'

Brigid turned around, grabbed Donna's hand and started walking towards the bar's front doors. As Donna stepped through the open doorway, Brigid looked around, smiled at Duncan and then blew him a kiss.

She smiled to herself. *Mission accomplished.*

CHAPTER THIRTY-FIVE

The following afternoon, Brigid arrived at Northwick Park Hospital in the uniform of a staff nurse which she had managed to acquire in a visit the previous day, along with her newly adapted ID. The hospital - a typically unattractive sprawling 1960s building of concrete and glass - served as the main hospital for that area of north-west London and was well regarded for its intensive care facilities.

Mo would have been proud of your planning, she said to herself. Having memorised where to find the Intensive Care Unit, Brigid walked confidently along the brightly lit hospital corridor towards the lifts. The only day that she could think of which could possibly match this one was when she pressed the button on Baqri's phone to blow up the men who had killed her father outside their favourite pub. That was without doubt the best feeling she had ever experienced in her life, as she watched the pure unbridled energy of the explosion instantly rip the car into small pieces, sending a huge plume of fire and smoke upwards. She liked to think - she desperately wanted to believe - that before her father's killers were pulled apart by the force of the bomb, that there was time for them to experience overwhelming terror and a level of pain beyond anything that they could possibly have imagined. For Brigid, this thought was like a comfort blanket and one which she had many times happily fallen asleep to - with a smile on her face. There had only ever been two men that meant anything in her life - her father and Connor. Both had been taken from her and now she would make things right again by killing the man who gunned Connor down. Brigid double checked the hospital floor plan fitted to the side of the lift and pressed the up button for the fifth floor and the Intensive Care Unit.

'Hey, Rosie. Funny seeing you here,' said a familiar but slightly gruff voice from behind.

'Hello, you!' said Brigid in her best English accent, and turning around. 'How's the head?'

'Urghhhhh!' replied Donna sticking out her tongue like a sick dog and in a manner befitting a person suffering from a severe hangover. 'Do you mean the throbbing ball of pain that sits on top of my shoulders?'

'Well, hun, I have to say that you drank like a world champion,' said Brigid, grinning.

'My head feels like it's had a battering from a World Champion, if that's you mean. Anyway, I thought you weren't due to start until Monday?'

'I'm impressed that you remembered that. Last night I don't think you would have even remembered your name.'

'Yeah, yeah. Whatever,' Donna replied with a smirk. 'I guess you're here to see lover boy?'

'I'm not sure what you're implying, Nurse Jefferies? As it happens, I am a true professional and thought it would be useful to check out where I will be working and even acquaint myself with a few of the patients. If I happen to bump into Dr Bradley on my travels then that would be fine as well,' Brigid said smiling and stepping into the lift.

'Well, you did a whole lot of bumping with him last night if I remember ... and grinding too,' Donna said with a suggestive grin, as she also stepped into the lift. 'I better show you up to ICU then - I'm on a break.'

The lift stopped briefly at two more floors on the way to the fifth floor with various hospital staff entering and exiting and Brigid found herself having to force a polite smile on each occasion and, at the same time, trying to conceal her growing irritation. Finally, the doors opened, and the pair stepped out into another typically bright clinical corridor and began walking in the direction of the ICU. Donna's constant chatter had now automatically been filtered out by Brigid's mind as she started thinking about the job that she was really there for. Feelings of both excitement and trepidation swept over her - she knew getting to her target and then escaping was going to be a challenge but at the same time she had a good plan and was confident of success. She always remembered Mohammed telling her that *to fail to plan, is to plan to fail,* and even though she always felt that he was as mad as a March hare, or at least very eccentric if one wanted to be kind, he was also a genius when it came to planning.

The ICU was certainly busy, with a constant stream of doctors and nurses crossing over each other, like a traffic scene in central Paris, as well as porters pushing patients on trolleys and the occasional visitor - most of whom looked slightly lost. Despite the initial impression, it was clear that the scene was far from chaotic, with a sense of organised calmness about the staff. As they approached the reception, Brigid recognised the figure of Doctor Duncan Bradley, standing side on to them and talking to a junior doctor. Duncan was now dressed in the purple scrubs of a consultant doctor, complete with a standard set of stethoscopes around his neck.

'Stay behind me,' said Donna, gesturing with a sweep of her hand. 'I think you're about to make his day, so let's give him a nice surprise.'

As Dr. Bradley finished his conversation, he felt a presence beside him and turned around. Standing in front of him and close up in his personal space was Donna Jefferies. Duncan, obviously confused by Donna's proximity, just frowned in response.

'Surprise!' exclaimed Donna, stepping to one side and revealing the slightly more petite Brigid standing behind her.

'Oh, my God,' said Duncan, genuinely taken aback by seeing Brigid. 'Rosie. What the hell are you doing here? I'm sure you told me that you were a nurse based at a hospital in Sussex?'

'Well, that's true but from Monday I'll be a nurse based here. So, I thought I would pop in and have a look at my new home. All I need is a good guide who will show me around. Don't suppose you know of anyone?'

'OK. So, I think my work here is done. I'll let you two play doctors and nurses then,' Donna said taking a step backwards and winking at Duncan.

'No worries,' said Duncan, in his typical Kiwi drawl.

'Wow. I mean, just wow. I can't believe we will be working together. I would be delighted to show you around, of course, Rosie. Sorry, I didn't even ask you what your last name was.'

'Oh, it's Leigh. Rosie Leigh,' replied Brigid pointing at her name badge.

'Rosie Leigh? As in the Cockney rhyming slang for tea?'

'Yes, I know. Spelt differently but my parents thought it was cute,' said Brigid.

'Well, I think they were right,' said Duncan trying to be charming. 'So, where would you like to see first?'

'I have to say that I thought you might be too busy to spend any time with me - you know with all of the casualties from the bombing.'

'Yeah, you would have been right a few weeks ago but now many of the patients have either recovered enough to be sent to a general ward or have, unfortunately, died from their injuries.'

Brigid said, 'OK then, how about taking me round some of the patients?'

'Right-o,' said Duncan, indicating with his arm towards a set of double doors to the side of the reception desk. 'Right this way, then, Nurse Leigh.'

As they passed though the doors and then walked briefly along the corridor, they reached a junction.

'So, if you turn right then you will go to the ICU ward but if we turn left and go through those doors there, then we have the private rooms. The fire exit, as you can see, is directly in front,' said Duncan.

'I can see an armed policeman through the glass of those doors. Why is there an armed policeman in ICU?' asked Brigid, looking left down the corridor but already knowing the answer.

'Ah, yes. Well, that's our VIP's room. Apparently, he is something to do with the secret service and helped thwart the recent terrorist attack which apparently would have been much worse if it wasn't for him.'

'Wow, what a hero,' said Brigid, with more than just a hint of sarcasm.

'Yes, quite,' Duncan continued, frowning slightly at Brigid's tone. 'Anyway, I'm not sure how he was involved as it's all very hush hush but the Prime Minister himself phoned the hospital's Chief Executive and asked her to ensure that the very best of care was provided. Actually, I'm not entirely sure how this guy is still alive. He was *so* close to the bomb blast and his injuries were *so* significant that, on paper, he should have died on the spot. But somehow he just won't die.'

'Bit like a cockroach, then.'

'Yes, I guess so,' replied Duncan, frowning again.

'Just a joke Duncan. Come on let's start with him.'

As Brigid approached Tom's hospital room, the police officer standing on guard outside turned to face them. Armed with an MP5 sub machine gun which was slung over his shoulder, he looked completely emotionless and simply nodded his acknowledgment to Dr Bradley. At 6' 4" tall along with a solid muscular physique and sharp crew haircut, Sergeant Mark Ricard was certainly an intimidating sight.

'This is Rosie - our newest member of the ICU nursing staff,' Duncan said smiling at the officer. 'Just familiarising her with the unit and all the patients. I can vouch for her personally by the way.'

'No problem, Doctor Bradley,' said Sergeant Ricard turning around again, placing his back to the wall. The policeman couldn't help but notice how attractive the new nurse was, however, with her blonde hair, bright blue eyes, tanned skin and what seemed like an amazing body underneath her uniform. He smiled to himself and then noticed a tattoo at the base of her neck as she walked past. A *Serch Bythol,* he thought to himself - remembering that his wife's best friend had one done when she got married.

Brigid could hardly believe it. Her plan had worked. She was in.

CHAPTER THIRTY-SIX

Ah, there you are, thought Brigid as she entered the room and saw Tom lying motionless in his bed, with numerous tubes connecting him to the surrounding pieces of equipment. She looked around the room, which was much larger than she had expected, and walked over to the window. She gazed out and briefly admired the view of Northwick Park Gardens. *That view's a bit wasted on someone in a coma.* On the wall was a flat screen television and, on a table, underneath she noticed that there was a DVD player which did not look like it was hospital property.

'Frasier,' said Duncan, pointing at the screen. 'Apparently, it's this guy's favourite comedy show of all time. The new Director of MI5 brought the DVD player down here personally along with the complete box set. Wired it up himself and gave us strict instructions to keep playing them nonstop. I normally wouldn't take instructions from anyone other than a more senior clinician but then he's the boss of the secret service and sounded like an aggressive Glaswegian, so I thought it was best just to go along with it.'

Brigid smiled at Duncan and then turned her attention towards Tom. A mere shadow of his former self, lying there motionless. *The man who almost casually walked down that street outside St Paul's Cathedral and ruthlessly gunned down Connor. Not so impressive now are you with all those tubes and wires attached?* she thought.

'We put him in an induced coma and, I have to say, we all expected him to die either straight off or during surgery. Incredibly, all his functions seem to be improving almost on a daily basis. This guy is as tough as old boots.'

'Why?' asked Brigid, genuinely curious. 'I mean, why hasn't he died?'

'Well, that's a really good question. I guess the best way to describe it is that he seems to be genetically and physically superior.'

'To who?'

'To pretty well everyone I've ever examined,' replied Doctor Bradley, shrugging his shoulders. 'We've had some time to study him now and he's the centre of many discussions between consultants and specialists here at the hospital. I'll give you some examples. First thing is that he has incredible bone density. You know when some people described themselves as heavy boned to explain their weight? Well, this guy really is. I doubt he's ever broken a bone in his life, and it also means that his vital organs are heavily protected - bit like having body armour. Another example is his blood, which seems to clot much quicker than normal but at the same time, it seems that his nervous system is de-sensitised. So, if you cut him then he won't feel a normal degree of pain - he may not feel it at all. Then he stops bleeding quickly too. If I was asked what the next step of evolution for mankind would look like, then I would say this is it.'

'But I assume that he wouldn't do so well if all the machines were switched off?'

'Well, if he was a normal man, then I would say that turning off his support equipment now would kill him for sure. All the heavy work is being done for him, of course, and that's why his body has recovered so much. But then again, he's not a normal man, so who knows if he would live or die. Right now, we're not willing to take that risk. I'm not keen on telling the angry Scotsman that we killed his agent,' replied Duncan slightly perplexed as to why an ICU nurse would ask such a question.

On a table to the side of the bed, Brigid noticed a small tray with some personal possessions including a watch, wedding ring, a set of keys with a fob attached and a mobile phone in a leather case. Beside that was a colourful bouquet of flowers in a glass vase and a packet of Buttermints.

'Oh, how lovely,' said Brigid sarcastically, walking over and picking up the sweets. 'I assume your wife must have sent these to you,' she said looking at Tom. 'Someone out there actually loves you, Frosty. Isn't that heart warming? And there's a *Get Well Soon* card underneath,' she continued, as she picked up the card and opened it.

Within a few seconds, Brigid's facial expression turned to one of visible annoyance.

'Oh, for fuck's sake,' she fumed, 'Are you kidding me?'

'What is it?' asked Duncan, walking over to peer at the card over her shoulder.

'The card is signed MB,' said Brigid in a disappointed tone and raising her eyes to the ceiling.

'Who's MB? Do you know this patient, Rosie? You called him *Frosty*?'

'Oh yeah. I know him alright. And MB stands for Mohammed Baqri,' snarled Brigid.

'Baqri? As in the leader of the terrorist group that just attacked London? The one that they're still hunting for?'

'That's the one.'

'That's a strange thing for him to do - I mean sending a *Get Well Soon* card to the guy who has just cocked up all of his plans,' said Duncan pointing at Tom._'Rumour has it that this guy here gunned down one of the terrorists outside St Paul's Cathedral. Well done him, I reckon. One less scuzzbag on the planet. They need to find that Irish girl as well. Apparently, she shot a load of people with an AK-47 - including a child. What a bitch,' said Duncan picking up Tom's medical file.

There was a long pause as Brigid looked down at the ground.

'Sorry, how do you know him again?' said Duncan, feeling slightly uncomfortable with the silence.

The red mist had once again descended on Brigid - not so much for being called a bitch (she had been called much worse things than that in her life) but for Duncan's assessment that her man was a 'scuzzbag.' She could physically feel her rage rising rapidly, like a pressure cooker, to the point where she could not control herself anymore.

'I know him because he's the bastard that killed my boyfriend - or scuzzbag as you like to call him,' Brigid quietly replied through gritted teeth and in her native Northern Irish accent. Slowly she lifted her head and looked at Duncan, as she reached into her nurse's tunic pocket.

'Jesus Christ,' muttered Duncan, as realisation struck, followed swiftly by an all-consuming feeling of fear and panic. 'Look, I'm sorry about what I said. Please. I'm *so* sorry ...' he continued as he started shuffling backwards towards the door.

'Oh, shut up Duncan. Shut the fuck up,' said Brigid, plunging a syringe into the side of his neck and swiftly expelling the contents within it.

Duncan stumbled two steps backwards before dropping to the ground in a seated position, holding the side of his neck where the syringe had entered - his eyes now huge like saucers.

'Now do you see what you made me do? This was meant for Frosty here and you made me use it on you. Guess I'm going to have to just kill him a different way,' said Brigid leaning over Duncan and talking to him like a child.

Duncan replied with a series of gasps as he tried catching his breath, the terror he was experiencing now very apparent.

'So, how should I kill this bastard? Now, I could just bash his head in with something ... or maybe slit his throat ... but, though that would be very satisfying, it might raise some questions when I leave - if I was splattered all over with his blood, I mean,' Brigid mused out loud. 'You're not being particularly helpful with suggestions now, are you Duncan?' she continued in a mockingly sarcastic tone.

Duncan's head was now starting to drop, and his eyes were rolling, as his body began to succumb to the poison. 'Did you honestly think someone like me would be interested in someone like you? Have you looked at yourself in the mirror recently, Duncan? So, just do me a favour and die quietly in the corner will ya?' said Brigid close up to his face, smiling at him as she spoke.

Brigid stood up and walked over to Tom's bedside. She looked again at the items lying on the table beside him. She then noticed that the leather fob attached to the car keys seemed like it could be opened. There inside she saw Tom's family photo. '*So, that's your wife,*' she thought, '*You did well there, Frosty. Strange there's no card or anything here from her though. So, perhaps she doesn't even know about this or where you are?*'

'Mohammed seems to treat this all as a game - a battle of wits,' said Brigid, as if expecting a conversation with Tom. 'He thinks that you're interesting. A bit of an enigma. But he's like a kid with a new toy. He's intrigued by you. For me, it's not a game. In fact, for me, it's pest extermination and now I'm going to snuff your miserable little life out. But before I do that, I need your help to find your wife.'

Brigid moved in closer to Tom and bent over to whisper in his ear.

'Oh yes. I'm not sure if you can hear me but I *so, so, so* hope you can. You killed the man I love, so I'm going to return the favour and kill the woman *you* love. I have to tell you that I did think, for a little while, about not killing you, Frosty. Why? Because I think killing you is far better than you deserve. What you deserve is eternal heart ache and suffering. I thought that if you recovered, you would have to live with the knowledge that you were responsible for the death of your wife. But now I'm here, I can't help myself - I really must kill you. And then your wife's next ... and I'm really going to make her suffer by the way. Just wanted you to know that.'

Brigid picked up the mobile phone that had been lying on the bedside table and opened the case. *Well, that's a hell of a phone you have there, Frosty. Still got some battery life. Must be MI5.* Brigid raised Tom's hand and then placed his thumb over the home button. She grinned as the main screen then appeared. She had wondered whether she would be able to read the numbers through the cracked glass but there it was nice and clear - 'Home'. *That's nice. Thought enough about your family to bother putting the number in to your Secret Service phone,* she thought. Having tapped the number listed on to her own mobile, she placed Tom's phone back on to the table. Brigid then picked up the wedding ring and key fob and placed them in her tunic pocket.

As part of her preparation, Brigid had gone through every step of her plan and considered where it might go wrong. Though she always considered Baqri to be a complete lunatic - albeit a charismatic lunatic - she was grateful for all the time he spent drilling the importance of planning into her mindset. *Next thing,* she thought to herself, *we need to make sure that we don't get disturbed.*

After flicking the switch on Tom's life support system to 'silent', Brigid switched off the machines one by one.

'Now die, you bastard,' said Brigid, with real venom in her voice.

As she stared at the Vital Signs Monitor waiting for the lines to flatten, something caught her eye. She looked down and to her astonishment, she saw Tom's fingers starting to twitch.

'You are kidding me. Really? OK then. Well, I've ready done this once already,' Brigid said as she removed a pillow from under Tom's head and then calmly placed it over his face.

But in response, Tom's twitching fingers turned to movement in his arms.

'Oh, no you don't!' she said with incredulity. 'Jesus Christ! What sort of fuckin' man are you? Just die, won't you?'

Harder and harder Brigid pushed down on the pillow until, in what seemed like ages to her, all movement gradually slowed and eventually came to a complete stop.

Brigid smiled as that feeling of complete satisfaction and elation returned.

Once again, she leaned down to Tom and whispered in his ear.

'Your wife's next.'

CHAPTER THIRTY-SEVEN

'It's Commander Malik here. Just checking on our patient and also to let you know that MI5 Director McGregor has just arrived at the hospital along with Captain Jax from the SAS.' Malik leaned forwards in his leather chair so that he could clearly be heard through the hands-free telephone system on his desk. 'I assume there has been no change in the condition of Tom Rivers?'

'Not as far as I am aware of, Sir,' Sergeant Ricard replied on the mobile phone pinned to his bullet proof vest. 'There's a doctor and a new nurse just checking on him right now as it happens.'

As the police officer was finishing his sentence, the door to Tom's room swung open and Brigid stepped out. She smiled at him almost suggestively before walking back down the corridor and towards the doors and fire exit beyond, which Duncan had identified to her earlier. Ricard's intimate thoughts about Brigid were interrupted by Commander Malik who had returned to his phone after a brief pause for thought.

'What new nurse, Sergeant?'

'Dr Bradley introduced her. She's a new member of the ICU staff.'

'What did she look like?' asked Malik, sounding slightly concerned.

'Blonde hair, blue eyes, dark tanned skin. Spoke with quite a posh English accent. Doctor Bradley seemed to know her quite well, if you know what I mean and vouched for her. Had one of those tattoos on the back of her neck - like a sort of Celtic knot.'

Commander Malik sprung out of his seat. His heart pounding.

'Where is she now?' Malik asked in an unusually flustered manner.

'She just left, sir.'

'God almighty, man. Do you not read the briefs? How do know that's not Brigid Doyle?'

'I'm sure it's not, sir,' replied Ricard, trying to sound confident but inside fearing that he had just made a mistake so huge and so unforgivable that it would certainly cost him his career.

'Why? Because she had managed to dye her hair blonde and speak with an English accent?' said Malik incredulously. 'I suggest that you check on the patient, Sergeant and I mean NOW!' he shouted down the phone.

As Brigid walked down the corridor, she could hear the start of the police officer's phone conversation behind her. Once she was on the other side of the doors, she quickened her pace towards the fire exit - walking as fast as she could, without actually breaking into a run. Ahead of her, she could see two signs - one pointing straight ahead for the ICU Ward and, above it, a green running man sign pointing to the left with the words 'Emergency Exit.' Her heart was now beating so fast and so hard that it almost felt like she should be able to hear it. The sound of her quickened footsteps on the concrete floor echoed loudly along the corridor and Brigid knew that she was on borrowed time.

'Hey, Rosie!' came a familiar voice from the corridor leading to the ICU reception.

'*Oh, Christ*,' thought Brigid, trying to ignore the call from Donna and continuing towards the stair doors. '*Just got to get through these doors, run down five flights of stairs and then I'm gone*,' she summarised in her mind.

Donna, however, was never one to be ignored. 'Rosie! Oi, Rosie!' shouted Donna down the corridor and then started jogging the short gap to catch her up.

'Don't you go ignoring me, girl,' she said with a smile and gently grabbing Brigid's arm.

'God. I'm sorry Donna. I was away with the fairies - didn't even hear you,' said Brigid, thinking on her feet.

'Well?' said Donna with a grin.

'Well, what?' replied Brigid before realising what she was getting at. 'Oh, yes. It's all good. Duncan's a great guy. I'm sorry Donna, I've got to run. I've just had a phone call and my poor old Dad's had a fall and I need to get over to see him at his care home,' she continued, sounding a bit frantic and having noticed out the corner of her eye that Sergeant Ricard had just entered Tom's room.

'Oh, your poor Dad. You know what? My Dad is ... '

'I really don't have time for this,' said Brigid.

Grabbing Donna by the arm, Brigid crashed through the fire exit.

'Rosie ... what are you doing?'

'I'm sorry,' said Brigid, putting both hands on Donna's shoulders and giving her a hard push.

Donna stumbled backwards but just managing to stop herself fully going over the staircase railings. As she tried pulling herself back up, she realised that Brigid had a hold of the bottom of her legs.

'God, Rosie. What the fuck? You nearly killed me. What are you ...'

Before Donna could finish her sentence, Brigid had lifted her by the ankles. Donna screamed all the way down until a thud confirmed that she had reached the bottom.

Brigid ran faster than she had ever done in her life. Down the concrete stairs she sprinted, as if her life depended on it - which she knew was no exaggeration. About ten steps from the bottom of each level, she would take a giant leap, followed by a scramble to her feet before continuing her escape. Above her she heard the emergency door slam open and then the voice of Sergeant Ricard as he leant over the balustrade and looked down the stairwell.

'Stop. Armed police. I said stop!' he yelled, seeing Brigid three floors below him but knowing that there was little chance that she would be complying with his instructions.

Finally, Brigid reached the bottom. There, to one side, lay Donna's crumpled body. Behind her, she could hear the heavy footsteps of Mark Ricard running down the stairs and the incessant chatter over his police radio. With one final sprint she was standing in front of the exit door. As if in slow motion, she placed her hands on the bar and deliberately pushed it very gently until the door opened. Then once outside, she turned around and pulled the bar off the door before slamming it shut. Brigid allowed herself a brief smile of self-congratulation before running to her car just twenty yards away in the car park. *'Perfect Planning,'* she thought to herself and remembering how she had loosened the push bar on her visit the day before. *'I wish you could have seen this Mo. I reckon you would have been proud.'*

Police Sergeant Ricard had now reached the emergency exit door but realised that he had no way to open it. He briefly contemplated using his MP5 sub machine gun but quickly discounted that idea - not knowing who or what might be on the other side. All he could do was to call-in the fact that he had lost sight of her.

Brigid's elation was, however, short lived. A slow circle of the car park and it became apparent that the police had reacted with incredible speed and much faster than she had anticipated. The entrance and exit to the hospital had been blocked off by police vehicles and even departing ambulances were being stopped and checked before being allowed to continue. The person responsible for this rapid police action was Commander Amir Malik who had immediately issued the order as soon as he had spoken to Sergeant Ricard and having had the foresight to keep a number of units near the hospital in the belief that Brigid would make an attempt on Tom's life.

Brigid sat in her car and contemplated her next move. She briefly considered trying to make her escape on foot but almost immediately decided that was not going to work - how far was she really going to get? Out of the corner of her eye, Brigid noticed a movement, quickly followed by the sound of squealing tyres. She looked to her side but even before she could select a gear, two police Range Rovers had raced across the car park and stopped straight across the front and rear of her car. Within seconds, four armed police officers were pointing their sub machine guns at her and demanding that she got out of her car and lie on the ground. She had no option but to comply. As she was halfway out, one of the officers unceremoniously dragged her out the rest of the way and threw her to the ground before pulling her arms behind her back and handcuffing her.

One police officer on each side lifted Brigid to her feet. In front of her stood a female police officer - a senior police officer she deduced from the crown rank insignia that sat on each of her shoulders. Brigid had seen the officer before somewhere - and then it came to her. The photograph she picked up in Laura's flat in central London. It was Shelley Carson - Superintendent Shelley Carson to be precise.

'Hello, Brigid,' said Carson drily. 'I've been looking for you. Brigid Doyle, I am arresting you on suspicion of murder and terrorism. You do not have to say anything unless you wish to do so and anything you do say may be given as evidence.'

Superintendent Carson looked at the two officers holding Brigid. 'Put Ms. Doyle in the back of my car,' she instructed. The two officers looked at each other.

'Ma'am, shouldn't we be calling for a prisoner van to transport her?' said one of the policemen.

'I'm sure you are aware of the grief that this person has caused me? It's taken weeks to clear my name. I intend to take her in personally and make sure she answers for her crimes. As far as we know, Mohammed Baqri could well be here as well, so I want the rest of you to do a sweep of the hospital.'

As Carson's Police Volvo S60 swept out of the hospital car park and through the roadblock, Brigid sat handcuffed in the back of the car and contemplated her fate. She had, after all, killed this woman's girlfriend. With that in mind, Brigid was surprised by how calm and controlled Carson was. *No wonder Laura was so interested in other women when her partner was such a cold, unemotional robot,* she thought to herself. Brigid looked out of the window but then after a few minutes started to get the feeling that something was wrong. *Why were there signs for Hendon and Brent Cross? They were travelling east whereas, surely, they should be heading south back into central London? Perhaps she was being taken to Hendon police station. But she was one of the most wanted people in Britain - why would she be going there? And the policeman was right. Shouldn't she have been taken in a secure prisoner van? Something was definitely not right.*

It was less than five minutes before the Volvo took another turn but this time into what appeared to be a park. 'Fryent Country Park' the sign said and now Brigid was feeling very uncomfortable. Carson was armed - she had seen her side

286

arm pistol - and so for what other purpose could she have for driving through a wooded park than to execute her? The car turned left and right and left again, weaving its way through the woodland paths until it came to a halt in the middle of the park. A dense area of woodland with no sign of any other person.

Carson stepped out of the car and drew her pistol.

'Get out,' she said, in a flat emotionless tone, opening the rear door for Brigid. 'Walk,' she continued pointing with her gun to a small grass trodden path leading deeper into the woods.

Brigid complied. Walking along the path, the scene was quite beautiful in an ironic sort of way. Dappled sunlight streamed through the occasional gaps between the treetops; islands of blue, white and yellow woodland flowers sat amongst the bracken like little explosions of vivid colour and there was even the sound of a woodpecker in the distance tapping away, as if sending out a morse code message to tell others of Brigid's imminent demise.

'One thing I would like to know is this,' said Carson walking behind her. 'Do you actually feel sorry for all the people that you have killed and injured?'

As it happens, Brigid felt no guilt, regret or remorse for her actions. In her mind, she had rationalised and justified every death and injury that she had caused – with the one exception of the young child. It was an inevitable and necessary consequence that people would die for what others believed in. Brigid did, however, see an opportunity from the question that she had been asked. *A careful response might help her catch her would-be executioner off guard or at the very least buy her some time*, she thought. She paused before answering.

'Of course, I do. I'm so sorry for what happened to Laura, by the way. It was actually Alim that killed her - I desperately tried to save her. I really did,' said Brigid, trying to lie as convincingly as she could.

'I'm not.'

'You're not... what?' replied Brigid, confused by the response.

'I'm not sorry about Laura. She was cheating little slut. It wasn't just you, by the way, that she cheated on me with,' said Carson in a matter-of-fact way.

Brigid was caught completely off guard by the unexpected comment from Laura's former girlfriend and just continued walking further into the woods, her mind now in a state of confusion.

'OK. That will do. Stop there,' said the voice of Carson behind her.

Brigid stood still and closed her eyes. A single shot to the back of the head and it would all be over. She started inhaling deeply and drifted into a state of partial serenity - waiting for the gun's hammer to fall.

Click.

She was still alive. Brigid opened her eyes. *What the hell just happened?*

'Turn around,' said Carson. 'Well, Brigid. It seems like you get another chance.'

Brigid could feel her handcuffs being removed and, as instructed, she turned to face Carson.

'Another chance at what?' asked Brigid, who was thankful to still be alive but now more confused than ever.

'A chance to redeem yourself. The failure to destroy the financial heart of Britain was, we thought, more than just a little disappointing.'

Brigid stood motionless, as she repeated in her head Carson's last remark.

'Jesus Christ,' said Brigid completely flabbergasted. 'You're a member of this organisation that Baqri mentioned - *The Collective*?'

'And your team's failure cost me, personally, an awful lot of money - as it has for many of our members. I had cashed in much of my lifetime savings and invested it based on a collapse of Britain's economy. So now, we want you to redeem yourself. Mohammed Baqri thinks that you will be useful for his next plan and to be fair, we have seen some impressive qualities in you. The assassination of Tom Rivers showed you have a natural talent for that sort of thing. Time to go and join Baqri, Brigid. Just to be clear, you won't get another chance if you fail again.'

'How are you going to explain my escape?' asked Brigid.

'Oh, that's all worked out. When they investigate, they will find that the handcuffs were faulty. You managed to grab my gun, directed me to these woods and then we had a struggle where you escaped. Unfortunately, it will mean a bullet wound to my shoulder. But that's just the way it is. You better be worth it, Brigid.'

'Are you actually going to shoot yourself?' asked Brigid, slightly taken aback.

'Well, we understand that your friend Baqri has a new plan. If it's anything close to what he has hinted at, then I'm going to be an incredibly wealthy woman and the money that I lost so far will look like peanuts. Has he told you anything about it?'

'Not much. Something to do with putting together a major weapon which he described as *devastating*. I get the impression that it will make the EMP that we used today, look like a child's toy by comparison.'

'Interesting,' said Carson.

'And are they really going to swallow your story? With me escaping and shooting you, I mean,' asked Brigid sceptically.

'Of course! The report on this incident will be exactly as we want it to be. This is really quite an easy one for *The Collective* to sort out.'

Brigid nodded. It was now apparent to her that *The Collective* was far larger and more intricate than she could have possibly imagined. She briefly wondered what sort of people around the world were members of this secretive organisation.

'If you keep walking straight on, you will find a blue Ford SUV. On the near-side back wheel are the keys and in the glovebox, you will find everything you need for your trip to North Korea,' said Carson pointing down the path.

'What happens if I get caught before I can get out there?' asked Brigid.

'You won't make it as far as being interrogated, if that's what you mean - so don't get caught.'

Brigid nodded, turned around and started walking away through the woods. As she did so, Shelley Carson took out her mobile phone and logged into a weather app - the same app that Sir Nicholas Meads had shown MI5 Director Iain McGregor weeks earlier. Brigid kept walking until eventually the Ford came into view and then the sound of a single gun shot rang out. She was on her way to re-join her mentor. But there was one more thing she had deal with first. Her revenge was not yet complete.

Meanwhile in Washington DC, Chief of Staff James McInnis was sat at his desk checking the President's agenda for the forthcoming NATO meeting and enjoying his second cup of coffee of the morning. A single 'ping' drew his attention to the mobile phone in his suit jacket pocket. He opened up the app, and then simply smiled and placed the phone back into his jacket.

'Everything OK, sir?' asked his assistant from the doorway, surprised by the rare show of emotion from her boss.

'Oh yes, Carol. Absolutely,' McInnis replied with another smile. 'I've just received a weather alert and I'm pleased to say that the long-range forecast is looking <u>very</u> promising.'

CHAPTER THIRTY-EIGHT

Almost a fortnight had gone by since Luna's unexpected visit from Iain McGregor on a sunny July morning at her house in the Buckinghamshire countryside. Every night since then, she cried herself to sleep and this seemed to extend to the daytime as well, where she had become a complete emotional wreck. Everything she saw, touched or smelt around the house reminded her of her dead husband. She would pick up one of his old jumpers, just so that she could smell his aftershave, and then she would remember his deceit. It was like a never-ending cycle of torment which went between feeling incredibly sad and depressed to overwhelming angry and confused.

Physically, Luna had always regarded herself as being lucky in many ways and in particular that comment was often made that she looked younger than her forty-one years - helped by a curvy but athletic build, above average height of five foot eight inches and a complete lack of obvious facial lines. Her failure to eat any meaningful food had, however, started to translate into some weight loss and she could feel her strength start to wain. A visit to the doctor a couple of days before, resulted in a heavy prescription of antidepressants and a stern warning that she needed to start eating properly. Further to her doctor's advice, she decided to drive herself down to the local supermarket where an unexpected meeting started a change in her feelings towards her deceased husband.

Luna found herself staring at the dairy isle in a complete mindless daze until she was abruptly brought back to reality by a man standing beside her.

'Luna Rivers?' he asked in a distinctly Bristolian accent but continuing to look at the food produce in front of him. Luna looked at him and nodded. 'My name is Simon Wheatley and I'm a reporter for the Guardian newspaper. I have some information on your husband that I think you will want to hear. Can you meet me at the Trattoria Italiano on the Uxbridge Road in Hayes at say 1 o'clock tomorrow? The owner is a friend of mine, and we will be able to have a proper conversation in a private area.'

Luna nodded and at that, the man turned towards the exit and walked out.

Even though her brief encounter with Simon Wheatley felt like something out of a Cold War spy novel, the invitation was one that Luna really couldn't refuse if she wanted to have any chance of some normality returning to her life. Though her previous meeting with Iain McGregor had answered many of the 'what' questions, the question of 'why' remained completely unresolved. *Why would Tom keep his alter ego from her for all those years? Why would he marry her, knowing that she didn't know the real Tom?* Feeling sceptical but also slightly intrigued, she decided that this meeting with him warranted a bit of an effort in her appearance, unlike her previous one with Mac. Now with make-up applied and a smart black skirt with floral blouse, she entered the somewhat larger than expected Trattoria Italiano at exactly the appointed time. Immediately, she was greeted by a very enthusiastic Mediterranean looking man wearing black trousers and an open white formal shirt. The owner she guessed.

'Luna? he asked in an Italian accent and with a huge smile on his face. 'Please come this way. Simon is expecting you.'

Luna followed him into a room with a long table and eight chairs which she assumed was used for private functions. She sat down, opposite the middle-aged man she had briefly seen the day before.

Well, another stereotype, she thought as she noted the journalist's slight build and side parted brown hair accompanied by elbow patched sports jacket, checkered shirt and faded blue jeans. The small rectangular pair of glasses perched on top of his nose completed the look.

'Thanks for meeting me Luna and I'm so sorry for all the theatricals at the supermarket - I know it seems overly dramatic and a little bit absurd for us not to be seen talking openly with each other. The thing is that when you discuss matters of national security, it tends to get more than a little attention from a number of parties, which we could do without. But I knew we could have a proper conversation here,' said Wheatley.

'You said you had some information on my husband?'

'I do. I guess you have been thinking a lot about him recently, so I'm not sure if you have any particular questions or how you want this to go?'

'Oh, I get it,' Luna said in an accusing manner. 'You want me to tell you everything I know and then you can publish it? Good try, Mr Wheatley. Unfortunately, the Secret Service has got to me first and I am not allowed to tell you anything or risk getting banged up in prison for the rest of my life.'

'That's not it at all, Luna. You don't need to tell me anything, but I can tell you things which may help. I know you had a meeting with the Director of MI5, Iain McGregor and I know that he told you that your husband was a special type of *invisible* agent and had been since before you met him. I guess you are probably angry at Tom for keeping it secret. It must have been a very confusing and upsetting couple of weeks for you.'

She paused and then nodded at him.

Luna said, 'OK. There are a couple of things that I still don't understand - they really don't make any sense to me at all. Firstly, how did Tom manage to keep it a secret for all that time? I thought we were incredibly close. I mean, we literally discussed everything, and I can never remember him keeping any secrets from me before. He's not the man I knew ... or thought I knew'.

'And secondly?'

'Well, the whole point of these agents is supposed to be that they are unknown - completely anonymous. But surely when they do a mission, wouldn't they lose that? All the other intelligence agencies would know who they are and that would defeat the object.'

Wheatley looked wide eyed at her, like a rabbit stuck in the headlights. The day before, he had thought about what he would say to her when they met but having failed to come up with anything sensible, he hoped that it would just flow out of his mouth when required.

'Sorry Luna, where are my manners? Can I get you a coffee or a tea or something first?'

Luna shook her head.

'Well, I think I better get one before I start,' Wheatley said but at the same time thinking to himself that he could really do with something much stronger. As he briefly stepped outside into the main restaurant, Luna noticed all the prints on the walls of the room depicting different landmarks and cityscapes around Italy.

God, Tom loved Italy, she thought. *The food, the people, the language, the culture ... can't believe we'll never go there again together.*

The door opened and Wheatley stepped back into the room, settled into his seat and placed a cup of coffee on the table.

'Right then. Here we go. What if I was to say to you that Tom didn't actually keep the fact that he was a secret service agent from you?' he said, attempting a positive and confident tone.

Luna stared blankly at him and then her face turned to anger. 'What?' she blasted. 'So, either MI5 have lied to me about him being an agent or they told me the truth and he was one and you're lying. That's the only two options that I can see. Or are saying that Tom told me, and I've forgotten that little fact?'

'There is one other option. What if he didn't know he was one?'

'How the hell do you not know that you are one? What, it just slipped his mind did it?' Luna blasted again. 'What a ridiculous conversation. I honestly thought you might want to help me, but I can see I was wrong.'

She stood up to walk out.

'Please Luna. Please. Give me just two minutes to explain what I mean,' Wheatley said, realising that his mouth had gone dry.

'Two minutes,' Luna replied firmly and then proceeded to sit back down but now with a furious look on her face.

Wheatley took a sip of his coffee, as much to relieve his dry mouth as for the need for caffeine.

'Special agents like Tom are useful for MI5 because they can live amongst the community for years and carry on a normal life. This means, for example, that non-friendly governments and terrorist organisations would perceive him as just another member of the public and even if they did do a background check on him then it would show a history of normal employment. You've got to remember that many terrorist groups are backed by, shall we say, unfriendly governments. So, when these agents do go active, they will have the very valuable advantage of surprise.'

'Yes, yes, I know all about that. The MI5 boss that visited me had already explained that,' said Luna, still with an irritated tone to her voice.

'OK, but the years or even decades of having these agents not active meant that there was a significant increase in risk that they might accidentally give themselves away or are somehow discovered. So, the perfect long-term agent is one that acts completely normally throughout his or her life because they don't realise that they are one.'

'You mean that Tom was some sort of sleeper agent?' said Luna more calmly.

'Well, more of a sleeper with a hint of selective amnesia,' Wheatley quipped with a nervous smile and then realised that Luna was not responding to his attempted light humour. 'What I mean is that, unlike Tom, most sleeper agents know who they are - they're just waiting for instructions. And the other thing is that they tend to be spies or maybe saboteurs - whereas Tom was a game keeper rather than a poacher. His purpose was purely for the defence of his country and its people - to be called up when the situation required the talents of someone quite exceptional. He was a bit like a *break glass in case of emergency* agent, really. Apparently, people like Tom are called Invisible Sleeper Agents or ISAs.'

'Actually, I can see why they would choose Tom. His protective nature was one of the things I loved about him - he was really quite chivalrous. But I still don't get why they didn't just use the agents that are currently active? I mean, why do they need to use one of these sleeper agents?'

Wheatley replied, 'OK. So, let's put it like this. Normal agents are perfectly fine in normal times, but exceptional circumstances call for exceptional solutions. Tom was an exceptional solution. He was highly trained in marksmanship, high speed driving, martial arts - basically everything to make him the ultimate defensive weapon. But his grades were off the charts.'

By now, Luna's face had changed to a combination of confusion and bewilderment and Wheatley decided it was best to give her a moment to process the information. There was just over a minute of silence in the room until Luna spoke again.

'So, basically ... what you are saying ... is that ... if they recruited someone, like Tom, who proved to be exceptional and they didn't have an immediate need for them, then they could effectively stick them in a freezer?' she said, almost thinking out loud.

Wheatley shuffled in his seat and adjusted his glasses slightly. It seemed that Luna was now in a more accepting frame of mind, and he was keen for this continue.

'Well, yes,' he replied in an encouraging tone.

'How were they able to wipe his memory though?'

'Well, his mind was conditioned rather then wiped and they did that when they recruited and trained him,' Wheatley replied.

'Conditioned? What, with some sort of chemical or electrical treatment you mean?'

'No, nothing quite as severe as that. You have to remember that he was a willing volunteer and so I gather they used a combination of hypnosis and other techniques to put those memories of being recruited and trained locked away at the back of his mind - in a box, if you will. To continue the analogy, when MI5 needed to use him, they could bring him in, unlock the box and send out one very talented agent. The conditioning also allowed them to normalise any other aspects of the agent that might otherwise have stood out. In the case of Tom, he had a number of particular gifts. The constitution of an ox combined with impressive physical strength, and a genius level of intelligence - an IQ of 165, I believe. I gather he also had an amazing ability to psychoanalyse people. So, they needed to make sure that these gifts didn't rise to the surface during his normal life - the aim, after all, was to keep him invisible. By conditioning him or her, they could ensure that the unwitting agent would more likely end up with a normal career. At the end of the day, they wouldn't want Tom to have ended up with a high profile.'

'Jesus,' said Luna. 'So, he was actually even stronger and more intelligent than he appeared? But they made his brain act like some sort of limiter?'

'Yes, exactly. Once unleashed though, quite a serious adversary and nasty surprise for any terrorist group or enemy of the state wouldn't you say? It also means that they could instill the importance of maintaining a high level of fitness into his subconscious. So, whenever they decided to call upon him, then he would be ready.'

Luna sat back in her chair in an effort to take in all that she had just been told. She could feel that numb brain sensation returning again like it had two weeks earlier with Iain McGregor, as she struggled to process the information.

Her mobile phone rang.

'Hello,' she said but only receiving silence in return. 'Look stop ringing me. Whatever you want, I'm not interested.' She pressed the 'end call' button and looked up. 'Do you know what? It doesn't matter what madness is going on in your life, you can't get away from nuisance calls.'

'Yes, the curse of the modern age.'

'I had another one like that this morning, on my way here. Just silence on the other end. What sort of person phones you and then doesn't say anything. Might be one of those automated marketing calls, I guess.' She smiled at Wheatley, who was by now feeling relieved that the level of tension had dropped.

'The thing is Luna, the man who you fell in love with and the agent who was killed in that bomb blast were the same person. He didn't really mis-lead you or pretend to be someone else. Apart from that bit, which was locked away in his mind, which even he didn't know about, he was the same guy. If someone had confronted him and accused him of being a secret agent, he would have laughed.'

'Do you know when they recruited him?'

'Well, I gather he decided to try out for the Royal Marines and went on a Potential Officers Course before he met you?'

'Yes, he told me that. Apparently, he passed but decided not to proceed any further,' said Luna, frowning.

'Passed with flying colours to be precise. His instructors at the Commando Centre described him as outstanding. They made particular mention of his relentless yet calm and controlled mental attitude as well as some exceptional skills such as his marksmanship.'

'So why did he decide that it wasn't the life for him then?' asked Luna

'He decided it wasn't the life for him because he was offered a different path. By MI5. You see, when he applied for the Marines, they tested him. He was subjected to medical examinations and blood samples were taken from all the potential recruits, which they said were just in case anyone became injured on the course. Their science boffins were then able to analyse, isolate and identify the superior genes that they were looking for. My understanding is that every person has forty-six pairs of chromosomes with about twenty-three thousand genes, and these are the blueprints for the body, or shall we say, an instruction booklet on how to build the person. If you are lucky enough to inherit superior genes then the result is likely to be ... well, someone like your husband. During the course, he was tested to his physical limits as you would expect for a potential Commando, but they also wanted to see how he would react under extreme pressure, and he unwittingly showed them that he had the psychological profile that they were after as well.'

'I'm sorry but I can't get my head around this. It's mad ... unbelievable. Incredible, actually. Where are you getting all this information? How do you know that it's all true?' asked Luna.

'The same source that told me about your meeting with Iain McGregor which has turned out to be correct hasn't it? My source must have some inside knowledge at MI5 and I assume that they feel you deserve to know the truth.' Wheatley paused for a few seconds. 'There is one more thing I should mention. You asked earlier about how it would be possible for these agents to stay completely anonymous if they carried out missions. You're right, of course, in that as soon as they complete a mission their identities are likely to be discovered. So, the answer to your question is that it wouldn't be possible and that in turn means that they are really a one time only solution.'

'Sorry?' said Luna. 'What do you mean by *one time only*? So, what do they do with them after they have completed their mission?'

'I believe that the type of mission they are sent on is regarded as being extremely dangerous - they're not expected to make it through,' Wheatley said in a quieter sympathetic tone.

'Are you saying that Tom was sent on a suicide mission?'

'No, not necessarily. But their priority and absolute focus is to complete their objective at any cost. An exit strategy would have been present, of course, should they survive. I'm sorry Luna and if it's of any comfort, I know they only use these agents for the most serious threats and when they don't think any other option is available.'

CHAPTER THIRTY-NINE

Just over a week had gone by since Luna Rivers' meeting with Andrew Wheatley from the Guardian newspaper at the Aroma Cafe. At last, she felt that some sense of normality was beginning to return to her life and certainly the information given to her that day had helped put her on the right path.

It was a Sunday evening and Luna settled back on the sofa with a mug of coffee and gazed at the dancing flames of the log fire. Tom had always said that given the choice between watching the television or the fire, the fire would win every time. Mesmerising was how he used to describe it and the strange thing was that Luna understood what he meant, particularly now that he was gone. In the background, Tom's favourite classical music was playing, and she almost felt like he was sat beside her again. She tried to hold on to that image for a while, not daring to look anywhere else or face the realisation that he was gone. *Not that we would have been listening to classical music, of course,* she thought to herself with a slight smile. Luna had never particularly liked classical music - with a few exceptions.

As she settled back into her chair, still with her mug in hand, the *Intermezzo* from Pietro Mascagni's *Cavalleria Rusticana* began to play. Tom claimed that it was one of the most emotional pieces of music ever written and insisted that the first dance on their wedding day should be to that. Luna had agreed not only because Tom was terrible at dancing to anything more contemporary but also because it meant she got to choose the music for the rest of the evening.

Luna closed her eyes as she remembered their wedding day and imagined that she was reliving it again. That long sedate walk up the Church aisle on the arm of her father, to see Tom look round with a huge grin on his face and a tear in his eye. She remembered how they both cried as they tried to say their vows and how they both roared with laughter later at their reception, as the Best Man mocked them for it. Luna smiled.

The reception had been held at an impressive country estate, complete with stunning landscaped gardens and a sweeping drive up to the imposing 17th century mansion. As she had slowly walked into the private function room with Tom to join their waiting guests, she gasped at the beautiful warm glow from the dozens of candles that adorned the walls and window cills. In the corner, a string quartet was quietly playing whilst waiting staff in white jackets were swiftly but calmly moving from guest to guest with champagne and canapés like swans swimming around a lake. Then later, after dinner, the string quartet began to play the *Intermezzo*. The waltz that they danced to was actually much more enjoyable than she had expected, and she always remembered Tom bowing and then taking her hand to kiss at the end. She responded by grabbing him and giving him a long passionate kiss on the mouth to the applause of their guests. The day had been perfectly romantic.

Luna's state of reverie was interrupted by the ringing of her home phone. She reached over to pick up the handset and, though clearly irritated, told herself to try and be polite with the person calling.

'Good afternoon,' said the woman's voice. 'Is that Mrs Rivers?'

'Yes, it is,' Luna cautiously replied and wondering why someone she clearly didn't know would be calling her on a Sunday.

'I'm so sorry for disturbing you but I thought you would probably have wanted me to. The reason for my call is that I have a few of your husband's personal possessions which I want to return to you. I'm so sorry but they seem to have been missed first time.'

'Oh my God,' said Luna, putting her other hand over her mouth, desperately trying not to cry. 'What possessions are they?' she asked after a brief pause, her voice quavering.

'It's his wedding ring and a key fob with a photo inside. Must be of you and your family. The problem is that I've gone and left your address behind at the hospital and can't remember the house name.'

The thought that her husband's wedding ring was going to be returned to her was such a poignant reminder to Luna that she was never going to see him again ... and it was just so incredibly painful. She told herself to try and not cry when she met this person from the hospital but deep down, she knew that she would. This woman might be able to tell her about Tom's final moments and, as painful as she knew it would be to hear, she had to ask. She didn't have to wait long until there was a knock.

Luna opened the door and there stood on the path in front of her was a slim, dark-haired female in a nurse's uniform. In her left hand, she was holding a small clear bag and inside that, Luna could see that there were a couple of objects.

'Hello, Mrs Rivers. My name is Rosie and I'm a staff nurse at the Northwick Park Hospital. These are the items that I mentioned on the phone,' said Brigid, holding up the bag in her hand.

As she saw the glint of Tom's wedding ring, Luna again held her hand to her mouth and then paused briefly to regain her composure.

'Hi Rosie. Thank you so much coming all the way down here. Have you got time to come in? I would love to have a chat with you about my husband.'

Luna showed Brigid into the sitting room and gestured with her hand towards the sofa.

'Please, Rosie. Have a seat. Can I offer you a cup of tea or coffee or something?'

'Thank you. A tea with milk but no sugar please,' replied Brigid, gazing around the room.

Beautiful honey-coloured oak beams adorned the ceiling of the sitting room and at the centre of the room, directly opposite the settee, sat a magnificent inglenook fireplace complete with black iron swans-nest grate, fleur-de-lis back plate and matching fire dogs on either side. The fire crackled away as the flames danced.

Brigid's attention was then drawn to the table beside her and all the photos that sat on it. In particular, the one of Tom and Luna on their wedding day grabbed her interest. *How nice. That would have been me next year, if your husband hadn't decided to kill my fiancé*, she thought. The photograph of Tom enjoying his wedding day, stoked her fire again for revenge.

'So, tell me Rosie, were you involved in the care of my husband at all?' asked Luna as she handed one the mugs that she had brought from the kitchen to Brigid and then settled herself down on the sofa next to her.

'Well, I was the primary nurse responsible for looking after him. Sorry, I should give you this,' said Brigid handing the bag with Tom's wedding ring and key fob over to Luna.

'So, can I ask if you were there when he died?'

'I was indeed. He passed away as I was watching him,' said Brigid before briefly pausing. 'I'm sorry but would it be possible to use your toilet?'

As Brigid got up and walked through the kitchen to the cloakroom, a mass of questions started running through Luna's mind - so many things that she wanted to ask about her husband's last hours. She opened the bag, took out the key fob and opened it up to reveal the photo inside. She remembered the day that it was taken very well. It was on holiday in Italy and just before their girls left to go to university for the first time. They had been having lunch at a local cafe and the girls had just endured a round of Tom's Dad jokes. They all roared with laughter as the girls begged their father to stop and that was when the waitress took the photo. Happy memories of much better times. Luna then took out Tom's wedding ring and having put it on her own middle finger, she turned it round and around with her thumb.

Eventually, in what felt to be much longer than it really was, she heard footsteps coming from the kitchen floor behind her. Luna put the two items down on the table beside her.

'So, how did he die, Rosie? I need to know,' Luna asked looking down at the floor, not bearing to twist around and look at her face. 'I hope that he didn't suffer. Was it peaceful? I have prayed that it was.'

'No. He died like a dog.'

'Sorry?' replied Luna, thinking that she must have misheard the nurse.

'He died like a dog,' Brigid repeated, her Northern Irish accent now very apparent. 'A feeble, pathetic, beaten dog. I can tell you this because I'm the one who held a pillow over his face as he struggled to breathe.'

'What the ...,' said Luna, as she tried to stand up.

Before she could even get out of her seat, Luna felt a cord around her neck from behind. It was the kettle cord and Brigid quickly pulled it tight whilst Luna gasped for breath - desperately trying to get her hands between the cord and her neck but to no avail. Luna then wildly struck out behind her in a futile attempt to stop her attacker, but her arms were now just flailing around helplessly.

'Yeah, I enjoyed killing him,' Brigid said taunting her victim and seeing Luna's resistance starting to fail and her life force fading. 'You see he killed someone I really cared about. We were going to get married next year but your husband killed him. So, I reckon that it's only right that you should die too. And do you know what? I don't even feel sorry about killing you. I despise weak women like you

'*Sob, sob. I prayed for him.* You're so pathetic. Time to die, bitch,' she said, tightening the cord around Luna's neck.

As Brigid finished her last words, Luna's face changed. Her arms stopped thrashing around and dropped to her side. Her breathing began to slow. Brigid pulled back on the cord harder and harder in an effort to bring an end to Luna's life but as she did so, something changed in Luna. An overwhelming feeling of strength and power now surged through her body - as if someone had just flicked a switch. Her mind changed from a feeling of fear to one of complete focus.

'You first ... bitch,' whispered Luna, leaning back and grabbing Brigid's hands behind her.

Before Brigid even had a chance to react, Luna had pulled her forwards and, in a move worthy of a world class gymnast, struck her in the head with an over-head kick. Brigid staggered back, shocked not just by the physical blow itself but the speed and skill by which it had been delivered. Luna leapt to her feet and swiftly vaulted over the sofa to land just in front of Brigid, who was still in a state of shock from what had just happened.

Luna stared intimidatingly at her - giving her just enough time to frown back in response before delivering a powerful kick to the chest and sending Brigid flying towards the kitchen door. Brigid scrambled to her feet, as she desperately tried to understand what was happening. She had seen the same look on Luna's face before somewhere. Then it came to her - it was the same look Luna's husband Tom had as he was walking towards Connor outside St Paul's Cathedral. Focussed, confident and relentless. Brigid threw punch after punch at Luna as she slowly walked towards her but each one was easily either blocked or deflected. It was now apparent to Brigid that she was hopelessly outmatched and that the woman whom she had initially described as weak and pathetic was actually anything but.

'So, you killed my husband, did you?' said Luna menacingly, as she picked Brigid up by the neck and flung her into the kitchen.

Brigid realised that she had, in a matter of minutes, gone from the hunter to the hunted. She knew that she had to find a way to turn the situation back in her favour and then she remembered that there was a block of kitchen knives on the wooden work-surface, near the kettle. Once again, she scrambled to her feet and then lunged towards the knife block. Having pulled out a large carving knife, Brigid stabbed and slashed at Luna who, on each occasion, managed to avoid the razor-sharp blade. She stabbed at her again but in a single quick movement, Luna slapped the knife out from her grip, sending it flying across the floor to the other side of the kitchen. Brigid turned to dive across and retrieve the knife but before she could so, Luna struck her again - this time with an opened handed punch to the face. Brigid staggered to the side and then dropped to her knees, putting her hand to her face and feeling a sharp intense pain from her nose followed by blood dripping down between her fingers.

'Tom was a good man and a great father. What could he possibly have done so bad that you had to kill him?' asked Luna standing over her. 'As far I am aware, the only people that he may have killed were terrorists who were trying to murder thousands of innocent people. So, I guess that means that your fiancé was a terrorist then ... and I reckon that also means that, since you've now developed an Irish accent, you're the other terrorist that they've been looking for. Does that sound about right ... Brigid?'

Brigid looked around – desperately trying to find a way to escape.

The phone in the lounge rang three times and then stopped. The answerphone cut in.

'Hello?' said a man's voice. 'Luna, if you're there, please pick up.'

The voice sounded weak but was, nevertheless, distinctive. Luna stood seemingly fixed to the spot, as if paralysed by the sound of the man's voice, and Brigid knew that this was her opportunity. Without a second thought, she jumped to her feet and ran towards the kitchen back door, frantically pulling at the handle and yet still expecting to be pulled back by her brutal attacker. The door flung open and to her huge relief she was out. She sprinted down the side path towards the road, her heart pumping faster than it ever done in her life. She had escaped.

Luna, however, had still not moved from her position and was just staring at the wall straight ahead. Only her mouth moved as she whispered a single word.

'Tom.'

CHAPTER FORTY

'How do you feel?' asked Iain McGregor.

Luna swung her legs around and sat up on the black leather recovery couch, briefly looking around the room. *Looked a bit like a doctor's surgery but must be somewhere in MI5 headquarters*, she surmised.

'Strong and focussed, Mac,' she replied. 'Strong and focused.'

'That's good to hear. As you will probably already have guessed, we have a significant threat facing us. In fact, *significant* might be a bit of an understatement and the threat seems to be aimed not so much at us but more at your mother country - the US of A. With that in mind, I assume that you are OK about a secondment to the CIA? They specifically requested you.'

'Sure,' replied Luna. 'Hey, I'll go wherever the bad guys are.'

'Excellent. Look, we've got a briefing due to start shortly in the Operations Room. Just to give you the heads up, the Director of the CIA will also be present. I believe you will be reporting directly to her for your mission.'

Luna stood up and nodded her agreement.

'You know I will want to see Tom, don't you?' said Luna, looking at Mac with her intense piercing green eyes.

'Absolutely. And I believe Tom could be invaluable to you on your mission with his knowledge of the terrorists, of course.'

'So, when can I see him?'

'How about now?' said Mac with a huge grin and nodding towards the curtained off area on the other side of the room.

Luna found herself momentarily unable to speak. She rushed over to the curtain and frantically pulled it back.

'Oh my God, oh my God … oh my God.'

'You sound like a deranged parrot,' said Tom, his eyes welling up. 'Hi, honey.'

Luna looked down at her husband in his wheelchair, flung her arms around him and then promptly burst into tears.

'I thought you were dead. Are you OK?'

'Well, let's see,' said Tom. 'I've been shot, blown up and then literally suffocated to death in my hospital bed. Apart from that, just another boring conference,' Tom said stroking the side of Luna's face. 'Hey, stop worrying - I'll make a full recovery apparently.'

'He will, Luna,' said Mac. 'Look I'm really sorry to spoil this moment but the meeting obviously can't start without you. My opposite number in the CIA really hates being kept waiting, so would you be able to wheel Tom across the hall please, Luna? You'll have plenty of time to catch up and compare notes later.'

'I could get used to this,' said Tom, looking back at Luna who had started pushing.

'What floor are we on again?' asked Luna.

'Sixth,' said Mac.

'Just checking,' said Luna smiling down at Tom.

As Luna exited the room with Tom, Mac turned around to look at Doctor Patel.

'Prisha, do you think Luna's OK?'

'Is she OK? That's hard to tell. Hopefully, yes.'

'Hopefully? That's not very comforting, considering we've just given her over to our closest ally,' said Mac, raising an eyebrow.

'It seems that the threat to her life caused a non-controlled unlocking of the subdued element of her psyche,' said Patel.

'That's not exactly what we planned, was it - to say the least.'

'You know what they say about best laid plans and all of that, Mac?' replied Patel looking across and shrugging her shoulders. 'Who was to know that Brigid Doyle was going to turn up and try to kill her?'

Mac sighed and nodded his agreement.

'As I've said to you before, the Sleeper re-awakening process is a major event that the brain has to deal with. A deluge of perceived new information about that person's life has to be processed and reconciled. Two weeks minimum is what a Sleeper needs under careful supervision. In Luna's case, she also had to deal with the apparent death of her husband. That's a lot for any mind to deal with in one go. If you remember, I was very specific with regard to Luna. The first objective was that we needed her to mentally accept the death of Tom. This meant giving her enough information so that she could move on with her life. Once she had a clear mind, then we could take her through a controlled waking-up process,' said Doctor Patel.

'And that's why I met with her and then went on to leak further details to my contact at *The Guardian*. Done in two stages as per your instructions. All designed to put her in the right frame of mind, as requested,' Mac interrupted, almost trying to defend his position.

'Yes, that's true and that was the right thing to do. It wasn't meant as a criticism by the way, Mac,' said Patel, trying to offer some reassurance. 'The part that neither of us had envisaged was that Tom would survive the bomb blast. All the doctors told us that there was no way he would live. But he did and then survived being suffocated in his hospital bed. That guy is as tough as old boots.'

'Yeah, constitution of an ox. Having said that he was still lucky that Jax got to his hospital room so quickly and managed to resuscitate him after Brigid's attack.'

'Ideally, we should have waited to see if Tom survived or not - before we started prepping Luna,' said Patel.

'I agree, Prisha, but at the end of the day, with the terrorists already planning their attack on America, we really couldn't wait any longer to see if Tom would pull through or not. The CIA wanted her re-activated immediately and don't forget she's really more their agent than ours anyway. We didn't have the time to wait and see what happened with Tom.'

Prisha Patel pulled up a seat beside Mac and then sat down.

'Tom and Luna are very close, aren't they? You never did tell me how those two got together. I don't suppose you had a hand in it?' asked Patel smirking.

'Might have,' said Mac grinning back. 'It was at the American ambassador's 4th July celebration party. Luna's Dad was a Counsellor in the American Diplomatic Corps at the time and my CIA contacts made sure that she was there at the party. The CIA had already identified her as having the right genetics, as we had for Tom, and so we agreed that this would be an interesting experiment. Just so happens that a handsome young Englishman was to receive an invitation from an old school buddy who knew someone at the Embassy and the rest, as they say, is history.'

'It didn't necessarily mean that they were going to be attracted to each other though, Mac.'

'No, but we hoped that the natural animal desire to find their strongest mate would come through.'

'There's one more thing, of course. Their twin daughters. Both Luna and Tom have exceptional genetics, making them far superior in many ways to the average person. So, the combination of their genes should result in something amazing,' said Dr Patel.

'That's my hope. We'll be looking to try and recruit the girls very soon, then hopefully it'll be over to you again to work your magic,' replied Mac. 'If we find that their genetics are superior even to that of their parents, then we need to continue strengthening it to the next generation after them. I have people already looking at potential suitors for the girls.'

'Mac, I have to say that I'm slightly uneasy about what we're doing here. Don't you think that there may be an ethics issue? You know, deliberately trying to produce genetically superior people. Wasn't that what the Nazis were trying to

'We're not trying to build a superior race to take over world, Prisha. Just stronger people to defend it. So far, we have used our resources to try and track down those people who have been lucky enough to have inherited superior ger through generations of their family. I think it's time to move on from luck and make it scientific. At the end of the day, job is to protect the public from all those nutters that would do them harm and I'm prepared to do whatever it takes,' sa Mac rising to his feet. 'Anyway, talking of nutters, I better g to this meeting and see what that lunatic Baqri is up to now

'Does it ever end, Mac? I mean this whole business of them trying to kill innocent people and us trying to stop them?' asked Patel.

Mac placed his hand on the door handle and paused fo few seconds before looking around.

'No Prisha, I don't think it ever does. This is the war th never ends.'

do?'
he

es
e
ur

d
et
,

a

t

AUTHOR BIO

T.J. Hawkins is a British author, born in Devon, brought up around Canterbury and now lives in the beautiful English Lake District. After leaving school, he joined the police and then worked much of his life in the licenced trade before becoming a professional in the property industry. Married to the lovely Sarah and a proud Dad. A keen cook with a very sweet tooth and loving everything Italian.

GET THE NOVELLA 'DARK AS NIGHT' COMPLETELY FREE!

Discover where it all began for the psychopathic villain of Sleeper.

Simply go to:

https://tjhawkinsbooks.com/subscribe

Plus advance notice of new books in this series with special discount days before the official release.

PERSONAL NOTE

I really hope you enjoyed reading my debut thriller, Sleeper. As an indie author, I rely heavily on recommendations for my book(s) to be seen. I would, therefore, really appreciate it if you were able to leave a review on amazon.com

Thank you!

Find me on:

www.tjhawkinsbooks.com
Instagram @tjhawkinsbooks
Facebook Facebook.com/tjhawkinsbooks
Twitter @tjhawkins